BLACK
CHALICE

"I HAVE BEEN *expecting you,*" *the monk said over the roar of the flames.*

Close to, the mutilation on the monk's face was even more severe than that of his brother outside. The scars had that same hard-white quality of age, but these were not restricted to his eyes. They spread all across his face, carving out his cheeks and opening his nose so his nostrils appeared to be nothing more than ragged holes in the centre of his face.

"And so it comes to this. Kill me if you will, knight. I shall not surrender the Devil's book to you willingly."

"I have no intention of killing you," Alymere said, the lie catching in his throat.

"Let's pretend that is true, shall we? You can use the last few steps to make peace with yourself before you strike me down."

"Silence," Alymere barked. His fist clenched around the hilt of his sword. It felt heavy in his hand.

"So that you may cut me down without my words pricking your conscience? No," the monk said, tilting his head slightly as though listening to the voices of the fire. "You are already too far gone for that, aren't you? The book already owns you."

"No-one owns me. I am a free man!" Alymere's denial was fierce but his words sounded hollow in his own ears. There were forces at play here that he could not understand. He shook his head, trying to clear the fog that shrouded his thoughts.

"Have you not wondered why the flames do not touch you?"
Alymere

An Abaddon Books™ Publication
www.abaddonbooks.com
abaddon@rebellion.co.uk

First published in 2011 by Abaddon Books™, Rebellion Publishing Limited,
Riverside House, Osney Mead, Oxford, OX2 0ES, UK.

10 9 8 7 6 5 4 3 2 1

Editor-in-Chief: Jonathan Oliver
Desk Editor: David Moore
Cover art: Pye Parr
Design: Simon Parr & Luke Preece
Creative Director and CEO: Jason Kingsley
Chief Technical Officer: Chris Kingsley
Malory's Knights of Albion created by
David Moore and Jason Kingsley

UK ISBN: 978-1-907519-66-6
US ISBN: 978-1-907519-67-3

Printed in the US

MALORY'S KNIGHTS of ALBION

The BLACK CHALICE

STEVEN SAVILE

Abaddon
Books

WWW.ABADDONBOOKS.COM

For Norman Carr, my grandfather

*A giant in my life, one of the best men I ever had
the pleasure to know, and the inspiration for the
Sir Bors de Ganis you are about to meet.*

ACKNOWLEDGEMENTS

THIS BOOK WOULDN'T be what it is without the help of some very talented and generous people - namely Greg Smith and Adele Harrison, first readers and good friends; David Thomas Moore, whose ruthless streak with the editorial red pen cut right to the heart of the matter without gouging the heart out of the story; and Jenni Hill and Jonathan Oliver. Between these three a writer couldn't ask for a better team on his side.

INTRODUCTION

FOUND IN A church vestry in 2006, the Salisbury Manuscript (British Library MS Add. 1138) is the only existing copy of *The Second Book of King Arthur and His Noble Knights*. Apparently a sequel to Thomas Malory's *Le Morte D'Arthur*, the best-known and most influential version of the story of King Arthur and his Round Table, the *Second Book* has caused enormous controversy throughout the academic world.

Following negotiations with the manuscript's owner, Abaddon Books won the rights to modernise and publish the stories for the mainstream press in early 2010. *The Black Chalice* is the first title to be released to the public.

For more information about the Salisbury Manuscript, this translation, and themes and notes from this story, see the Appendices at the rear of this book.

ASPIRANT

ONE

BETRAYAL WAS THE furthest thing from Alymere's heart as he crossed the drawbridge into Camelot.

His journey had lasted for a week and a day more. He wore his father's mail shirt. He didn't feel like a knight. He felt like a boy in borrowed clothes pretending to be a man. But as he crested the rise and saw Camelot laid out before him, all of his doubts left him. This was where he was meant to be. This was his time. He breathed in deeply, savouring the taste of the air as though it were his very first breath. Today he was born again. It didn't matter that the dirt of the road was grained into his skin, nor that the fine mist of rain, cold against his cheeks, couldn't wash it away. All of the miles, so heavy in his legs just a few minutes ago, slipped away with his doubts and he found renewed vigour and walked a fraction taller. It was all he could do not to run the final mile to his new life.

Before him, the sun crept slowly down toward the rooftops of the castle's seven sandstone towers before finally slipping behind the tor upon which Camelot stood. Alymere drank it all in: the slate rooftops of the town sheltering behind the high wall; the still blue waters of the lake that formed part of the castle's natural defences and the stone bridge that spanned it; the curls of mist rising from the water; the colourful tents on the training fields before the walls and the pennons snapping in the breeze; the Maypole in the field; the two men riding their horses up and down the flattened track while others crowded around, goading them on faster and faster; the women like ants marching from the gateway to the water's edge clutching pails and linen. This was Camelot, the beating heart of the greatest castle in all of the kingdom.

Seeing his approach, one of the riders steered his mount toward Alymere. The warhorse's powerful gait ate the ground between them. As he neared, the rider pulled back on the horse's reins; the horse reared, kicking at the air, but there was no doubting the fact that the rider was in absolute control. Alymere felt the ground shiver as the hooves came down. The rider leaned forward in the saddle, eyeing him curiously. He was a big man, broad at the shoulder, with wild black curls and wilder eyes. Beneath the curls there was a distinctive scar on the big man's forehead.

"What brings you to Camelot, son?" the man rumbled, as though stones grated deep in his throat.

"I have come to serve, Sir Knight."

"Have you indeed?"

He nodded earnestly, suddenly all too aware of his scuffed boots, the threadbare weave of his homespun trousers, and the patch his mother had sewn into the hip where they had torn. He thought for one sickening moment the knight was about to suggest a place could be found for him in the scullery, but the big man continued. "What skills do you have, boy? I see a mail shirt, but no sword. I see a maiden's favour but no sign of fluff on your face, nary even a whisker by the looks of things. Unlike me." He grinned as he stroked his jaw; at least Alymere thought it was a grin, it was hard to tell through the thick beard. "Peasant's hose and a nobleman's shirt. You are a veritable mass of contradictions, lad. So, perhaps it is best if you tell me who you are?"

"Alymere, sir."

"Well that explains everything then, doesn't it?"

"I don't follow, sir."

"Then you must lead, young Alymere," mischief sparkled in the big man's eyes. Alymere found himself liking him immediately. "Then you must lead. To Camelot! And best not tarry!" He spurred the horse and drew back on the reins, causing the majestic creature to rear up once again. This time the warhorse snorted great billows of misty breath before its hooves came drumming down. It wheeled away, kicking up mud and dust from the road, and cantered toward the foot of the hill below. The horse was easily twice the size of any Alymere had ever seen. The knight looked over his shoulder, definitely smiling now, and called, "Come on, lad, that means run!"

Despite the fact that he had been on the road for so long, despite the fact that hunger gnawed away at his belly and he couldn't recall his last proper meal, despite the fact that every muscle in his body cried out in protest before he had taken a single step and his head swam dizzyingly before he managed a dozen, Alymere did as he was told. He chased the big man all the way down the hill to where he waited. As Alymere half-ran, half-stumbled the last few yards, concern crossed the rider's face and he swung down from his mount. He caught Alymere with one tree-trunk of an arm before he fell, and steadied him.

"Easy, lad. Easy." He held Alymere, peering deep into his eyes. Whatever he saw there satisfied him. "Let's get you up on Marchante, shall we? First time in Camelot, you should pass beneath the keystone arch like a knight, not a knave, riding tall rather than stumbling and skulking, don't you think, Sir Alymere of the Contradictions?"

Alymere nodded gratefully, even as he protested, "I can walk, sir," causing the big man to chuckle.

"I can see that, lad, but humour me. It wouldn't do for you to fall flat on your face as I introduce you to the king, now would it? Not unless you're planning to offer your service as his new fool, of course? I suspect Arthur appreciates a good pratfall as much as the rest of us. Can you juggle burning clubs, Alymere? Have you got the gift of tongues? Can you tell a joke to make the toes curl or sing a ballad so sweetly maidens swoon?"

"No, sir."

"Then you'd better mount up, lad. Because I doubt you'll be ousting Dagonet any day soon."

And so Alymere accepted his help into the saddle and allowed the big man to lead him the final few yards of his journey across the drawbridge and into Camelot. To be here, finally, was overwhelming. It was more than simply keeping a promise to a dead man. It was the fulfilment of years of sacrifice and privation. Nobility might have been Alymere's birthright, but the big man had been correct. The boy was a mass of contradictions; disenfranchised since his father's untimely death, he had been raised in poverty and privation, yet schooled in chivalry and honour; landless despite being firstborn and by rights heir to his father's estate, he had seen it taken by his uncle while he and his mother, Corynn, were cast out and forced to live on scraps. Every day for years he had been mercilessly mocked as a poor 'knight' by the children of the village, because he lacked even a sword to call his own, yet had a squire who drilled him day and night, using makeshift wooden weapons to instil discipline into his arms. Baptiste had been his father's squire, but more than that, he had been his friend. He had stayed with the family long beyond what was required by duty or honour, making sure the boy Alymere knew his father, if only through stories and recollections, and – as he grew into a man – honoured his memory. But Baptiste had been in the ground three weeks now. Sickness had taken him. He was simply too old and tired to fight it off. Alymere had learned one final lesson from the old man that day, the hardest of all that life had to offer a young man: everyone leaves.

His head swum alarmingly and he was forced to clutch the pommel as he leaned in the saddle.

Even on his deathbed, Baptiste insisted on maintaining his role as Alymere's teacher, offering one last story. He had heard it before, of course, many times, but it was a good story and to think he would never hear it again pained him, so he listened intently rather than beg the old man save his breath. They both knew this was going to be the last time that they shared a tale, and Alymere was determined to glean every last morsel of understanding from it. It was a simple enough story of how a broken link in a mail shirt had saved his father's life, by catching on his mount's barding and breaking his stride. That single missed step saved his life. One more step and the arrow would have struck him instead of the horse, and Alymere would never have been born. As he finished his tale, Baptiste begged him to draw the travelling chest out from beneath his cot. In it was his parting gift, Alymere's inheritance, the ill-fitting mail shirt he wore on his back. It was the only thing of his father's he possessed. The favour he wore was his mother's, given before her death. There was no sweetheart waiting for him back home, because there was no home waiting for him.

This moment, riding into Camelot like a true knight astride what was surely the most noble horse in all of the kingdom, was his father's reward, Baptiste's reward, and his mother's, for all of their sacrifices and their faith, though none of them were alive to share it with him.

The big man led Marchante by the reins, occasionally stroking the horse's long neck and offering a reassuring word.

Alymere struggled to take it all in at once. A single apple tree grew in the centre of the courtyard, laden down with fruit. A young man sat at the base of the tree, one foot crossed over his knee and his hands crossed behind his head. He appeared to be dozing. Alymere wondered how he could possibly sleep with so much going on around him. Market stalls, filled to overflowing with foods and fruits of every colour imaginable, lined the left side of the courtyard, striped canopies casting long shadows over the dusty ground. The fine mist of rain made the world appear so much more alive. He heard the clang of a blacksmith's hammer and the hiss of steam from water being poured onto coals and the wheeze of bellows. Somewhere off to the right, he heard horses. There were so many people. They crowded around every stall, haggling and joking and laughing, each voice rising above the other, the noise making his head spin. A woman was at the well, drawing up water. Somewhere else a church bell chimed, calling the faithful to prayer. The sheer smell of humanity was overpowering. But Alymere just breathed it in, savouring it.

Camelot.

A stablehand moved to take the reins from the big man as they neared the row of stables.

"See to Marchante, there's a good man."

"Of course, my lord. Will you be requiring him again today?"

"No, Merrick, I think we've had more than enough excitement for the time being."

"Very good, Sir Bors."

Bors de Ganis surrendered the reins and helped Alymere to dismount. The stablehand led the horse away while they walked together through the courtyard toward the keep itself. "I almost envy you, lad, seeing her for the first time. Tell me, is she everything you dreamed she'd be?" the knight asked, as they climbed up the few short steps to the great oak door.

Alymere didn't need to think about his answer. "Everything and more," he admitted, though even an hour ago he hadn't known quite what he expected.

At the door they were greeted by two armoured guards who drew sharply to attention as they recognised Bors. The men eyed Alymere curiously and seemed disinclined to let him through until the knight said, "Be so good as to inform the king that Sir Bors de Ganis and Sir Alymere de Énigme seek an audience. You might want to tell cook to prepare a feast; I suspect Arthur is going to want to show his visitor far more respect than you currently are."

Alymere found himself smiling as he caught the Norman joke: Sir Alymere the Puzzle. They heard the title, and saw his threadbare hose, and obviously didn't know quite what to make of either. Bors made a brusque 'hurry along' gesture when neither of them rushed to do his bidding. He seemed determined to find gentle fun wherever he could.

"You really don't want to make me ask you twice," Bors said, reasonably enough, but there was a steel beneath his tone that brooked no argument. One of the two men nodded sharply, spun on his heel and rushed off into the labyrinthine passages of the keep. He returned a few minutes later, flustered and flushed.

"The king will receive you in the aviary, Sir Bors. He bade me tell you he never could resist a good puzzle, and is most looking forward to whatever delights you have to stretch his mind."

"Excellent. Follow me, Alymere, we're off to meet the king." Without waiting to see if he was keeping up, Bors strode off into the many passageways of Camelot. Alymere hurried to catch up, nodding apologetically to the guard as the man moved aside. Inside, the castle was no less spectacular than outside: here, rich tapestries depicting the wild hunt hung from walls, while between them torches guttered in metal embrasures, casting fitful shadows deeper into the maze. Bors, six steps ahead of him, moved with the easy familiarity of someone at home. Alymere rushed to catch up with him as he navigated the twists and turns. The deeper into the castle they journeyed, the more soot-stained were the stones around the iron embrasures, and the darker the crannies and crevices between the huge stones. The quality of light changed subtly. Very few chambers in the heart of Camelot appeared to be blessed with natural light, if this brief tour was anything to go by. Alymere gawked as he walked, staring at the pages and scullery maids running about their business and at the imposing figures of the knights and fighting men they encountered. Bors nodded politely to every single one of them, no matter their station, Alymere noticed, and each and every man, woman and child they encountered seemed genuinely pleased to answer the big man's smile.

They paused at the foot of a narrow, winding stair as a pretty-faced maid came down the last five steps in a bustle of skirts and, as she reached the bottom, offered Bors a coquettish smile, fluttering her eyelashes playfully. She said something Alymere didn't quite catch, which earned her a gentle slap on the rump from the knight. "Alas, my lovely, as much as I would dearly love to take you for a bit of rough and tumble, my heart belongs to another."

The woman shrugged with mock-sadness and said, "Same as it ever was, my lord."

"Indeed, sweet lady. But we both know my love is a jealous love, and she owns me body and soul, Katherine, and ever was it so." Alymere could feel the comfortable familiarity of the exchange, and couldn't help but wonder how many times they'd danced the same dance, because this surely wasn't the first time.

"How about this little man all dressed up in his finest armour? Is his heart taken, too?" The maid asked, turning the full force of her smile onto Alymere for the first time. He felt his breath catch in his throat. It wasn't that she was beautiful - she was comely, in a homely sort of way, he realised, but the word *beautiful* was not one he would have ever used to describe her. She was not some fair maiden, but neither was she some foul hag – but rather, when she smiled something happened behind her eyes. Something came to life back there. It took Alymere a moment to recognise it for what it was: mischief. It was the most disarming thing he had seen in his young life, and in that moment, under the influence of her eyes, he would have done anything she asked.

"Ah, that, sweet Katherine, is a sad, sad tale. A tragedy indeed," Bors told her.

"Is it now?" the woman's smile broadened and Alymere felt every nerve and fibre of his body thrill to the sound of her voice.

"Oh, for sure. My young friend here, Sir Alymere of the Wounded Heart, took to walking in the Dryads' Wood when his one true love was taken by the pox, and there, in the throes of grief, he happened upon one of the wretched, shrewish, tree sprites who tricked him into one kiss to betray everything he ever held dear. Alas, he was not himself, and fell victim to her charms. Everyone knows – well, everyone save for poor foolish Alymere here – that the wood nymphs cast their mischievous magics in the heat of a kiss. It's a poison as deadly as any venom, that's what it is. In that moment, as their lips touched, she claimed his soul, forcing him to forget his one true sweetheart, whose favour he still wears, though he cannot recall so much as the curve of her lips as she smiled or the twinkle in her eye as she breathed out his name –"

"Why do I think there's a joke about wood coming up?" the woman said, cutting Bors off mid-flow.

The big man laughed. It was a joyous sound that rumbled deep in his belly and shook his entire body as it broke free. It seemed as though his laughter filled the whole of Camelot. "Because age has turned you cynical, lovely Katherine. Because you've no romance in your soul," Bors said.

"Or perhaps I just know you too well?" she offered.

"There's always that," he agreed, "But you must admit I have a gift for tall stories."

"I would never dream of arguing with a gallant knight such as yourself, good sir. I am but a humble girl who scrubs and cleans. What would I know of wood nymphs and lovesick fools?" She curtseyed to the big man, and then to Alymere, looking up into his eyes as she did. "But I'll say this much, 'tis such a pity," she said. "You're far too pretty to be saving yourself for a bit of dead wood." She winked at Alymere then.

Flustered, he bowed clumsily in return, but she was already bustling off toward the kitchens.

"Watch yourself around that one, lad," Bors said after the maid left them. "She's more dangerous than anything you'd meet on any battlefield, trust me, and with a damned sight less honour; a woman who knows just how to stop your heart dead with a single look, a single smile, a single word. So let this be lesson one, my young conundrum. A true knight must be pure of heart and mind, always, and it's damned hard to be pure of anything if your head is full of that woman. And that, young Alymere, is the wisdom of Bors de Ganis. Do with it what you will."

Alymere really couldn't tell whether the big man was joking, or deadly serious. There was no reading his mannerisms, no deciphering his tone of voice, and Alymere wondered which of them was truly the enigma. The stairs climbed through the full height of the seventh tower, high above the rooftops of Camelot, to the aviary. Every fifteen feet or so, arrow slits offered glimpses of the town below, the rooftops getting further and further away until it felt as though they had climbed all the way to the clouds themselves. They passed seven heavy oak doors, each leading on to some other landing, some other passage or chamber, before stopping at the eighth and final door at the top of the stairwell.

Bors knocked once, rapping his ham-hock of a fist on the oak.

A moment later the door opened, and through it Alymere saw the rich red of the sky, so close he felt as though he were truly part of it as he followed Bors out onto the rooftop. "Breathtaking, isn't it?" Bors said. Alymere had never seen the land from such a height.

"This is what it must feel like to be God Himself," he barely whispered, "looking down upon all of creation."

Bors nodded approvingly. "Look at this and tell me how a man could ever give his heart to another."

Alymere moved toward the parapet, more and more of the world opening up before him. The first thing he saw was simply the colours. There were so many shades, even in a single field. Every leaf bled into every other leaf, becoming part of the mosaic of creation, and yet somehow remained utterly unique.

"Albion. Have you ever seen anything quite so beautiful?" Another voice asked.

Alymere turned to see a man emerge from one of the coops, a hooded falcon tethered to the leather wrist brace on his left arm. He was taller than Bors by three fingers, blonde where the knight was raven-black, beardless with a pitchfork moustache that grew past his chin, with the most beautiful, piercingly blue eyes. Where Bors was barrel-chested, this man was wiry and compact. He was older than Bors, and not by a little; the years he'd lived lined his face. And even over those few paces he moved with the confidence of true power. This was Arthur Pendragon, he realised. This was the king. *His* king.

"No, sire," Alymere said, realising some sort of answer was expected of him.

But, as Arthur stood before him, it was the king who found himself lost for words. He looked as though he had come face-to-face with a ghost. All colour drained from his face, leaving his complexion waxen where moments before the sting of the wind had made it ruddy. "Can it be? Truly? After all this time?" The king asked, caught between reaching out to touch Alymere's face – as though to confirm he actually stood there – and flinching away from the apparition stood before him. He shook his head as though he couldn't quite bring himself to believe the truth of his own eyes.

"I believe so, my liege," Bors said. For the first time there was nothing jocular about his tone. Alymere didn't understand what it meant. "Roth's blood runs strong in him."

Why were they talking about his father?

"It's uncanny is what it is," Arthur said, not taking his eyes off Alymere for a moment. "It's like he's found his way back through the veil to come before us again in the flesh. I understand why you called the boy a puzzle."

"Indeed, sire."

Arthur snapped out of his reverie. "Well, Alymere, son of the forgotten knight, whatever are we to do with you?" There was unexpected gravity to the question. Arthur, unlike Bors, was not merely filling the air with words.

Alymere had practised this moment many a time on the road. He knew exactly what he intended to say, and how he hoped to say it: like a true knight, with humility and honour, underpinned by courage. He assayed a deep bow and spoke to the stone floor. "I have come to serve in any way that I might, sire."

"Have you now?"

Straightening, Alymere nodded earnestly.

"How do you suppose I might put you to work?" Again, it was a serious question. Already, in these few moments, Alymere believed he had seen the true nature of the king. There was nothing in his demeanour that spoke of folly or frippery. There was no smile as he asked, "Do you have any skills to speak of?" The question mirrored Bors' earlier one, but Arthur did not seek to answer himself.

"I am strong and hardworking. And I learn quickly."

"I am sure you do, lad. But the sad truth is I have stablehands and kitchen boys aplenty. Is there someone in Camelot who would speak for you? Someone who might offer you a bed, or employment so those idle hands don't make the work of the Devil?"

Alymere did his best to hide the crushing disappointment that came with the answer, and what it most likely meant for his aspirations. "No, sire. I do not know any who live within the castle."

Arthur did not answer for a moment, instead he gently adjusted the falcon's tethers. The bird ruffled its wings, seeming about to take flight, but then settled comfortably again on the king's wrist. "You know no-one here and yet you chose to serve in Camelot rather than on your uncle's estates? A curious choice."

"Not so curious, sire. My uncle would rather I were dead with the rest of my kin and I would rather not die quite so young."

"Hold your tongue, boy," the King of Albion admonished him, the sting of his words twice as hard as any blow might have been. He lowered his head. It had not been like this in his imaginings.

"Sorry, sire, but denying the truth helps no-one. In the months since my protectors have entered heaven I have come to understand precisely what my life means to my uncle."

Again there was silence between them, Arthur Pendragon weighing his next few words very carefully. Finally he asked: "And what *does* it mean? I should very much like to understand."

Alymere met the king's ice-blue eyes and held his gaze. "It is simple, sire. While I live I am a threat to the estates and holdings he calls his own. I have a prior claim to the title. I am the rightful heir to all that he has stolen, not least the title he usurped from my father. And now I have come of age. I am no longer the boy to be watched, I am the man to be dealt with. I have come to serve and swear fealty to the crown and honour to Albion now so that when I return to claim my birthright you will know who I am and will take my pledge that I have acted only in the name of what is just and right."

"Those are serious words, boy. Serious words indeed."

"Aye, they are. And by God, I like this lad," Bors said, his grin returning. "He's his father's son, by Christ is he!"

"Be that as it may," Arthur brushed aside Bors' declaration, "your uncle is one of my knights and I cannot hear words of treachery spoken within these walls. This is Camelot. Do you take my meaning, boy?"

He didn't know what he had expected the king to say, but

every time he had acted this meeting out in his mind, the king had never sided with the bastard, Lowick.

Alymere nodded, feeling sick deep in his gut.

"Good. Time will bring what time will bring, and fate is a fickle mistress, so who knows, perhaps one day I will take your pledge, or then again maybe I never will. That is not for us to reason. You are here now and we need to work out what to do with you."

"Yes, sire. I am willing to do anything to prove myself, my lord."

"Did your father's man – what was his name?"

"Baptiste, sire."

"That's right. Tell me, did Baptiste see to your training, boy?"

Alymere nodded. "Every day, sire."

"The martial arts? Sword and shield? Lance? Maces and morning stars? How broad was your education? Do you know your letters?"

Again, Alymere nodded, though in truth it was difficult to call the bits of broken wood they sparred with anything other than branches. "Yes, sire. I have read the Holy Book chapter and verse. I can write and reckon. We only had practice weapons, sire, but I believe Baptiste did his best to see to that aspect of my education as well. He raised me to be my father's heir."

"I would expect no less. Did he school you in the Oath?"

Alymere nodded.

"Tell me, then. I would hear it from your mouth."

Alymere closed his eyes and began to recite the lesson Baptiste had drilled into him over and over, the Knight's Code. The code by which his father had both lived and died. The words were ingrained upon his soul. "A true man must never do outrage, nor murder. A true man must flee treasons of all kind, making no room for treachery in his heart. A true man must by no means be cruel but rather give mercy unto him who begs it. A true man must always give ladies, gentlewomen and widows succour, and never must he force himself upon them. A true man must never take up arms in wrongful quarrels for love or worldly goods.

"Though never will a true man stand by idly and watch such evils perpetrated by others upon the innocent, for a true man stands as last bastion for all that is just. A true man is the last hope of the good and innocent. A true man must hold fast to this code above all things. Only then might a true man do honour to Albion and stand as a true knight."

Bors nodded, appreciatively. "Well said, lad."

"Are you a true man, Alymere son of Roth?" the king asked.

"I believe so, sire." Alymere told him.

Arthur stretched out his hand. It took Alymere a moment to understand, and then he gripped the king's hand, trying to grapple with what, exactly, the gesture meant.

"Good, because I have as much need of false men as I do stablehands and scullery boys. Welcome to Camelot, Alymere," Arthur said, releasing his hand. He turned to Bors. "See to it that he is fed, then take him to the armoury and equip him for the practice fields. Come dawn, run him through his paces. We will talk again when you are done."

It was a dismissal, but Alymere found himself asking one last question of the king. "Forgive me, sire, but might I ask, did you know my father well?"

"Know him well? As well as any might know another. That is to say, I counted him as a friend. Does that answer satisfy your curiosity?"

Alymere nodded. "A little, sire. I find it hard to remember him."

"That is understandable. It has been a long time, and memories fade, especially for the young. But I will tell you something now, young Alymere: this day you give me the opportunity to do something I should have done many years ago, and that is to honour the memory of a good friend. For that, I thank you, and in your father's honour I pledge now that I will make a place at the Table for you if you prove yourself worthy. It is the least I can do."

Alymere did not know what to say to the king's promise. He felt the emotions broiling inside him. He struggled to find the words. Any words. Finally, he made a pledge of his own. "I will not disappoint you, sire."

"It's not me you would be disappointing, boy."

TWO

THE COMING DAYS brought three surprises, each greater than the last, and only two of them pleasant.

The first came in the form of simple generosity. Random acts of kindness are things to be treasured, as they so often come when most needed.[1] In this instance the kindness was nothing more than a few words, reminiscences about his father, but that didn't diminish the impact it had on young Alymere. There was something immediately comforting and familial about the hour spent in the company of Maeve, the ruddy-cheeked cook, and the scullions. He felt as though he belonged; it was something he hadn't felt for a long time.

Maeve sat him at the big table and fed him chunks of cheese and freshly-baked bread with a thick buttery crust, the remnants of a haunch of venison – really little more than a few bites left on the bone – and a mug of honeyed mead. It wasn't exactly a meal fit for a king, but after more than a week on the road the mead might have been ambrosia and the meat nectar. Grease ran down his fingers and smeared his chin as Alymere worried away at the meat stuck between his teeth. His belly ached long before he had finished feeding his face. He couldn't help himself; he ate like it might be his last meal, because that was how he had always eaten, bolting the food down.

[1]Malory, like many of his contemporaries. is given to interjecting in his prose with moralising narrative asides like this one.

Maeve's hands were never still. She kneaded dough, shaping oat cakes and loaves for the morning. She stoked the oven's fire. She sliced and diced and peeled without looking down at the vegetables she threw into the stew pot. She had the bold air of a seasoned veteran, although her weapons of choice were the cleaver and rolling pin. She was the absolute and uncontested mistress of this place.

And all the while she didn't stop talking.

She maintained a stream of cheerful babble in between shouting instructions at the scullions and scattering them left and right with culinary purpose. The focus of her conversation was reminiscences of his father. This was where the kindness lay. She could simply have cut off a hunk of bread from the loaf and a slab of cheese and been done with it, but instead this busy woman chose to talk about the only thing they had in common. She seemed to know everything about everyone in Camelot, as surely all stories made their way down to the kitchens eventually when hungry bellies brought fighting men below stairs. She had a hundred recollections of Roth, from his first day in the service of the king when he was little older than Alymere was now, to his proudest moment, taking his seat at the Round Table side by side with Sir Kay, Gawain, Bedivere and the others. Her pronunciation of their names was distinctly Gallic. Indeed, everything she said, as she diligently worked away, was touched by her foreign tongue. He found it strangely comforting to know that he was not the only refugee in the castle; that the old woman had not only made it her home but had become a vital part of the place. To hear these stories, and within them, glimpse his father's life through the eyes of a stranger had to be one of the most precious gifts he had ever been given.

Dusting the flour from her hands, Maeve started to tell him how his parents had first met, in that very room, with the help of the brothers Percival, Lamorak and Aglovale playing Cupid, but then, seeing Bors return, she promised to tell the story another day, but only if he promised to tell her a few stories of his parents' life after Camelot. It was a promise he was only too happy to make.

He left with Bors.

The second surprise came in the armoury.

Bors unlocked the heavy oak door and slipped the brace beam, pushing it open, and Alymere followed him inside. The room itself was somewhat smaller than the kitchen, and replaced the scents of cooking with the metallic tang of mail and goose grease. All manner of swords were stowed in racks along one wall, from single-handed broadswords polished to a shine, through hand-and-a-half bastard swords and great two-handed longswords to short one-handed stabbing blades for close combat. Three windows filled the armoury with the dying light. Motes of dust turned lazily in the dwindling shafts of sunlight. One shaft struck a breastplate, transforming it from simple metal into something breath-taking. There were twenty-five such harnesses around the room, but only one captured the sun. Alymere walked across to it and placed his hand over the heart, feeling the sun's heat thrill through him. It was almost as though the empty metal were alive, as though somehow it held the spirit, the essence, of the warrior it protected.

Bors moved to stand beside him. "I do not think Lancelot would take kindly to your greasy hand-print in the middle of his chest, lad. So best not touch. Just between us, those Bretons can be a touchy lot and they're not exactly renowned for their sense of humour. Put it this way, lad, it'd be a crying shame if I was picking bits of you up off the practice field come sunrise because of one of Maeve's greasy roasts."

Alymere recoiled, pulling his hand away as though suddenly scalded by the metal, and stood there staring in horror at the greasy outline of his palm planted in the middle of the breastplate and then down at his treacherous hand.

Bors dropped a rag into his hands and chuckled, but Alymere was too mortified to realise what he was meant to do with it until Bors said, "There's leather strips in the bucket over there. I suggest you make it shine, lad. But clean the grease off your hands first or you'll be at it all night."

By the time he was done with the buffing rag the breastplate was gleaming. He had been so consumed by the task that he'd not noticed Bors searching the sword racks, picking out a single-handed broadsword and working the whetstone along the edge to hone its bite. When he was satisfied with it, he set the sword aside and turned his attention to all manner of shields – kites, bucklers and heaters – stacked up in the racks, again taking his time to gauge the size and weight before making his choice. He discarded the bigger, sturdier shields in favour of a relatively thin wooden heater overlaid with leather. It would withstand a number of solid blows without encumbering Alymere, allowing him freedom of movement on the battlefield. It would most certainly do for the practice field tomorrow. He laid a simple pair of leather gauntlets on the table beside the sword and shield, and finally he chose a helmet, a simple cervelliere skull cap, rather than a bascinet or more elaborate closed or great helm. There was nothing either embellished or decorative about any of the equipment the knight had selected; it was all chosen for its functionality.

Alymere set aside the leather buffing cloth and saw the equipment that had been set aside for him.

"Try this for size," Bors said, tossing the helmet over the table to him. It nestled snugly on Alymere's head, flattening his wayward hair as he secured it in place. Bors helped him pull on the leather gauntlets. He stood back. "Let's have a look at you then, shall we?"

Bors looked him up and down without a word. He didn't need to say anything. Alymere was all too conscious of what he must have looked like in his mismatched armour and too-big mail shirt.

"I'm sure we could find you a shirt that you'd fill out, lad. Something that doesn't make you look quite so much like an orphan playing dress-up."

"No," Alymere said before he could stop himself.

If his refusal surprised the knight, he didn't let it show. Bors merely inclined his head slightly, as though considering a problem, then cast about the room and found a leather belt to cinch the long mail shirt at his waist.

"Better. Now there's just one thing missing. We'll make a knight of you yet, lad."

And with that, Bors gifted him the second surprise. There was a soft knock on the armoury door, and a moment later Katherine, the feisty serving girl they'd met on the stairs, entered the room. She carried a tabard draped over her arm, and on it was a familiar crest: a leaping white stag on a black engrailed slash across a white cloth.

"It's not much, but it seemed appropriate," Bors said, taking the tabard from the woman and offering it to Alymere. Suddenly Alymere knew what the knight had been doing while he ate in Maeve's kitchen. He didn't know what to say. What words could he offer, save *thank you?* The gesture went beyond simple kindness. In giving him his father's tabard Bors had, in no small way, given him part of his own identity back. "It was your father's." Bors explained needlessly. "Put it on, lad, and let's see what you really look like."

Alymere pulled the tabard on over his head. Bors nodded approvingly, then helped strap the heater onto his left arm and handed him the sword.

"Come here, Katherine, and tell me, what do you think? Have we made a knight of him or does the poor lad still look like some waif we dragged from the fields?"

The maid came to stand beside the knight and took his measure, looking Alymere from head to toe and back to head again. Her smile was genuine when she said, "He looks most noble, sir."

"He looks nothing short of his father's ghost, come to haunt these hallowed halls once more," Bors said. "If I didn't know better I'd think it so. The likeness is uncanny." He made the sign of the cross over his chest, then grinned that infectious grin of his.

To the maid he said, "Thank you, Kate. You can leave us now."

She curtseyed and slipped out of the room, closing the door quietly behind her.

Then the big man turned back to Alymere. "Come on then lad, away to bed. You've got a big day ahead of you tomorrow."

And that was more true than either man could have known, for tomorrow was where the third surprise would reveal itself.

THREE

"MOVE YOUR FEET!" Bors' voice boomed from the side-lines.

Two dozen spectators manned the ropes around the combatants, knights and their squires come to see how Alymere acquitted himself. A smattering of applause rippled through the onlookers. It wasn't for him.

"Get your guard up!" another voice added helpfully.

The others sucked in their breaths as one, as the crack of wood on wood reverberated across the practice field. The rhythm of the fight changed, growing faster and faster, the blows merging into a single sound as the echoes hit the high walls of Camelot and folded back on the practice field.

"Better, lad!" Bors encouraged. "Keep your eye on him! Watch the way he moves! Read his body! That's it, lad. That's it!"

But for all the encouragement, the blows kept coming without any hint of letting up, and there was no way he could hope to ward them all off. Alymere was outmatched in every way: his opponent was a head taller, and faster of foot and eye both, blessed with a longer reach, and quite simply more accomplished. Had this been a real fight, out there on the field, there would only ever have been one winner, and the fight would have been over a long time ago.

Alymere had known he was going to lose before they had traded more than a dozen blows. What he had not understood was that this in itself was the true test. Sometimes it was not how one won, but how one lost that revealed most about a man's character.

Alymere gritted his teeth against the pain as another blow rapped off his knuckles and his practice sword went spinning from his hand. It hit the dusty ground and rolled to a stop more than ten feet away. He clenched his fist, shaking his hand as his eyes darted toward the fallen weapon. The momentary distraction earned him a sharp jab with his opponent's sword in the stomach. The blow was hard enough to knock the wind out of him. Unbalanced, Alymere's feet scuffed the dirt as he stumbled back a step, trying desperately to get away from the next huge swing.

Instead of finishing the bout as he had every right to, his opponent inclined his head toward the fallen sword, allowing Alymere to retrieve it.

That stung more than the initial rap across the knuckles.

Alymere swallowed his pride and stooped to pick up the sword. His opponent's next blow nearly took the wooden blade straight back out of his hand again, but he managed to roll his wrist with the impact and cling onto it. His hand was numb from the cracks it had taken in the last few minutes and his knuckles were bloody.

They came together again, wooden swords clashing.

His opponent darted in, delivering three quick blows, the third of which nearly took his head from his shoulders. Alymere felt the displaced air rush over his face as the blade missed by nothing more than a whisker. His mind raced. Baptiste had drilled the need for a cool mind in combat into him over and over; fear, doubt, all served to undermine the fighter, and all were a more fearsome threat than the opponent's sword. A fighter had to keep his mind clear, to become one with the sword in his hand, transforming it into a natural extension of his arm.

He was too aware of the onlookers, too worried about the outcome of this fight. His mind, like his body, was on the back foot, reacting instead of acting. When he needed it most, all of the poise, all of his training abandoned him, the mocking voice of doubt filled his head with thoughts of failure and exile, of losing everything he had let himself hope for.

Raw instinct took over.

And for a few minutes more he matched his opponent blow for blow, but always fractionally too slow to work any sort of advantage. He was tiring quickly. Every new swing, block, thrust and parry drew on his dwindling reserves of strength. He was breathing hard, sweat running down his face and into his eyes. He blinked it away, but it stung nonetheless. His father's mail shirt weighed heavily on his shoulders, slowing him down.

The bystanders had stopped with their shouts of encouragement, or he had stopped hearing them.

"You're predictable," his opponent said matter-of-factly as they broke once again. They circled each other warily. The man, Alymere realised sickly, was barely out of breath. "Your body announces your intention whenever you so much as think about countering. You over-compensate, you lean, putting too much weight on your right foot. It's obvious if you know what to look for. It'll also get you killed." The man's wooden sword darted in, cracking off Alymere's shoulder. The impact forced several of the chain links into his skin. He felt blackness well up, threatening to drown him. He backed up a step, doing his best to shake it off, and brought his own sword to bear, aiming a scything swing at his opponent's skull. The wild swing was easily dealt with. It was never meant to connect. It was only meant to buy him a few precious moments of respite, and in that it succeeded. "You're quick, I'll give you that, but you're crude," the man said. There was no hint of mockery in his voice, but still Alymere flinched at the words. The words stung, but only because they were true. "You don't read my body, you're so intent on the sword, so you are always reacting and on the defensive, instead of watching my body, reading my intentions, predicting and countering accordingly. There's no doubt you've got some skill, but as I said, you're crude, and your mastery of the sword is lacking. In short, there is much yet you need to learn."

Alymere swallowed hard, his pride urging him on. "And you

talk too much!" he said, throwing himself forward. He slashed at the air between them wildly, once, twice, three times. The man skipped away from the blunt sword, rocking back on his heel as the third swing whistled past his face.

Alymere had let himself get riled, and in turn had left himself exposed.

The man came on again, smiling this time.

Alymere grunted, expecting a blow to the chest, a jab or a thrust, something to take advantage of his imbalance, but instead, going against everything he could reasonably have anticipated, the man dropped to one knee as though ceding the bout.

Alymere hesitated, and his opponent whipped his sword around to crack off his ankle, bringing stunned tears to his eyes. Alymere threw himself to the ground, scrambling away before the wooden sword could smack down across his shoulders.

Another furious blow swept in, this one coming in high, with the blazing sun behind it. He mistimed the parry and took the full weight of the blow on his forearm.

This time, when the sparring sword went spinning away, his opponent offered no concession. He closed the gap between them quickly, reversing his blade to deliver a stinging rap across the side of the skull that left Alymere's ears ringing and his eyes watering.

"Enough!" someone bellowed from the side-lines. Alymere didn't recognise the voice. He sank to his knees gratefully and lowered his head.

The wooden sword lay in the dirt a few feet beyond his reach. Trying to focus on it, he shook his head. A wave of nausea rose up inside him, and the horizon canted treacherously, the world and his grasp on his place within it rushing away from him. He fell, reaching out blindly to catch himself, felt the welcoming impact, and tasted the dirt on his tongue. He lay still for a moment, trying desperately to gather his wits, then lifted his head.

He saw the man's back as he walked away from him, leaving him lying in the dirt, and felt impotent fury rise up like bile. Without thinking, Alymere leaned forward, scrambling in the dirt until his fist closed around the sparring sword, and surged to his feet, closing the gap between him and his opponent in five unsteady steps. Even as the crowd shouted out its warning he delivered a savage blow across the back of the unsuspecting man's shoulders, driving him down to his knees.

Before he could deliver the *coup de grâce*, Bors came between them, crushing Alymere in a huge bear hug and forcing him to drop the practice sword. Others gathered around the fallen squire who had been his opponent, helping him.

Bors growled, "You will never do that again. *Never*. Do you understand me?"

Alymere was shaking. He stared down at his bloody knuckles, trying to understand what he had done.

"There are no answers there, lad," Bors said, his tone softening, but only slightly. "The king was watching, and half the knights of Camelot, and what you showed them was that you don't know when you're beaten. That makes you dangerous, lad. Courage is a good thing; spirit is a good thing. Being able to dig deep and fight on even when you're hopelessly outmatched is a good thing. There's no shame in being beaten by a better man. But listen to me now, because I may never say a more important thing to you: there's nothing but shame in striking an unarmed man, and from behind no less."

It was the disappointment in his voice that cut Alymere. It was worse by far than the anger. In defeat, Alymere had revealed more about himself and his nature than a hundred victories might have. He pulled his father's tabard off over his head and screwed it up in his fist. In less than a day he had brought shame to it, to his father, to Baptiste and to everything he held dear. He had let them all down. He lowered his head, unable to look Bors in the eye as he said, "I'm sorry."

"Then maybe there's hope for you yet."

FOUR

THE THIRD SURPRISE awaited Alymere in the Great Hall that night.

He had spent the remainder of the day with Bors. The big knight worked him to exhaustion and beyond, pushing him every step of the way. They ran for miles across the open ground, side by side, Bors urging him to dig deep and find another burst of speed, to stretch his legs, to push on, and then, bathed in sweat, they stripped to the waist and began sword practice. Bors tried to explain how the body moved, demonstrating the most common moves he was likely to face so Alymere could learn to read his intentions before the blows came. Bors delivered cuts and thrusts, urging Alymere to watch his legs and torso for tell-tale signs of where his strength was being directed. It was enlightening. And as the day wore on, Alymere began to make sense of what his opponent had meant, but making sense of it and being good at it were two distinct things. When Bors put him through his paces an hour before sunset Alymere was disarmed again and again and again, the knight sending his wooden blade spinning with a roll of the wrist or a rap on the knuckles. Each time, though, Alymere came a little closer to anticipating the move before it caught him.

Bors seemed pleased as they packed up their things.

As they walked back through the bailey into the castle it seemed almost as though the morning's bout had been forgotten and Alymere walked tall, new-found pride in each step. He belonged here. He might not be the knight his father had been, and he might still have a lot to learn, but neither was he the boy who had embarked upon this journey only a few days ago. He had changed.

One of the guards drew Sir Bors aside as they approached. Alymere couldn't hear the words being exchanged, but Bors returned with a face like thunder. He pushed open the great double doors, grinding them back heavily on their iron hinges, and strode into the hall. In that moment there was no doubting Sir Bors's nobility. He commanded the room and seemed to stand a head taller as he swept down the central aisle toward the great Round Table that dominated the middle of the vast chamber. Alymere hurried five steps behind him, eyes everywhere as he tried to absorb it all. He had imagined this room, but never in his wildest dreams had he come close to the reality of it.

Huge kite shields hung around the wall, a hundred or more, each painted with a distinct crest. Baptiste had schooled him in the coats of arms of all the noble families of Albion as well as those of Breton and beyond. Ignorance, the man had always maintained, was worthy of scorn, nothing more. So now, as he walked into the Great Hall, Alymere found himself naming the devices in his head as his gaze moved from one to the next; Sir Dodinal the Savage and the brothers Sir Balan and Sir Balin, Sir Helian le Blanc, Sir Clariance, Sir Plenorius, Sir Sadok, Sir Agravaine of Orkney and Sir Ywain of Gore among so many of the others. It was a humbling sight; one that reminded him very much of his place. Here he was, surrounded on all sides by the shields of every knight who had ever taken the vow of fealty to Arthur; of every knight who honoured the tenets of chivalry and upheld them to the highest order; of every knight who had risen to take a seat at the fabled Round Table through the years since its formation. Here, in this room, was the true history of Albion.

And among them, Alymere saw his father's leaping stag on the wall. He swelled with pride at the sight of it, side by side with the likes of Galahad and Kay and, perhaps the greatest of them all, Lancelot du Lac.

It did not last.

There were two men in the chamber. Arthur himself, seated at the great oak table, the other with his back to Alymere. There was something uncannily familiar about the man, he realised, as he knelt before the king. Arthur rose to stand over him. He said something, but the words did not carry.

Bors stopped shy of the men, and turned to face Alymere. The big man blocked his view of the two men behind him. "This is your second test, lad, do not fail yourself," he said when Alymere was close enough to hear his low-pitched warning. "Not when the sting of this morning is still so keenly felt."

Alymere did not understand what was happening.

Bors stood aside to let him approach the king.

He walked slowly down the aisle toward Arthur's chair.

Again, Alymere was struck by the familiarity of the penitent's shape, even with his head down and shoulders stooped, although it wasn't until the armoured man rose and slowly turned to face him that he recognised who it was. In that moment the world ceased its turning, and then the man broke the silence.

"Nephew," he tilted his head slightly in place of a bow. "You truly are my brother's ghost, standing in his old clothes. For a moment I could almost believe..." His voice trailed off and he shook his head slowly, in seeming disbelief. "Remarkable."

Alymere's mouth refused to obey him. In his mind he offered the simple acknowledgement – "Uncle" – in response, but shock would not allow him even that little dignity. He tried to cling on to Bors' warning, not wanting to fail twice in the eyes of the king in a few short hours. But it was hard. He could not move. He could not talk. He stared at his uncle's face, looking for murder in those cold grey eyes. He saw only gentle mocking amusement, which was in its way far worse.

Arthur rose from his seat. "Well met, Alymere. I trust you have had a good afternoon with Sir Bors?"

"Yes, sire," Alymere said, unable to take his eyes off his uncle.

"Good," the king said. "Upon learning of your intentions to take the oath and pledge yourself to Camelot, your uncle rode day and night, arriving but a few short hours ago. He was keen to bear witness to the ceremony."

"Your father would be so proud to see you now," Sir Lowick said, and Alymere's mind reeled. He wanted to scream. He felt as though he had been punched in the throat. He couldn't breathe.

"Kneel, lad," Bors urged, placing a meaty hand on his shoulder. Alymere felt his legs buckle. He stumbled forward a step and sank to his knees. The big man stepped back as the king moved to stand before him.

Arthur drew the huge blade, Excalibur, from the sheath at his hip and held it over Alymere's head like the threat of execution. "I asked you privately if you knew the Oath, but now, in this most sacred place, the heart of Camelot and in turn the heart of our great nation, and before blood witnesses, I would hear you swear to uphold it. Think hard before you do this, boy, for believe me, I will hold you to every part of it. These are no rash promises you make today; with these words you bind yourself to me and to Camelot for the rest of your days. Do you understand the importance of such a pledge?" Alymere nodded. The king held his gaze. He thought for a moment he glimpsed a flicker of pity there, but it was gone before he could be sure. Pity, because surely Arthur knew what Alymere would have to forego to uphold the promises he was a being asked to make, and pity because there was no way he could refuse to make those promises, either. "In making the oath you swear to set aside personal disputes and live by the Oath of Pentecost," the king explained. Again Alymere nodded his understanding. There was nothing else he could do. This was why he had come to court. "Then, Alymere son of Roth, tell me, do you swear to hold life sacred above all else?"

"I do so swear," Alymere said, trapped by that simple promise. The king was no fool. In demanding his oath he was bound now, and all thoughts of justice for his father, of reclaiming his birthright, were stymied. To raise a sword against his uncle now would be tantamount to treason and raising his sword against the king himself.

As though reading his mind, Arthur continued, "Do you swear that treason shall have no place in your heart and that you will honour and serve the will of Camelot above all others?"

"I do so swear," Alymere said, raising his head proudly. If he could not honour his father by reclaiming his home, he would find another way. There was always another way.

"Do you swear that you will offer mercy to all deserving of it?"

"I do so swear."

"Do you swear that you will offer succour to those in need if it is yours to offer?"

"I do so swear," the words came easily to him now.

"Do you swear never to take up arms in wrongful quarrels for love or worldly goods?"

"I do so swear."

"Do you swear never to stand by idly whilst such evils are perpetrated by others upon the weak and innocent?"

"I do so swear."

"And do you so swear to be noble, worshipful and just in all things?"

"I do so swear," Alymere concluded.

The king withdrew Excalibur and sheathed the great blade without the tip of the sword touching so much as a hair on his head. He bade Alymere rise. "I will hold you to this oath, Alymere, for now you are no longer the son of Roth, but a son of Albion. And as such you are my ward in your father's absence. Think on this oath when you retire tonight, boy. Think on what it means and how it will change your life. For when first light comes you will enter into the service of your uncle, Sir Lowick." Arthur raised a hand to forestall any argument. "I would have you serve him faithfully as squire and learn what it means to be a true man and worshipful knight. There is much yet you need to learn – you have shown us that – and accordingly, you shall be bound to his service for two years and a day; then, when you are released, you are to present yourself here for judgement. Should you be found worthy, you shall be asked to renew the oath you have just sworn and invited to take your father's seat at the table, as is your birthright. If not, you shall be given a hot meal and released from your oath to make your way in the world alone. Serve your uncle well, learn from him, and in that way you will serve both your king and your country. That is my judgement. Do you accept it?"

And with those few words Alymere's world was wrenched out from beneath him.

He reached out to steady himself.

Now he understood what Bors had meant by his first test.

He wanted to scream, *Why? Why would you do this to me? Why would you give me to him? Is this to be my punishment? A death sentence?*

If this was the path to righteousness and becoming a true man, he did not know if he had the strength to take the first step, let alone to walk the path to its end.

He didn't know what he'd expected; to imagine that Arthur might simply finish the oath with the words "Arise, Sir Alymere!" and congratulate him was naive, especially after the morning's events, but this was cruel. This felt like the greatest betrayal imaginable. After everything he had told him, how could the king make him swear his oath and then deliver him unto the usurper like this?

It was all he could do to nod, but Arthur pushed him to answer, "Yes, sire."

The great chamber, the castle beyond it, the bailey and the courtyards and practice fields, shed every illusion of homeliness in favour of its true cold stone face. No matter how desperately he had tried to convince himself otherwise, he didn't belong here.

"Thank you for this chance to honour my brother's memory, sire," his uncle said, his delight obvious as he offered his hand to the boy. Alymere shook it off, gripping instead one of the high wooden backs of the chairs beside him. All colour had drained from his face. The chamber reeled around him. He was breathing too quickly and too shallowly, and couldn't catch a proper breath. "The past shall remain where it belongs, I have no dispute with the boy. My blood flows through his veins, after all. We are kin.

We stand together, we fall together. I shall see to his education as though he were my own son. When he comes before you next he will be worthy of the knighthood, this I swear." Lowick bowed low.

"That is my hope," the king said, gravely. "There is much for him to learn, and more to unlearn from what I have seen, but he has courage, some skill and no small heart. All of which he will need if he is to rise to claim his father's seat."

SQUIRE

FIVE

"Everything matters. Everything is significant. Everything you say, everything you do, everything you think, everything you feel. Everything matters, all of it, every little thing, because when they are all brought together, they become you. But of equal importance, lad, are the things you don't do, the things you don't say. If you forget all but one thing that I teach you, let this be the one thing you remember. We are the sum of all these things." Sir Lowick said, tightening the buckle on his great destrier's saddle. It was a familiar lesson.

Alymere drew his wet cloak tight around his throat. The heat was leeching out of his body. Corkscrews of breath wreathed out of his nostrils as he wrestled with his own mount.

It was grim outside of the stable doors.

The blizzard had been blowing for days. The world was white. The snow was so thick, the world ceased to exist a few feet in front of his face. The skeletal limbs of the nearby trees were bowed under the burden of snow. The short walk from the house to the stable had been hellish; fat flakes of snow swirled about in his face, in his eyes, in his ears, and in his mouth as he tried to breathe. Head down, they floundered through the snowfall, the insidious cold soaking through to their skin in just a few paces. The thought of willingly riding out into the storm was insane, and yet that was precisely what his uncle intended they do.

Alymere was dressed in layer upon layer of tightly knit

woolens beneath his mail shirt, as well as a heavy travelling cloak and hood lined with rabbit fur, and still the cold found its way through.

The wind cried out in a hundred different voices, each more plaintive and mournful than the last. Together the voices made the most haunting sounds as they rushed around the immovable stone of the stables. Alymere saw to his own horse, adjusting the blankets beneath the saddle. No one in their right mind would willingly set out into the heart of the storm. Even inside the stable the cold was ferocious.

The susurrus rush of snow sliding from the roof above them spooked the horses. It took Alymere several minutes of soothing and whispering to calm his mount, whereas his uncle's destrier settled almost immediately. The snow blustered in through the stable's barred windows. It was still cold enough inside the building that it settled, leaving a shallow mound of white banked up against the wall.

Alymere was long since past the point of challenging his uncle's will; if he wanted to ride out, they were going to ride out and no amount of protesting from him would make a blind bit of difference. They were well into their second year together. The first time he had questioned Sir Lowick, he had earned a swift slap with the back of the knight's hand across his face, and the second, and the third, and the forth, fifth, sixth, seventh, until he was broken of the habit and merely acquiesced. But, like the most stubborn stallion, he was a long time breaking. Alymere let his dislike for the man fester, but resisted allowing his anger to show through his mask of servility. He was the willing apprentice. He did not understand why the knight was delivering those back-handers until much later in their relationship, and not once did Sir Lowick take the time to explain why he had raised his hand to his nephew every time he voiced dissent or disagreement. His word was law. It was that simple, as far as the knight was concerned.

Hence, when Sir Lowick insisted they ride out, ride out they did. Duties could not and should not be shirked. Both the Stanegate

Road and Deere Street traversed their lands, the crossroads deep in the heart of the old forest, and several mile houses on the great wall fell under their protection. These had to be patrolled; bandits and robbers preyed upon travellers. Although surely the inclement weather ought to be more of a deterrent than two men on horseback riding the road could ever be? Alymere did not argue, though. He finished getting his horse ready, then mounted and rode out into the storm.

Try though he might, Alymere found it more and more difficult to nurture his dislike of the man, though little things still prickled away at him. It had been so much easier during their first weeks together, with his uncle's fist doling out lesson after lesson, but once he'd learned to bite his tongue, they'd begun to learn about each other. There was a lot about the knight that felt weirdly disconnected from the stories Baptiste had told him, making Alymere all the more unsure about their provenance. What could Baptiste stand to gain through lies? In the meantime, Sir Lowick had been good to his word, taking his young nephew under his wing and picking up his education where Baptiste had left off. More surprisingly, he had allowed the boy to have his mother's body moved to join his father's in the estate's chapel. Little gestures like that made him seem almost human. And those moments were exacerbated whenever he caught sight of his uncle from a certain angle, or the sun lit his face just so, and Alymere would imagine he could see his father looking back at him. It was hard to believe – or to continue to believe – that Sir Lowick could be the monster he had grown up thinking him to be. But that didn't mean he was kind, only that he was fair. There was a difference. That was another lesson the knight imparted, with something akin to delight at times.

The cold hit him with stunning force the moment he rode out into the open. He ducked his face out of the wind, drawing the thick fur of his cloak up over his mouth. His eyes watered, and the tears froze on his cheeks. Alymere turned his horse, the great beast churning up snow as it side-stepped away from the stables. The white seemed to roll out endlessly in front of him, two feet deep and more in places. The horse couldn't stand still for a moment. It walked on the spot, as though it didn't trust the ground beneath its feet. Great curls of steam billowed out of the horse's flared nostrils.

Alymere leaned forward, soothing the animal's neck, stroking its mane and calming it. The horse whickered at the air and churned its hooves through the snow, digging out its own grave. Alymere was all too aware of the raw strength beneath him. If the horse panicked and bolted there would be nothing he could do about it.

Sir Lowick rode out behind him.

"Come on, lad. Think of it this way; the sooner we're about this damned business the sooner we're home wrapped up beside the fire." He spurred his horse forward and set off at a canter through the snow.

Alymere spurred his own horse on, and set off after him.

Their tracks from the manor house to the stable were already blurred and indistinct as they filled with fresh snowfall. Snow pelted his face and wormed its way down his neck and back. But it wasn't so much the snow as the wind that was the worst of it. Without the freezing cut of the north wind he might have been able to weather the storm. He willed himself smaller in the saddle and kept his head down, concentrating rigidly on the horse's mane. It didn't help.

They rode for the north wall and the mile houses along it. Each one would offer brief respite from the elements, a fire to warm their extremities at, and a few minutes' shelter from the wind. But the nearest one was nearly twenty minutes' hard riding across inhospitable countryside.

He looked up. The snow blew under his hood, soaking his hair. In seconds the fat swirling flakes had filled his eyes. He tried to blink them away but it was a losing battle. He had no real idea where he was, beyond the very general idea that, providing the horse hadn't strayed from the path, he had to be somewhere between the manor house and the wall, but it was all too easy to imagine that they might have been turned around in the blizzard and be riding off into the white oblivion where, in a few hours, his blood would freeze in his veins and his heart would stop. The world was that disorientating. What should have been a twenty-minute ride had turned into a snowbound odyssey. With the cold clawing into his nose, his ears, his throat, down into his gut and burning into his lungs, Alymere felt like a lost spirit – a ghost that never made it home.

The snow came high up around the horse's fetlocks, exaggerating its canter into a seasick gait.

His nose started running, only to freeze in the scruff of his scraggy beard.

By the time they arrived at the first mile house he had lost the feeling in his face and fingers. He spent ten minutes huddled over the brazier, rubbing his hands briskly together and trying to massage feeling back into his cheeks while Sir Lowick took the warden's report. It was a waste of time; ten minutes later he was back out in the snow.

It was the same at the second and third mile house, and although both were considerably closer than the manor house, the ride between them took longer, twenty minutes becoming thirty as nature turned more and more hostile. Alymere couldn't imagine bandits out on the road, but more to the point he couldn't conceive of any innocent traveller making a journey north *or* south in this savage weather.

The territory around them began to change subtly as they rode deeper into the wild. The forest brushed up against the wall. The hills became higher, the valleys wider.

The fourth mile house gave the all clear.

And the fifth.

The time they spent huddled over the braziers increased with each mile house, finding it more and more difficult to drive the ice out of their bones. Alymere could no longer feel his hands or feet, and his face felt as though it belonged to someone else, a mask crusted over his own. He was looking forward to a few minutes thawing in front of the brazier.

The sixth mile house was different.

It was dark as they approached. It took him a moment to realise the implications of that.

There was no welcome fire burning in the brazier.

Sir Lowick stamped the snow off his boots as he entered the room. It was cold; an old cold, deep-rooted in the stones. The fire had been dead for some considerable time; days, maybe. It was also empty. There should have been two wardens. There were plenty of signs of habitation: bed rolls, blankets, cooking pots hard-crusted with food, tallow candles burned down to the nub, and more. So the wardens had been here, but they were long gone. That made no sense. They wouldn't abandon their posts. Not willingly. The thought sent a shiver down Alymere's back, independent of any chill.

He rushed over to the fire grate. The wooden logs had burned down to curls of grey-white charcoal, and ash had gathered beneath them. By the looks of things, the fire had been left untended to burn out. Alymere reached into the grate hesitantly to confirm what he already knew: there was no lingering warmth.

Behind him, Lowick grunted. "This isn't like Markem. He wouldn't just wander off. What are you thinking, lad? Talk to me. What does the room say to you?"

Alymere straightened and stood. He rubbed the last residual traces of charcoal between his fingertips, dusting them white. He looked around the room, at the unwashed pots and at the unmade bedding, and then back at his fingers, trying to think it through. The evidence was all there, waiting for him to interpret it. "They left in a hurry, this morning or yesterday morning."

"Good. Talk me through your reasoning?"

"The bedrolls have been slept in. It could just be slovenly housekeeping, but the mile house is small, so it's likely that the wardens would tidy their rolls away for the day when they were done with them."

Lowick nodded. "But why have you discounted them being drawn away in the middle of the night?"

"Two reasons. One: the fire. They would have banked it to preserve the wood. There are only a dozen logs left in the woodpile and they wouldn't want to have to go foraging, plus anything they did find would have to be dried out if it was going to burn. And two: the pots."

"Go on?"

He picked up one of the pots to demonstrate his reasoning, and ran his fingers around the inside of the rim. "There's a crust of food dried into the pans, meaning they ate but didn't have time to clean them. It's like the bedrolls. They'd clean them after they used them, simply because they'd need them again the next time they were hungry. Not cleaning them is more than just slovenly habits. It's an indication that they were disturbed."

"Good."

"There's no food left in their bowls though," Alymere followed his reasoning through to its logical conclusion, "so they had time to finish their meal. By the looks of what's left," he flaked it off with his fingers, "it's oats, or porridge, so definitely morning."

"Well done, lad. That kind of keen eye will serve you well, as will your analytical mind. The world talks to us all of the time – all we have to do is listen. What else can you tell me?"

Alymere scanned the small room, looking for some tell-tale sign that he'd missed, some small irrelevancy that was anything but. "There's no sign of a struggle," he said eventually, "so they went willingly."

"That's the one. Two men, veterans who've been guarding the wall between them for the best part of fifty years willingly abandoned their post in the middle of the storm of the century. What does that tell you?"

He thought about it for a moment. There was only one logical conclusion he could make. "They knew whoever it was."

"More than that, they trusted them," Sir Lowick finished. "That's the only thing that makes any sense. Last night or the night before someone came here begging for their help. They knew them, and more, they trusted them, because obviously they didn't think twice about helping them."

"And they didn't return," Alymere said.

"And they didn't return," the knight echoed.

SIX

"WHERE DID THEY go?" Alymere wondered aloud as he stepped back out into the snow storm. The wind swept away his words.

He studied the ground.

Any footprints that might have been there even a few hours ago had been masked by the latest fall of snow. He knelt, hoping to see any slight difference in the lie of the snow as though it might still give away the ghost of footprints long since buried. It was hopeless. There was nothing to indicate anyone other than he and his uncle had come or gone from the mile house. He rose again. The chill he felt this time had very little to do with the elements. It was as though the two wardens had simply ceased to be, spirited away by demons under the cover of the snow without a trace.

"We've got to make some assumptions now, lad. Whoever came out here had to have walked, meaning they couldn't have come from far away. The nearest settlement is a good two miles or more due south –"

"But that doesn't make sense, because anyone in trouble there would turn to their neighbours first, and the manor is closer than the mile house, anyway."

"Exactly. So if not the settlement, where?"

"The next mile house along the wall?"

The knight shook his head. It was a reasonable suggestion, but there were protocols in place for sending messages down the line from mile house to mile house along the wall. Signal fires were much more efficient – he stopped mid-thought and ran around to the side of the mile house, floundering in the snow that had drifted up against the walls. He waded toward the iron brazier. It was still covered. He pried the iron lid up. What he saw confirmed his suspicions. The logs were still banked up. It hadn't been lit. Had there been trouble at the next mile house Markem would have lit the fire to pass the warning down the chain. Markem was a decent soldier; if they were under threat he would have lit that fire. He hadn't. It was as simple as that. So what else could have lured the men away from the mile house?

By the time Alymere joined him at the brazier they had both arrived at the same conclusion: the wardens hadn't been summoned east because they hadn't lit their beacon. Whatever had drawn them away from their post wasn't a threat – at least not to the wall itself. It was something they believed they could handle alone.

"The threat wasn't martial," Alymere said. He had a quick mind, and was a step further along in his thinking than his uncle. "In point of fact, I don't think there was a threat at all."

"Now you've got my attention, lad. Explain it to an old man who's not quite as clever as you. Why would two experienced soldiers desert their post?"

"There's no sign of a struggle inside, and they haven't lit the warning fires outside. The absence of both of which suggests strongly that they were lured out with honey rather than driven out with a stick. Admittedly they could have been dragged off by an army and we wouldn't be able to tell in this snow, but I don't think so. I think they went out to help a traveller in distress. It's the only thing that makes sense. The conditions make travel almost impossible." He started to run with the idea, extrapolating a story that would explain precisely why the two men had left the mile house untended. "A woman turns up at the mile house begging for help, because her cart has overturned and her father's trapped beneath, with a broken leg and freezing to death. It has to have overturned because that would explain both men leaving the mile house. It would take both of them to right it. It's an easy enough scenario to imagine."

The knight nodded thoughtfully. "Bait the trap with honey," Lowick agreed. "But who in their right mind would be on the road in weather like this?"

"Someone who had to be somewhere."

"Or," the knight said, "or there's no cart at all. Think about it. There doesn't have to be one, does there? You can't see the road from here. The message, along with the damsel in distress, serves the exact same purpose as an actual overturned cart. It gets them out of the mile house. But to what purpose? What would anyone stand to gain from having this place empty for a day?"

"It would give them time to rob it."

"That it would, but there's nothing here worth stealing," the knight said, shaking his head. Something didn't sit right about this whole thing, but he wasn't sure what. Not yet, but he would work it out. For now he would trust his gut instinct. Doing so had kept him alive thus far. "And, think about it, they haven't robbed the place, have they? Whatever they wanted it for has to have happened by now. But there's no sign anyone has been in there since Markem left."

"True. Could their intention have been to pose as wardens for real travellers heading this way?"

"That would make more sense," the knight reasoned, "but that is assuming it was the mile house they wanted and not the wardens themselves. One thing's for certain, we're not going to find out standing around here freezing our backsides off. If we're right, the answer is out there on the road waiting for us."

"And if we're wrong?"

"I don't want to think about that," Sir Lowick said, trudging through the snow toward his horse.

SEVEN

ALYMERE RODE BLINDLY into the blizzard.

The road took them into the fringe of the forest, the trees providing some small respite from the harsh weather, if not the extreme cold. He found himself thinking how easy it would be to become disorientated and lost, and from that, how easy it would be to stumble, turn an ankle, and fall, and end up freezing in the snow. How long would you last? In a matter of minutes the shivering would become uncontrollable, in an hour the cold would creep into your bones; in two, or three, you'd slip into a drowsy torpor, and you'd never wake up. It would be an almost pleasant way to go, he thought, then shook off the thought. It was an all too seductive idea and once it had a foothold in the back of the mind it would keep whispering away all the while as the world grew colder.

Sir Lowick was a man with a mission. He pushed his huge warhorse on, urging the animal to gallop faster and faster, headlong into the snow. Alymere, more cautious and on a less sure-footed animal, had long since lost sight of the knight in front of him, but he could hear his destrier's heavy hooves in amongst the other sounds: the whistle of the wind through the leaves, the rustle of the snow-laden branches as they stirred, the chafing of the leather saddle against his hose, the crunch of the snow beneath his horse's hooves, and the muffled sound of his own breathing dampened by his fur-lined hood.

It was darker here, beneath the canopy of trees. Sunlight cast silver coins across the road in front of him like an offering over the snow that Sir Lowick's warhorse had churned up. He caught a glimpse of movement off to his right, but even as he turned to get a better look it had gone, disappearing back into the deeper woods.

Alymere rode on, alert, his eyes darting everywhere at once. Given the discovery of the abandoned mile house and the suspicion that the wardens had been lured away, a deep sense of unease began to take root deep in his craw.

He saw it again as the road bore to the right two hundred paces on, but no more distinctly than the first time. It moved quickly, whatever it was, with an animal grace. He was left in no doubt that the thing was shadowing them. It seemed to be running parallel to the road – which had become more of a track the deeper they travelled into the forest – keeping itself always just out of sight.

He saw it again twice more before he realised what it was: a red hart.

It was a big majestic creature with ten points on its antlers, making it almost certainly king of the forest. That such a noble beast followed them rather than fled at their approach was curious in and of itself. Even as the thought crossed his mind, the hart bolted, disappearing into the forest.

Alymere drew his travelling cloak tighter about his shoulders and hunched down in the saddle, keeping low.

A red hart.

They were deep into his father's lands, his father who had been known as the Knight of the Leaping Hart, and it had been ten years since his father's death. Ten points, ten years, a leaping hart running alongside them on the road. Could it be an omen? If it was, could he afford to ignore it? Alymere made the sign of the cross over his chest.

As he came around the next corner, the track opening up before him, Alymere was surprised to see the hart standing there, head high, staring him down as though in challenge. The huge beast's ribcage heaved, expanding and contracting with the rhythm of heavy breaths. Wraiths of white coiled out of its flared nostrils, conjuring ghosts between them. But this was no ghost or vision, Alymere realised, staring at the hart as it stared back at him. It was very much alive.

He slowed his horse from a canter to a stop, no more than twenty paces between them. The last thing he wanted was for the hart to bolt again, but for some reason he was absolutely sure it wouldn't.

Alymere felt the change in the weather around him; the lessening of the snowflakes, and the easing of the pressure of the cold in his lungs. The change was subtle but noticeable.

He dismounted, walking slowly toward the hart.

The proud creature didn't turn tail and run; at least not immediately. It watched him curiously. As he neared it pawed at the snow with one of its front hooves, and dipped its head to aim at Alymere's chest. For one heart-stopping moment he thought the hart was about to charge him down and he imagined the agony of those points driving through his father's mail shirt and into him. But it didn't. The hart tossed its head to the left, seemingly gesturing for him to follow as it rocked back on its powerful haunches, turned, shifting its immense weight, and sprung into a flurry of motion. The hart's hooves kicked up snow as it bounded away into the trees.

For a moment Alymere stood in the middle of the road, his horse behind him, the hart disappearing in front of him, trapped in indecision, and then he ran after it, pushing his way through the hanging branches. They cut at his face and pulled at his cloak as he forced his way through them. He didn't care, even as a briar thorn tore open his cheek and drew blood. If he slowed down he would lose the hart, and he wasn't about to let that happen. If pressed, he couldn't have said why, but he knew that it was imperative he follow the animal. It was as though he had no conscious choice in the matter, some unseen force impelling him, and all he could do was stumble and flounder deeper and deeper into the forest, always trying to run faster, pushing at the dragging branches and tripping over snagging roots.

The hart was always there, just in front of him, darting and weaving gracefully through the tangled wood.

It was playing with him. He never gained so much as a pace on it, and it never drew away more than a dozen before it looked back to be sure he still followed.

Alymere blinked back the sting of cold tears from the bitterly cold air and plunged on. The sounds of the forest changed, dampened by the press of snow on the canopy of leaves above. Less and less light filtered through, but the little that did speared down in shafts of golden sunlight. The ground was dusted with snow but nothing like the two-foot deep drifts that lay on the fields. Alymere pushed back his hood, sacrificing the warmth it afforded for some semblance of peripheral vision. The forest was alive with movement.

He caught sight of a flurry of black off to his right: wings. After the initial shock at the explosion of movement and sound, Alymere realised it was nothing more sinister than a bird startled into flight and trapped beneath the canopy, unable to rise into the sky. The bird darted between branches and trunks, finally settling on a thick limb in front of Alymere, halfway between him and the hart. It was a crow, he realised, although it was larger than any crow he had ever seen.

The crow ruffled its feathers as he approached, its beady yellow eyes watching him intently. Alymere felt distinctly uncomfortable under its scrutiny. For the second time since leaving the mile house he made the sign of the cross over his chest. The crow threw back its head and burst into a raucous caw that rang out through the trees. The echo folded back on itself over and over again, making the caw seem to last forever.

As the sound finally faded, the hart bolted.

Alymere launched himself after it again. He glanced back over his shoulder once, to see the crow staring down at him. The bird loosed another mocking caw. Alymere was left in no doubt that the crow was laughing at him on his fool's errand, but he ignored it and ran on. He was lost, the hart leading him a merry dance deeper into the wood. He wanted to stop, to turn back and follow his tracks back to the road before they blurred away beneath more snow, shed by falling branches, but retreat wasn't an option. He was committed. He had been ever since he had taken the first step into the forest. The forest was a primeval place; strange things happened within its sanctuary, of that Alymere was in no doubt. The red hart was a portent, and a powerful one at that... could it be his father's spirit guiding him now? The thought sent a thrill through young Alymere's blood, reinvigorating every muscle and fibre in his body. He pushed himself harder, running faster, ignoring the sting and cut of the trees. He wasn't about to let the hart escape him. Not now. Not if it had been sent by his father.

The crow flew behind him, darting ahead occasionally only to circle back through the tree trunks and up behind him again as the bizarre procession wound its way deeper into the heart of the primeval wood.

The press of the trees began to thin. He saw moss growing on one side of the trunks, and knew from his uncle's teaching that he could use such knowledge to find his way back out of the forest. It was as good as a mile marker and a signpost for charting the passage of the sun.

And then the forest opened up into a grove. The red hart stood in the centre of it, drinking from a crystal blue pool while the crow settled on a dolmen that seemed to form a gateway on the far side of the clearing. For a moment Alymere thought he caught sight of another place through the stone arch, but the illusion was broken as a woman stepped through it into the grove. She was breathtakingly beautiful, with a garland of summer flowers tangled in her hair. Sunlight streamed down all around her, bathing her in its radiance.

But it wasn't the woman that stopped Alymere dead in his tracks, nor the sight of the crow bursting into flight in a flurry of wings to settle on her shoulder a moment, but the shift in temperature. It was as though he had stepped out of the heart of winter into the warmth of spring in a matter of a dozen paces.

She wore a simple white dress that hugged her body. Her long black hair cascaded down her back, with rings of daisies woven into the curls. A blush of colour filled her cheeks as she smiled at him. It was a smile to fire the blood and stop the heart at the same time.

Alymere felt a thousand urges welling up inside him all at once, each one undeniable – lust, hunger, adoration, protectiveness – but more than anything, seeing her, being near to her, he felt alive.

The Spring Maiden stood beside the red hart, stroking its glossy pelt, then knelt, cupping her hands in the water and offering it to the majestic animal. The hart drank from her hands. Alymere had never seen anything like it in his life and doubted he ever would again.

Had he not been so taken with her beauty he would have seen the reflection she cast in the water. In the truth of the pool she was anything but beautiful. In the water the flowers in her hair became corpse blossoms, the blush in her cheeks gave way to grey, cracked and withered skin, and her eyes, so full of summer, darkened and became sunken hollows set deep in her pinched skull. Her glossy black tresses reflected back as thin clumps of grey hair and patches of psoriasis-crusted scalp. The beauty mark on her left lip was a wart in the water. Her simple white dress which hugged her like a long lost lover was transformed into the black shift of a crone in mourning. Where youth and beauty gazed into the pool, death looked back out of the water. But Alymere was young, his heart naïve. He saw only beauty.

And when the Crow Maiden opened her mouth, her words were every bit as seductive as her borrowed demeanour.

EIGHT

"ALYMERE THE UNDECIDED," the Crow Maiden crooned, her voice breathy. He found himself taking another involuntary step toward her. She offered her cupped hands to him as though offering him the chance to sup from them as the hart had done, but even as he took a second step the water trickled between her fingers. It splashed on the dirt, muddying the soil between her toes. "Alymere, Destroyer of Kingdoms. Alymere, Killer of Kings. Alymere, Champion of the Wretched. Alymere, Saviour of the Sick. Or will it simply be Alymere, son of Albion? All of these futures I see before you, though none of them are writ on your flesh and bones indelibly. You could be all of these and more, or none of them. So which is it to be, young Alymere?"

He fell to his knees.

The sudden movement startled the crow into flight. It launched into the clear blue sky in a fury of feathers, cawing raucously as it climbed higher.

She laughed then, a beautiful sound, although her laughter echoed the crow's cawing perfectly.

"There is no need to worship me. I am not your goddess. Arise, young Alymere. Arise."

"How do you know my name?" he asked. It was the most obvious question, and one he could find no rational answer for.

"I know everything about you, Alymere Orphan-Knight."

"I am not a knight," he said, fastening on to the obvious fallacy in her words, reminded of Sir Bors's jests when first he had set foot inside Camelot so many months ago.

As the Crow Maiden said, "You will be. That is your destiny; to rise and take your father's seat at the Table," he knew she was right. "But more interesting, surely, is the question, what *else* do the Fates have in store for you? What other days and hardships, what other triumphs and tragedies await the Undecided? Do you want to know?"

Before he could answer, the Crow Maiden's mouth split into a broad smile. Had he looked closer he would have seen her crooked yellow teeth, but he only had eyes for youthful beauty and no time for the decay beneath. She said, "No matter, I couldn't tell you even if you did," and he believed her. "So much is dependent upon so much else. But know this, Alymere: you have been marked. You are an actor on the world's stage. You have it within you to make the world dance to your whim, should you choose. All you need to do is make a decision, set your first foot on that path to any of the many futures that await you."

"I don't understand," he said, looking up at her. She really was heart-stoppingly beautiful. The way the sunlight touched her face; the way her eyes sparkled, so full of mischief and fierce intelligence; the way her rich red lips parted and the blush touched her cheeks; the way her dress clung to the swell of her teardrop breasts and the curve of her hips. What he felt inside went beyond desire. Like the forest itself, it was primal.

"And neither should you. Not yet. But you will."

He wrestled with the emotions warring within him, trying desperately to exert some small mastery over them. "Why did you bring me here?" he asked. "Surely not just to taunt me with riddles I cannot hope to understand? Was it to *not* tell me my future? It seems like great lengths to go to merely to impress me with your beauty." The more he spoke, the more he found his confidence returning, as though the simple act of questioning her somehow unravelled a little of whatever enchantment she had woven around the grove.

"So young and yet so wise, you are. Perhaps I should call you

Alymere the Knower, or Alymere, Arbiter of Truth? That has a certain ring to it, don't you think? Could that be your destiny?"

"I don't know what I think, my lady," he said, finding his manners at last. "Perhaps you should tell me?" The harshness of his own words surprised him. He lowered his gaze, ashamed. No sooner had he found his manners than they deserted him once more. She did that to him. She unnerved him.

"Do you know who I am, Alymere?" the Crow Maiden asked. He shook his head.

"Then I should tell you, don't you think? You shall call me Blodyweth,[2] though I have many names. I think I like this one best, so it is only right that you should know me by it. It is such a pretty name, don't you think?"

He nodded, again slightly lost in her nearness. He was inexperienced in the ways and wiles of women, and such was her heady fragrance that he found himself intoxicated as she drew closer to him, drunk on her beauty and the perfumes coming from the garlands in her hair. No amount of flirtation – nor, for that matter consummation – could have prepared him for the effect the Crow Maiden was having upon his soul.

"This place is my sanctuary." She spread her arms wide to encompass the entire grove, the rippling pool, the stone arch and all of the trees. Not her *home*, but her *sanctuary*: her safe haven. "It is sacred to me, but more, it is sacred to Albion itself. It is the very heart of the old country. There is power here. The old ways are strong in the earth. No doubt you have noticed winter's reach does not extend quite this far into the Summervale."

"Are you a witch?" He blurted out the question, not answering her.

She laughed again, not unkindly. Above her, the crow heckled

[2] Probably a distortion of *Blodeuwedd*, the treacherous "flower maiden" of the *Mabinogion*. Whether Malory imported the character from the *Mabinogion*, which existed in Welsh in his time, or from a now-lost third text is uncertain. The variant spelling is most likely for the benefit of a Norman readership, although it may be intended as deliberate within the narrative, the distortion of the name indicating a darker twin – interestingly, in the *Mabinogion*, Blodeuwedd is associated with an owl, not a crow – or a disguise.

with its ear-splitting caw. The sound echoed around the grove, sounding as though it travelled miles before folding back in on itself. It was a disconcerting sound. "Hardly, but if it helps you to think of me that way, by all means, I shall be a witch for you. All you need to understand is that winter cannot touch the Kingdom of Summer."

For a third time Alymere made the sign of the cross, though this time it was greeted with derision.

"That will not help you here," Blodyweth told him, enjoying his discomfort.

"What do you want from me, witch? Speak plain," Alymere said, finding his courage.

"What do I want from you?" the Crow Maiden smiled again, though this time the veneer of perfection cracked subtly, hinting at the hag that lurked beneath the pretty little maiden. In that instant he caught a glimpse of death in her eyes and it chilled him to the marrow. Yet still it wasn't enough to break her spell on him. "It is not what I need from you, it is what the land needs from you, what your king needs from you, and what, most of all, you need from yourself. All three are in grave peril, young knight. That is why the hart brought you to me."

Three black feathers fell from the cuff of her dress, turning and turning again as they fell down to the ground. One of them landed between her toes and seemed to melt back into her skin, but Alymere was oblivious. He gazed up, full of longing, at her face.

"What would you do for your king?" She asked.

"Anything," he said without hesitation.

"What would you do for your land?"

A trickier question, being a much more nebulous concept, but again he offered the same answer, "Anything."

"What would you do for me?" He had expected her to ask what would he do for himself. She didn't. He offered her the same answer again without thinking.

"Anything."

"As it should be," she said.

TEN

"Every possible fate is woven together like threads to form something more, something greater. Each thread of fate becomes the warp and weft of the tapestry that is this life. Imagine being able to unravel each thread, to be able to pluck it from the weave and recreate the pattern in any way you so wished," the Crow Maiden said. "That is what we are, single threads."

Alymere didn't understand. It didn't matter. He didn't want her to stop talking. He just wanted to listen.

"Some parts of the pattern must never change, and others are more... malleable," she continued. "I know you will claim your father's seat at the Round Table, that is woven into the tapestry and cannot be changed, but the rest," the Crow Maiden's smile was gentle, "you are a dangling thread, Alymere the Undecided. I cannot tell you the future because you haven't decided it for yourself."

She could see he didn't understand, so she took one of the flowers from her hair and told him to watch as she plucked the petals from the daisy one by one. "He loves me," she said, blowing the white petal away from her fingertips, "He loves me not." And another petal was blown away. "He loves me." Again and again until the flower's stem was denuded. The final petal left her lips to the promise of: He loves me. "It's a children's rhyme, but it demonstrates the fact that, whilst it seems that nothing is decided, from the moment the flower began to bloom whether he loved me or not was always going to be dictated at this point of time. It was decided, even though I hadn't so much as pulled that first petal away. It is the stem that never changes. Without it, the flower couldn't exist. And like most of us, the flower only wants to be loved."

He watched the way her lips moved, willing to believe every word they said.

She took a second flower from her hair, a bluebell this time, and crushed it between her fingertips. "But not all beautiful things are cherished." Her words – love, cherish, beauty – conjured an image in his mind of some peaceable kingdom, a place of love and beauty, tranquillity, harmony. A place like this, he realised, looking around the grove. What had she called it? The Summervale. He felt the warmth settling on his shoulders, as though intensified by her words. He began to sweat beneath his thick travelling cloak and his mail shirt. He unclasped the hook fastening it around his throat and let it fall to the ground. He was still too hot. He pulled at his mail shirt, starting to lift it over his head.

"Think on this," the Crow Maiden said. "Some strands of the tapestry exist merely to mar it; almost as though there is beauty in the imperfection."

Alymere cast the mail aside. He felt so much better for having his skin bare, more in touch with the world around him, closer to it. "You are speaking in nonsense words. This is no tapestry," Alymere thumped the ground. "This is Albion. This is a forest, that is a lake. Those are oaks and if I pluck this strand of grass and rub it between my fingers it doesn't all come undone. The oaks are still oaks, the stones still stones and the lake is still a lake. The world doesn't work like that."

"Then let me speak plainly to you," she said. "These oaks, these stones, this lake, all of this – everything you can see, everything you can't, all of it – is in danger. These are the petals on the flower, and you, Alymere, you are the stem. Should you fail they will all wither and die."

"How can I fail if I don't know what I am supposed to do?" he said.

She placed her hand flat on his chest. Where he saw soft fingers he felt long talons sinking in deeper and deeper in search of his heart.

"Tell me," he pleaded. "How can I serve you?"

Instead of answering him, the Crow Maiden gathered the hems of her dress and drew it up over her head. She stood naked before him.

"There is one thing you can do for me," she said.

"Anything," he said eagerly.

"Love me," she said. "Love me unconditionally, body and soul," and opened her arms to him. Alymere couldn't help himself. He stood on unsteady legs and stepped into her embrace. She whispered into his ear, crooning soft words, sweet deceits. "If you can do that, you can do anything."

"I can do that," he promised.

Only when he was lost inside her did the Crow Maiden dare whisper, "Do you love me?"

"Yes. Yes."

"Tell me again, what would you do for me?"

"Anything," he said breathlessly.

Her smile widened, turning predatory. Alymere could not see the cracked and broken teeth in the cemetery smile. He had his face buried in the nape of her neck, tasting her sweat and breathing in her sex.

"Anything?" she whispered in his ear.

"Yes," he said, all the promises in the world were nothing though, until he spilled his seed, sealing the pact between them.

ELEVEN

THEY LAY TOGETHER on the soft grass, spent.

For all the pretty words she had used, there really was beauty in that moment. Beauty and peace.

She owned him then, body and soul.

Alymere rolled onto his elbow. He looked down at her, seeing finally that there was nothing innocent about her nakedness. There was a look of utter contentment on her face. He smiled.

The hart stood at the edge of the clearing. It wasn't alone. It seemed almost as though all of the creatures of the forest had come to witness their coupling. He saw dozens upon dozens of birds, all manner of them, lining the branches around the grove. He saw foxes and badgers and voles, rats, moles and ferrets hiding in the shadow-fringe of the trees, watching. It was the most unnerving thing he had ever witnessed. Not one of them moved. Not once did their gazes waver. They only had eyes for him.

"You could do one more thing for me," she said, not looking at him.

"You need only ask it," he said.

"Do not be so eager to make promises you cannot keep," she chided him lightly.

"There is no promise I cannot keep," Alymere said earnestly. "There is nothing you could ask of me that I would not willingly do, without a second thought."

Blodyweth shifted slightly in the long grass, and turned to look at him.

"You really mean that, don't you?"

"With all of my heart."

And with that rash promise, he took his first step on the road to becoming the man he was always destined to be. He was no longer Alymere the Undecided.

"Be my champion," she said. "Save me."

Alymere traced a finger down her cheek to her lips, and leaned in and kissed her. "No-one will harm you while there is a breath in my body."

"You are so sweet, my little knight," the Crow Maiden met his kiss with her lips and for a moment they chapped and hardened, betraying her true age, though again Alymere was too lost in the moment to notice the disparity between what he saw and what he felt. "My fearless and brave hero. Lying here in your arms like this, I almost believe that you could protect me from anything."

"On my life," Alymere swore, leaning in to kiss those lips again.

"But you cannot save me, the bones are already cast. No-one can."

"Hush," he said, pressing his finger to her lips. "Didn't you just say nothing is writ in stone?" He teased a flower from her garland, and held it between two fingers as though it were the most precious thing in the whole world. "He loves me, remember?" He scattered the petals with one breath.

And for a heartbeat her resolve crumbled, the cunning of the crow creeping to the surface for all the world to see, in her eyes and in her predatory smile, as she drew him closer and said, "Hold me." He did. And because of that, he missed the truth.

"That is not such a hard promise to keep," he said.

"If only it were so easy," the Crow Maiden breathed in his ear.

"Talk to me, Blodyweth. There is nothing you can say that will scare me away. I am yours." It was said with all of the earnest honesty of youth; the same sort of youth where mountains are there to be climbed and fears to be conquered.

"I know," she said, soothing him. "I know, my sweet, sweet

knight." When at last he began to doze sleepily in her arms, and she judged him receptive, she whispered: "Our fates are entwined now, just like our bodies. You are my champion. I love this land as though it were my own flesh, and her rivers flow through my veins like blood, and you love me, don't you?" he nodded. "Here," she tore a strip of fine linen from her discarded dress, tying it around his forearm, "so that I am always close to you, wherever you may be. Close your eyes, my love. Rest, dream of me."

He did.

And while he slept, she planted the suggestion in his mind:[3] "Do this one thing for me, Alymere. Find the blind monk whose skin is impervious to blades and steal the Devil's book[4] from his hands... do not fail me, or all of this will be lost. Promise me now, make this the one promise you keep."

He grunted and shifted in his sleep.

"Promise me," she insisted, letting go of her beautiful face. Feathers fell from her lips to tickle his. He sighed, his lips parting.

"Promise," Alymere said sleepily, sealing his fate once and for all.

The Crow Maiden leaned down and kissed him like lovers do. His mouth opened to take her in. Finally she broke away from that last kiss and told him, "Follow the smoke. When the time comes, you will understand. You must be strong. True. If there is a weakness in you, he will exploit it. If there is evil in your heart, he will stoke it, and all will be lost. Stay true. Save me, my champion. Save me, or the Devil take both our souls."

[3]Literally, "She caste a thoghte into his mynd as he slepyt."

[4]From the description, the *Codex Gigas* (also known as the Devil's Bible), which is currently at the Swedish Royal Library and can be viewed with permission of the curators.

TWELVE

Sɪʀ Lᴏᴡɪᴄᴋ ꜰᴏᴜɴᴅ Alymere naked and shivering in the snow, his clothing scattered around the clearing. His eyes had rolled up inside his head and he appeared to be in the grip of some manner of fit or seizure. He knelt beside the young man, cradling his head in his arms and holding him firm until the convulsions had passed.

He fetched his cloak and wrapped it around him.

"Come on, lad. Come on," he repeated over and over, turning the demand into a mantra, willing Alymere to come back to his senses. He was sweating despite the cold. Some sort of fever sweats. He smoothed the matted hair away from the lad's brow. There was a scrap of linen tied around his forearm. Lowick couldn't tend to Alymere here. He put all thoughts of reivers[5] and missing guards from his mind. One thing at a time; he needed to get Alymere to a fire, and get some warmth back into his blood. Anything else could wait.

He started to gather the discarded clothes and dressed his nephew, pulling his undershirt and shirt on over his head and his hose on one leg at a time. His mail shirt lay in the soft mud where the melt had soaked into ground, softening it up. Lowick

[5]Literally, "rayders from Scotland." Border reivers didn't exist in Arthur's sixth century, but were very active in Malory's fifteenth. William Matthews, at California University, places Malory in Yorkshire, which would make the reivers a prominent part of his world; I suppose that the "Scots" referred to many times in this story are at least inspired by the raiders of Malory's own time.

thought long and hard about leaving it there, but knew that out of the cover of the trees where the blizzard was still raging any extra layers could be the difference between life and death. The mail would serve to lock in what little heat his body generated, so the added burden of it couldn't be measured in pounds and ounces.

Besides, the boy would be wretched if he woke to find it had been left behind in the forest.

The knight man-handled his nephew into the mail shirt and gathered him into his arms. Following their muddy tracks back to the road, Lowick carried him the mile and more back through the trees.

The horses were tethered where he had left them.

When his nephew hadn't caught up with him down the road he had turned his horse around and come looking for him. He hadn't known what he expected to find, but certainly not this. Alymere's mount was loose, but well-trained. It hadn't strayed too far from where Alymere had left the road, and the knight had been able to find his tracks and follow them. "Thank the Lord for small mercies," Lowick grunted as he hoisted Alymere up into the saddle. He draped his nephew's limp body over the animal's back, checked he was indeed still breathing, so grey and pallid was his complexion, and then draped his own cloak over his nephew's back before climbing into the saddle himself.

With the reins of both horses in his hands, the knight spurred his mount into motion, and led them back out of the trees into the cutting wind and swirling snows.

He knew this land well – he had ridden it every day for the forty-seven years he had been on this earth – but even so, with the snow storm raging, it would have been all too easy to get turned about and lose his way. The cost of that, though, was beyond anything he was prepared to pay. Shivering against the freezing cold, and with his head down against the icy sting of the snow as it abraded his cheeks, the knight guided the horses back through the blizzard to the abandoned mile house.

He threw the door open and staggered into the room, laying

Alymere down on one of the unmade bedrolls closest to the fire, and then threw off his gloves and knelt at the hearth. He set about banking up the coals quickly and fed two new logs into the grate. He fumbled with the tinder, trying to get a spark. His frozen fingers refused to obey him as he struggled to light the fire and get some blessed warmth into the place. It wouldn't light. Again and again he sparked the tinder but couldn't get a flame to catch.

The answer, of course, was in the brazier outside; the knight braved the storm one last time to gather two logs from beneath the brazier's cover. They had been soaked in oil to withstand the elements, and to light no matter how harsh or hostile the conditions. They had to. Lives depended upon it. He tossed them into the grate and knelt, fumbling with the tinder. It sparked the third time of asking and the fire caught on the fourth spark. In a matter of minutes the fire was cracking and sap snapping and popping in the logs as it burned, filling the small room with warmth.

Lowick stripped out of his own armour, and then did the same for Alymere. What had kept the heat in outside only served to keep the heat out inside. Alymere's shivers lessened as the warmth filled the room, but he didn't stir.

Lowick had set his sword down upon the small table, within easy reach.

The knight paced around the cramped room, frustration eating away at him. What had possessed the lad to leave the road? Snow madness? He had heard of such things, when the cold was so great it froze the blood in the brain, but surely the onset of any such madness demanded more time in the cold for it to worm away inside a man? He cracked his knuckles and stretched out the bones in his back.

He needed to think.

There was much about the day that the knight had no liking for, not least the fact that his guards were still missing. Had they too succumbed to snow madness? Was it some sort of sickness that his ward had contracted in this very room? Was bringing him back here a mistake? Would he succumb to it himself? A thousand thoughts and more raced through his mind, clamouring to be heard, each of them more strained and panicked than the last. He needed to focus. To think. He had not been able to find any trace of the guards out on the road, which, he was beginning to suspect, boded ill for them. For two miles up and down the road he hadn't been able to find sight nor sound of an overturned cart or a wagon with a broken axle or any other travellers in trouble. That didn't discount the idea that the missing men had been lured out exactly the way Alymere had surmised.

Mercifully, he hadn't found any sign of reivers either.

He pulled up the small stool and sat, leaning back against the wall of the chimney breast, savouring the warm stones on his back.

Once, during the darkest part of the night, when the lad had tossed and turned most violently during his fever-dreams, the knight knelt and said a prayer, offering his own life in return for Alymere's if that was what was demanded. A life for a life. It was the old way. He didn't know how he would live with himself if the boy didn't make it. It would be like losing his brother all over again. And it didn't matter how strong he was, how great his skill at arms, he could vanquish every foe he faced on the battlefield and it wouldn't matter, because he couldn't fight disease or sickness. He couldn't save his brother and now he was helpless to save his brother's son.

All he could do was pray, and hope that the God that looked after foolish young men with hearts the size of lions was listening.

The knight didn't move from his bedside vigil until Alymere woke with the coming of the dawn.

THIRTEEN

HIS DREAMS WERE plagued with visions he could neither cling to nor understand. In them, he dreamed he was a blind man battling demons or a demon battling blind men, his focus shifting from one set of eyes to another again and again as the battle raged on. And these were proper demons, devils even, barbed tails, forked tongues and all. Again and again, the Crow Maiden's imprecations that he follow the smoke, find the blind monk and bring her the book, turned over in his mind. Always, as the fight was won, his foe was vanquished in a flurry of wings and feathers as the blind man or the demons transformed into black birds, crows, rooks, ravens, and scattered before him.

He woke sweating and feverish.

His uncle knelt at his bedside, head down in prayer.

Alymere coughed, hard.

The knight looked up, met his eye and said simply, "Thank the maker. You gave me a fright there, boy. What the devil were you thinking?"

Alymere eased himself up onto one elbow, but even as he did the world reeled around him and he sank back into his pillow, groaning. It was no kind of answer, but he couldn't answer, because he had no idea what his uncle meant.

The last thing he could remember was the red hart standing in the middle of the road.

Both Alymere and Lowick flinched as a crow flew up against

the window, battering the streaked glass with panicked wings. There was something familiar about the bird: a vague memory that evaded him in the clear light of morning. He lay back in the bedroll, trying to remember how he had got here. "Sorry," he said, finally finding his voice. Meaning *Sorry, I don't understand; sorry, I don't know; sorry, I can't tell you.*

The knight shook his head, "Not good enough, lad. Words are cheap. You nearly got yourself killed running off into the forest like that. It's nothing short of a miracle that I found you." The words were harsh, but his manner masked genuine concern. Alymere didn't understand what could have happened to warrant it.

He tried to move again, easing himself into a sitting position. He didn't say another word for a full five minutes whilst he gathered his wits. He rubbed at his right eye and temple, trying to get the blood flowing. The horizon slowly stopped canting and settled. He breathed slowly, regularly. It was only then that he noticed the strip of linen tied around his forearm and remembered how he had been given it, and, more slowly, by whom.

And with that memory came the rest: following the hart into the trees, the maiden herself, making love to her, and finally his promise, which had bled into his dreams. But for the life of him, Alymere couldn't recall anything after that. He had no recollection of leaving the Summervale, nor of the fact that the glade itself was not a sanctuary of summer but rather a trick of the mind and that as the so-called summer faded and the sun went down on it he was left lying naked in the snow in the thick of the forest, winter wracking his body. The last thing he remembered was the maiden kissing him like lovers did, her tongue licking along his teeth and lips, and whispering, *"Follow the smoke. When the time comes, you will understand. Do not fail me, or the Devil take your soul."*

"Do you believe in the otherworld, uncle?"

"Do you mean do I believe in magic?" Lowick asked, his brow furrowing as he considered the question. "There are more things in this life that I can understand or account for. Whether they're magic or not, I don't know. Why do you ask?"

"I think I saw a sign," Alymere said. "A red hart."

"And that's why you took off into the forest?"

"Don't you see?" He reached for the tabard the knight had draped across the chair before the fire. "A leaping hart."

"A white hart, lad. There's a difference. You're reaching."

"Still –"

"Look at the evidence. Discard the fanciful, the wishful thinking, and what have you got? Apply your mind to it like any other puzzle. Be dispassionate, rational, logical."

Alymere didn't answer him, but that didn't mean he was not doing exactly that; picking through his memories in search of the truth. He wanted to believe that it was his father's animal totem that had led him to the maiden and the Summervale, because that would make finding the blind monk so much more meaningful, but wanting didn't mean that it was. It just meant that he was trying to find some sort of reason where there was no reason to be found. He didn't argue with his uncle. Instead, he clambered out of the bedroll and, beginning to dress, asked, "Did you find the men?"

"No," Lowick said, but it was the way he said it, part dread, part resignation, that conveyed the full extent of his expectations. That they still hadn't returned meant the missing men had been out in the snow for at least two full days now, but most likely three. Three days out in the bone-freezing cold. Three days with the mile house abandoned and the wall vulnerable. Nothing good could come of that.

Alymere belted his tunic and stuffed his feet into his boots. He felt woozy and light-headed, but more than anything he felt hungry. It had been more than a day since he had last eaten. He looked around the guard room, saw again the dirty pots, but this time realised what he didn't see: food. There was no food in the place. He couldn't believe he hadn't seen it before.

"We spent so long thinking about what was here we didn't ask ourselves what was missing," he said, rummaging through the pots. "There's no food." The knight looked at him as though he were speaking in tongues. "Think about it. They weren't lured out by anyone; they went in search of food."

"By Christ, you're right," Sir Lowick said, making the sign

of the cross over his chest as the blasphemy slipped from his tongue. It was the most telling thing they hadn't seen, and offered one rational explanation why the men had ventured out into the snow. What it didn't explain was why they had allowed their victuals to run so low in the first place? Neither did it explain why they hadn't sent word along to the next mile house to beg rations to see them through until the knight and his squire made their rounds and could send for proper supplies, nor did it account for the fact that one of them hadn't simply returned to the estate whilst the other maintained their watch. There was something that was just wrong about the whole thing.

That was when a second alternative occurred to him; that their food supplies had been tampered with.

It made sense of a couple of the *whys*. Tampering with the rations would explain why the rations had run out – or rather why they had been allowed to. Simply put, the men hadn't been any the wiser. As far as they were concerned they had supplies to last out the worst of the winter.

"I'll be back," Sir Lowick said. "Be ready to leave as soon as I return."

With that, he donned his cloak and, drawing it about him, pushed open the door and plunged out into the storm. The snow had hardened into hail, which bit into his cheeks as he floundered through the snow to the side of the building. He pulled open the wooden doors of the shed that served as a pantry for the main building. The place was bare. On closer inspection he saw the black shadows of the scorch marks on the walls where fire had claimed the oats and other victuals the men had stored out here in the cold cupboard. Someone had burned the lot. Only the fact that the shed was stone and isolated from the main building had saved the entire mile house from going up in smoke.

Grunting, he threw closed the wooden doors and trudged around to the stables to see to saddling the horses.

Knowing that hunger was no doubt behind their desertion made all of the difference. Without doubt, he had been looking for the men in the wrong place.

When Alymere emerged from the dwelling wrapped up against the cold, without looking up the knight asked him, "If you were hungry, where would you go?"

"The nearest settlement," Alymere said. It was the most obvious answer, and sometimes the most obvious answer was the right one.

"Exactly. We've been looking for them in the wrong place. We assumed they were going to help someone else, not themselves. Saddle up, lad. The road waits for no man."

They rode out, the knight urging his mount into a gallop before they were halfway across the open field. Alymere spurred his horse on. The animal was grateful to be given its head. The nearest settlement was five and some miles south, close to the crossroads where the Stanegate Road met Deere Street, deep in the heart of the valley between the Tyne and the Irthing. Stanegate wound and wandered more than other Roman roads, but offered reivers easy passage deep into the southlands.

The stretch of road from the wall down as far as the crossroads was known colloquially as The Maiden Way.

They rode in silence, heads down, hunched low over the necks of the racing horses, spurring them on to greater and greater speeds despite the treacherous footing the road offered. The wind whipped at Alymere's face. In front of him, Sir Lowick's cloak billowed out behind him like some black wraith looking to snag him and haul him down out of the saddle. The forest raced by on either side, shadows and phantom forms pulling at Alymere's eyes again and again, but not once did he catch sight of anything even remotely resembling the red hart running along beside them.

He knew rationally that his uncle was right; a red hart was a long way from a white hart in terms of symbolism and meaning. White reflected purity, while red equated to guilt, sin, and anger. It conjured images of blood and sex. His mind raced, avoiding the most obvious explanation and the Crow Maiden's parting words, and instead wanting to believe that somehow his father was still with him, watching over him. There was comfort in it. It was as simple as that.

Up ahead, the road widened.

It took him a moment to realise that what he was seeing wasn't snow but rather smoke through the trees ahead, and the maiden's words came back to him: *"Follow the smoke..."*

"Smoke!" Alymere yelled, his voice torn away from his mouth by the blustering wind. Lowick looked back over his shoulder to see Alymere pointing to the curls of smoke rising from the distant trees, and like Alymere before him, seemed to take an age to distinguish the smoke from the snow and recognise it for what it was, but when he did, he spurred his horse on, urging it to go faster still. Hooves thundered on the road, the two of them riding like the hounds of Hell themselves were snapping at their heels.

Because smoke meant fire, and fire meant suffering, torment, and pain. Because, like the hart, fire was red.

FOURTEEN

THE THATCHED ROOFS of the ring of homes had caved in beneath the heat. The straw had curled, withering, while the edges charred, and finally the entire structure collapsed, the flames leaping higher.

Alymere's horse shied away from the fire and smoke, snorting and kicking as it pranced sideways, refusing to go any closer to the burning buildings.

As he watched in horror, the fire quickly consumed the wattle walls, blistering the whitewash daubed on the façades.

The heat coming off the huts was staggering. It battered him. He felt his mouth dry and the inside of his throat shrivel as the heat intensified and it became progressively more difficult to breathe.

The horses refused to go any nearer to the flames.

Beside him, the knight swung down out of the saddle and rushed toward the closest building. He didn't look back, didn't hesitate. The door hung on one rope hinge, as the other had burned through. He pushed it out of his way and plunged into the fire. Alymere was slower to react, not through fear but because of what he saw lying in the snow a few feet beyond the door of the second hut: a body, though it was barely recognisable as such. It lay curled up, one arm outstretched, clawing at the snow. The entire body was charred, the clothes fused to its back and legs where they had melted into the skin. Licks of steam rose off blistered flesh where the snow cooled it, and blood had begun to congeal. Slain.

But that wasn't the worst of it.

Not even remotely.

Alymere swung down from his horse and walked toward the ruined body, sick to the stomach.

As he neared, it became more and more difficult to deny the truth of his own eyes. The body in the snow was that of a child. Alymere caught himself saying the words of a prayer as he knelt beside the body. It was impossible to tell whether it had been a girl or a boy, the damage wrought by the blaze was so complete.

His eyes stung, and not just from the smoke.

He wiped away the tears with his left hand.

The smell, the sickly sweet stench of burning meat, stuck in his throat.

Alymere felt his gorge rising. He turned away from the ruined body, gagging, and retched violently. He dry heaved again and again, doubling up as the spasms wracked his body. There was nothing in his stomach to bring up but bile.

Gasping, he wiped his lips with the back of his hand.

What he had seen, he would never forget. That small body, broken and burned in the snow, would forever shape his fate, and time and time again affect decisions he made from that moment until the day he died.

It was only then that he became aware of the screams: there were people trapped inside one of the buildings, begging for help.

This time he didn't hesitate.

Alymere pushed himself to his feet and ran toward the burning building.

Every step took him deeper into the heat.

He pumped his arms and legs furiously, driving himself on even as the heat strove to batter him back. He felt it burning the skin on his face and hands as he came within touching distance of the fire.

And still he didn't stop.

He threw himself into the flames.

FIFTEEN

THE SHEER HEAT was overwhelming. All around him the building burned, flames leaping and writhing as they found something else to feed them. He could barely see for the smoke. It clawed at his lungs. Each successive breath became harder to draw than the last. The smoke clotted around the ceiling, rising. Alymere dropped to his hands and knees and crawled forward into the flames.

He couldn't see anything beyond a few blurred outlines.

The shadows were alive, dancing and gyring to the whim of the flames.

He crawled forward, calling out, "I'm here, I'm here," over and over to give whoever was trapped behind the curtain of fire something to focus on. Not that they could have heard him above the roar of the flames, which crackled and spat and hissed, filling the silences ahead of them with their implacable hunger.

The air was so thin that he needed three breaths to swallow what amounted to a single lungful of air. It tasted foul. Bitter. Acrid.

But the noise was the worst of it. It was like a thousand madmen had crawled inside his brain, cackling and laughing, intent on making him one of their number.

Above him, something cracked with a sound like broken bones. He started to crawl back, pushing desperately at the hard-packed dirt, but as a single shaft of light speared through the collapsing roof, he saw them hunched up against the furthest wall – a mother cradling her child in her arms – and threw himself forward. An instant later the ceiling joist gave way, splintering through the heart as a dozen cracks tore through the rings and the dry wood caved in beneath the load it bore.

Alymere threw himself to his left, rolling away from the burning beam as it thudded into the ground where his back had been just a heartbeat before. He didn't have the luxury of celebrating his fortune; breathing hard, he rose to his hands and knees, and then into a crouch, and shuffled forward. The smoke had blackened, but with the roof gone it billowed up freely into the sky. That should have provided some small relief for his lungs, but it didn't. As the roof collapsed the flames leapt higher with more air there to feed them.

Alymere was on the wrong side of the fire now, but there was no way he could retreat. The flames filled the door and all of the space between. They were insatiable. Everything would burn, including him. There was no way back. All he could do was fight his way deeper into the fire. He couldn't allow fear into his mind. It would sear his strength away and finish what the smoke had begun. No. He had to reach the woman. His world was reduced to that simple necessity. He had to reach the woman.

He felt his skin tightening where the heat drew every ounce of moisture out of it.

He licked at his lips. It didn't help.

He ducked his head, gasping at the dead air, then plunged on, fighting his way to the woman's side. All around him the fire raged on, gathering intensity as it found fresh fuel to burn.

Alymere knelt beside the woman. Her head was down, her chin resting on her breastbone, and there was no strength in the arms holding her child. He placed his hand against her cheek, but there was no way of knowing if her warmth sprang from life or the fire. Her face was at peace which, given the maddening noise and the sheer overwhelming heat of the fire, was damning.

Alymere tried to wake her, but it was hopeless. He clutched at her shoulders and shook her – and then again, more forcefully – but failed to elicit so much as a groan.

Her hand fell and lay limply at her side.

The fire was only feet away. It had raced across the bed and spread to the blanket box at its foot. The family's few clean linens burned. And the more the fire was fed, the thicker and less breathable the smoke became.

He had to get them both out of there.

Alymere pushed himself to his feet and looked around.

There was no way out.

It was as simple as that.

The flames closed in around him, darting toward him again and again, and his cloak caught. The fire raced up his back toward his hair. Alymere couldn't breathe; his head swam and colours sparked across his vision. He fumbled with the cloak's clasp, his hands trembling. The metal clasp broke between his fingers and he threw the cloak into the fire before it could spread to his other clothes.

Gasping and coughing, Alymere stumbled forward and lost his balance. He reached out blindly for the wall.

He knew that if he fell, he wouldn't get up again.

The fire had done so much damage that he punched clean through the thin wattle wall as he tried to steady himself. He wrenched it free, the jagged edges of broken branches cutting into his wrist as he did, and then started kicking and punching frantically at the wall, trying to batter it down.

It splintered and split beneath his furious onslaught, and smoke streamed all around him, pouring out into the clear blue sky above. He didn't stop. He lashed out over and over again until his lungs threatened to seize up on him, and doubled up in a fresh coughing fit. This time he couldn't clear his lungs. The bile and black stuff flecked his lips and stained his tabard. When he finally stopped coughing long enough to see through the smoke and spots swirling across his vision, Alymere could see a narrow shaft of daylight where he had torn through the binders and the branches beneath. He wiped his mouth with the back of his hand, smearing the black soot across his face and looked around for something to use to make the breach wider, but anything that might have been useful was already burning. Now that he had opened the wall, the flames had a way into the wood beneath the daub and the whitewashed lime and the fire was in, devouring the brittle branches and the weave of dry twigs. Alymere could hear the sighs and groans as the timbers within the walls shifted. In a few minutes everything was going to buckle and fold as the walls came crashing down.

Alymere threw himself at the wall, using his entire body weight to drive the wattle back. It splintered further, parting around him and, in some grotesque parody of birth, he stumbled out into the snow on the other side. His momentum sent him stumbling and sliding to his knees, skinning his palms as he fell face-first into the snow. The cold hit him, hard, driving what precious little breath he had out of his lungs. He lay there for a moment, face-down and gasping for air. The snow felt so good against his skin, offering the briefest of respites from the heat of the conflagration, but he couldn't savour it, not with the woman still trapped inside the burning building.

Alymere pushed himself back to his feet and turned. There were people around him, battered, bruised, lost in shock. None of them spoke. The silence they shared between them was the quiet of desperation. There could never be words enough to fill it. He turned his back on them and stumbled toward the building.

His legs tangled and betrayed him less than five steps later. He fell to his knees, and then forced himself up again, gritting his teeth against the agony suffocating his lungs. Tongues of flame licked out through the wall. He couldn't see anything beyond them, but that didn't stop him. She needed him. He would not let her down.

Every subsequent step was harder. The scorching heat engulfed him. The smoke was so thick now that he was essentially blind and forced to find his way by memory and touch – where he could bear the contact with anything within the blaze.

He fumbled his way toward where he remembered her being.

She hadn't moved.

Sure that she was dead, Alymere dragged the woman out.

SIXTEEN

PEOPLE RUSHED TO help him.

He felt their hands steadying him and heard their voices, but couldn't make sense of anything they said. Alymere could barely stay on his feet. He saw his uncle striding toward him, face grim. He was carrying another body in his arms. Alymere laid the woman down in the snow and sank to his knees beside her.

One of the women came forward, reaching out for the baby.

Tears and soot stung his eyes as the woman took the tiny infant in her arms and cradled it to her breast, soothing it and stroking the fine wisps of hair back from its scalp. She slipped a small finger between the baby's lips, hoping it would suckle. It didn't. Next, she pinched the baby's cheeks, hoping the nip would succeed where the suckling instinct had failed. It didn't. The woman's expression didn't falter. She swung the baby around in her arms and delivered a sharp smack to its bottom, once, twice, and on the third the baby's cry filled the silence.

Alymere turned his attention to the mother, but there was nothing he could do to save her.

SEVENTEEN

OTHER THAN THE child Alymere had saved, seven people survived the reivers' raid on the village, all of them women.

In a few harrowing minutes an entire community had died.

The men's bodies were lined up in the snow, some of them barely recognisable from their injuries. Only three of them had died in the fire. The others had been butchered by the Scots' swords. Beside them lay the smaller bodies of six children and the woman Alymere had dragged from the flames.

So few survivors out of all of those families. Seven women who had lost everything.

Alymere couldn't begin to comprehend their grief. Generations cut down, grandparents, fathers, mothers and children. It was senseless. All he felt was rage at the men who had done this. It was like a vile black canker in his heart that threatened to overwhelm all else. He wanted to lash out, strike something, someone. He wanted vengeance for these helpless women and their fallen families. Surely that was what it meant to be a knight, wasn't it? To protect those who could not protect themselves, and when that failed, to give their ghosts justice? What had they done to deserve this? The answer was, of course, nothing. There was nothing anyone could do to deserve a fate like this.

And yet not one of them had wept as they gathered the dead and cleaned them. The tears would come, of course, when the horror subsided and the reality of their situation set in. Only

Alymere had cried. He did not feel any less of a man for it. The dead deserved no less from him.

Sir Lowick took no part in the funeral rites. He rode out in search of the reivers before they could cover their tracks.

Alymere had wanted to ride with him, but knew that his duty was to stay with the women while they built funeral pyres, although consigning the dead to more flames seemed almost repugnant to him. He saw the need for the ritual, though – it was more about the living than the dead – and he knew the choice of pyre over plot came down to the fact that none of these women intended to stay in the ruins of their village. And why would they, when all they had for company were the ghosts and constant reminders of what they had lost today?

No-one talked while such grim work needed to be done. Each looked after their own.

Alymere busied himself with physical work, hacking down branches for the women to build the pyres. And he kept on hacking away at the barren branches long after his muscles began to burn. His face contorted with pain as he pulled the tangled wood free and dragged it over to the growing bonfires. Over and over again, the mindless repetition of it freeing his mind to think of nothing.

But, of course, all he could think of was the body of the burned child and all of those other bodies lined up in the snow. There was no respite.

The wood piles grew higher and higher until, with the sun lowering in the sky, he helped each of the women in turn bear their loved ones over to a pyre so that their spirits could be laid to rest.

One by one the women applied burning torches to the wood piles until the ring of bonfires blazed all around them.

At last, when all of the fires were lit, the oldest of the women sought him out. "Would you say a few words, my lord?" she asked. He couldn't look her in the eye. He knew she was right; they deserved no less from him, but he didn't know what he could say about these people beyond platitudes. He had never met them before in his life. He inhaled a deep breath and held it, letting it fuel his blood. "Something to send them on their way to their maker so that He might know they are coming?"

But when it came down to it, he had no deep wisdom, no kind words, only a profound and infinite sadness for what had happened to these people. So that was what he said.

He took the time to stand beside each pyre, to learn the names of the dead and to hear a story or two about each of them so that they might live on, for another night at least.

And he cried silent tears for the widows and the orphans.

Before he left each funeral fire he made a promise to the ones left behind. There would be justice for the ones they had lost.

Even as he swore that promise he recalled the last few words of the Crow Maiden as she begged him to save her, and knew, on some instinctive level, that this was part of what she needed him to save her from. If his time bonded to his uncle had taught him anything, it had taught him to think. There was no such thing as happenstance. Coincidence was nothing more than a hidden chain of cause and effect waiting to be unravelled. The reivers hadn't simply come marauding south, intent on death and burning for the hell of it; they moved with a purpose. He thought it through: first they breached the wall, taking out the wardens without raising the alarm, which was no mean feat, and then they had struck deep into Sir Lowick's protectorate, leaving devastation in their wake. *They seek to horrify*, Alymere reasoned, thinking about the human cost of their raid, but something, some ill-formed doubt niggled away at the back of his mind, and he found himself thinking it was more akin to smoke and mirrors – tricks – there was grim purpose to their advance, and there was nothing random about those they had chosen to spare. They were looking for something; not food, and they hadn't taken any of the women, so, something else...

The Devil's Bible, he thought, staring into the dancing flames. Why else had Blodyweth drawn him into the Summervale? Why else had she made him swear his promise to save her and then bid him follow the smoke? They were linked, like chains that weighed on his soul. The Scots sought the book. Their purpose didn't matter.

The Crow Maiden had asked him three questions: what was he prepared to do for his king, for his land and for her, and he had offered the same answer to all of them, anything and everything. Failure meant the land would fall, the king die, and whatever magic sustained Blodyweth in her kingdom of summer would fail. And somehow all of these fates were bound to this book, this bible.

All of this was for a book? He remembered something Baptiste had been fond of saying: a little knowledge is a dangerous thing. Now, in this dead village, he thought he saw what his friend had meant by those words.

He remembered something else Baptiste had said, his lesson on the quality of mercy. Watching the fires burn themselves out, he was far more interested in the quality of retribution than anything even vaguely merciful. An eye for an eye. A tooth for a tooth. A life for a life. There would be a reckoning, he would see to that.

When the pyres had burned out he shepherded the women back to the manor house, where at least they would be dry and warm. They had precious few belongings to gather, and offered no objections. They followed him, trudging wearily through the deep snow, as they left their lives in the ashes behind them. Gwen, the woman who had taken the baby from his arms, hugged him hard. She was the last of them to enter the great house. She looked at him, down to his feet and back up to his eyes, and said, "God help them if you find them, my lord."

"Indeed," he said, coldly. The way he said it frightened him. It was absolutely detached from the young man he had been when he woke up that morning. "But even with his help they are damned."

"I do not doubt it for a moment," she said, sadly.

He couldn't understand her sadness; he would, but only when it was too late.

Once the women were quartered in the Manor, Alymere rode out to join his uncle. The storm had abated, but, with midday fast approaching, it was still bitterly cold. But the cold was inside him, in his soul, so that was hardly surprising.

EIGHTEEN

THREE MORE SETTLEMENTS burned on the road before them.

More dead were laid out in lines on the hard ground. More widows and orphans left behind. The senselessness of the slaughter sickened Alymere.

The smoke led Alymere and Sir Lowick toward the coast and the storm-tossed sea.

Long before the spires of the isolated monastery on Medcaut[6] came into view, Alymere knew where their journey would take them. There were other settlements the raiders could have hit, but nowhere else they might find a blind monk and the Devil's Bible, and Alymere didn't doubt for a moment that the reivers sought the book.

He spurred his mount on, leaning forward in the saddle, his right cheek pressed to the horse's mane, and urged the animal to run faster and faster as they broached the hilltop. Coming over the top he saw Medcaut and the monastery little more than a mile or more ahead. And what a sight they were, with the harsh whitecaps of the sea roiling and surging as they climbed up the pebbled beach and broke on the cliffs beyond them. Medcaut rose up like the hands of a drowning man.

---

[6]Probably Lindisfarne, off the Northumberland coast. The island appears as *Medcaut* in Nennius's *Historia Brittonum*, the earliest source of the Arthur legend. Andrew Breeze suggests that the name derives from the Latin vulgate *Medicata Insula*, "healing island," after the island's reputation for medicinal herbs.

Medcaut was a tiny tidal island linked to the mainland by the Pilgrims' Way, a stone causeway that was submerged twice a day beneath the North Sea. The monastery was a place of pilgrimage for the sick who hoped to find remission from their suffering; not that there would be any succour today. Snow capped the rooftops and lined the high monastery wall.

But that was not what had Alymere driving his heels into his horse's flanks again, harder still. Great wreaths of steam billowed out of the animal's flared nostrils as it raced down the hillside, hooves drumming on the hard-packed winter earth. The wind tore at his face and at his cloak as it billowed out behind him. At his side, Sir Lowick roared his fury and spurred his warhorse on, pulling away in front of him. For a moment Alymere couldn't tell where the horse's misted breath ended and the smoke began.

The entire west wing of the monastery, including the cloister bell tower, was choking in thick smoke. Great black clouds of it belched up into the blue sky. For a moment, Alymere imagined he could see faces in the clouds – the faces of the dead they had cremated along the way. And then he saw the first licks of flame lash over the wall as the fire climbed higher and higher.

Alymere rode over the dunes and down onto the beach, the ground shifting beneath the horse's hooves as it negotiated the loose shale and finally, as it reached the water's edge, the sand. Alymere urged his horse on and, side-by-side with his uncle, plunged into the sea. The great whitecaps splashed up around their horses' bellies before they were more than a dozen steps into the water, making it impossible to go any further.

They stared at the smoke and the flames.

It would be hours before the tide turned. The causeway was more than two miles in length, curving like a Saracen blade through the bay to the rocky promontory where the monastery burned.

There was nothing either of them could do. The sea kept them back.

But it also served to trap the reivers. There would be a reckoning, cold comfort though that was, for the monks of Medcaut.

Impossibly, Alymere was sure he could hear their screams across the water; hundreds of voices crying out. They swelled within him until all else ceased to exist. He swung down from his horse and splashed deeper into the water until the waves were lapping around his throat. The mail shirt weighed him down, threatening to drag him under. There was no way he could strike out and swim all the way to the island. It just wasn't possible. Of all the lessons that he might have learned at Sir Lowick's side, this one – that he could not save everyone – was the hardest of all to learn.

"Forgive me," he said, the wind whipping away his words and carrying them off over the sea. Whether they reached the dying monks or not he had no way of knowing. Not that their forgiveness could have eased the burden on his soul. He sank to his knees and let the water wash over his head, hoping, at least, to drown out the voices.

But even with the waves crashing down over his head there was no relief.

He held his breath until it burned in his lungs.

The saltwater stung at his eyes.

Then, finally, as the pain in his chest grew too much to bear, he opened his mouth and breathed in mouthful after mouthful of water, taking it down into his lungs until it filled him.

He struggled then, thrashing.

He felt his uncle's grip on his shoulder as he hauled him up to his feet, and came up out of the sea in a plume of spray.

Lowick dragged him out of the water and back up to the beach, and drove the water out of his lungs. The stuff frothed at his lips and dribbled down his cheek. He coughed, spluttering up a mouthful of saltwater, and again, harder this time as the knight pushed on his ribs, pushing down over and over until he coughed up every last drop.

And then he screamed.

In that sound Lowick imagined that all of those others could be heard at last, making Alymere a conduit to give voice to their suffering.

He lay on his back, the sea lapping almost tenderly around him, waiting for the ebbing tide to retreat, and knowing that every minute that passed with him staring up at the darkening sky only served to damn the island's inhabitants all the more completely.

"The tide will turn, lad. Best to rest up so we can ride out when it's full-dark."

Alymere did not move.

"There's nothing we could have done," the knight said.

"We could have ridden harder," Alymere said bitterly. "You could have woken me instead of leaving me to sleep all night through. We didn't have to stay to burn the dead or escort the women back to the house. We didn't have to do any of those things, and if we hadn't, we could have done *something*."

"It is pointless to think like that, boy. We had to do all of those things. I couldn't wake you, you were dead to the world. We couldn't leave those women to mourn alone; it was our duty to protect them, and when we could not protect them, to see that they were cared for. We owed that much at least, if not more, to their dead. This conflict you feel warring within yourself is only natural. You would be no sort of man if you did not feel it. But don't talk to me of 'doing something,' boy. We did everything we could. The one thing we cannot do is turn back the tide."

But Alymere knew he was wrong; they could have done *something*.

Even if they had reached the coast an hour earlier, it might have been enough to beat the tide.

And for want of an hour all of those lives were lost.

Where was the justice in that?

The justice, he realised, was in the sword that hung from his hip.

He pushed himself to his feet and stood for hours at the water's edge, watching the sun leave the sky. The tide would turn. Already it was beginning to retreat, shrinking back from the beach to reveal more and more of the causeway. An hour, maybe two at the most, and it would have pulled back far enough to make the crossing safe.

The fires still burned behind the monastery's high walls. They would rage 'til dawn.

His sword was patient. Alymere rested his hand on the pommel, drawing some small comfort from it.

The reivers would not leave Medcaut.

That much he promised the dead.

He took no pleasure from the promise, but in it Alymere learned something new about himself – he was a man of his word.

NINETEEN

THE NIGHT WAS only a few hours old when the tide started to turn in earnest.

Alymere had not left his waterside vigil, despite his uncle's insistence that they rest before the coming fight. The strength of vengeance sustained him, though he would never admit it. He knew that should it come to it, his arm would not fail him. The spirits of every single one of the fallen would support his sword arm, lending him the last of their strength. Of that he was utterly sure.

The older man was certain there would be a battle, but as the hours passed Alymere became less sure. It was not that he feared the fight, no matter how many warriors waited across the water. No, the longer he watched the monastery burn the more certain he became that the reivers had not only trapped themselves on the island, but had almost certainly penned themselves inside the burning monastery, turning the high walls into their own prison. The causeway was the only way off Medcaut, and with Alymere and Sir Lowick waiting for them at the end of the road there was no way they could have escaped. There was a justice of sorts in that, Alymere thought, watching Medcaut burn.

And if the fire didn't claim them, then they would.

The knight said very little to him during those two hours. He did not seek to comfort him, but neither did he try to stoke the fires of his anger. He simply allowed Alymere to be. This too was part of his training, allowing him the space to master himself.

The young man knew that how he handled himself over the next few hours would define the rest of his life – either in terms of demons he carried with him or in demons he laid to rest. What Lowick did not – could not – know was that there was only ever going to be one outcome from the night's trials. Alymere already knew the kind of man he was going to be.

So as the fire spread, he imagined it burning the raiders as well as the monks. Separated from its heat, Alymere could only watch with grim fascination and marvel at its appetite as the flames scorched the sky red.

Eventually the two men saddled up and rode out, the water still around the horses' fetlocks as they negotiated the slippery stones of the Pilgrim's Way.

It was the longest two miles of his life.

He recalled another exhausted ride he had made, this time to Camelot, looking for an entirely different kind of justice for his father. He had been wrong then, believing that the man at his side was responsible for all of the ills of the world. The king had known that, and hence his 'punishment.' He had ridden to Camelot sure he was right, sure the king would see the justice in his suit and confer his father's nobility onto him. Arthur had done nothing of the sort, of course. He had seen into the heart of the hot-blooded youth and sought to find a way to quench that fire and turn him into a man worthy of his father's nobility. He knew all of this now, but as he rode up to the monastery gates, what he *knew* ceased to matter. It was what he *did* that counted.

The horses would go no closer to the flames.

Beside him, Sir Lowick dismounted, strode up to the wooden gates and pounded upon them with his mailed fist. It was a curiously pointless gesture given the flames behind the gates, but that did not deter the knight. He called out, "Holy men of Medcaut! If you are able, open the door in the name of the king!" but the cry brought no response.

The knight drew his sword and nodded solemnly to his charge.

"Now we bring justice, boy. May your sword be true, your aim honourable. And may you live to see tomorrow."

With that, the knight charged down the door. Medcaut was not a fortress; it took Sir Lowick four blows with his shoulder to splinter the wood, and two more for him to tear the timber loose of the frame supporting it.

Alymere saw the flames through the splintered wood, dismounted and followed his uncle inside.

Left unchecked for hours, it had torn through all of the easily burnable parts of the monastery, the straw on the stable rooftops, and much of the stables themselves, twisting and charring the wooden stalls until only blackened spars remained, and even those were crumbling and breaking down. More of the monastery was ablaze: the apple blossoms looked like dying men; the stained-glass windows of the lower chambers had shattered under the heat; the stone of the great building itself was seared black, tongues of flame licking out of the broken windows. At the farthest edge of the compound, up against the wall, the Abbot's house was ablaze.

It was like something out of Hell.

Lowick crashed through what remained of the door and burst into the courtyard. He looked right then left, taking stock of the situation quickly. Alymere stepped in behind him, his own sword tip wavering as he saw the silhouette of a hooded monk in one of the upper windows of the main building.

The fire lit the air behind him, making him look, momentarily, like some shadowy angel with flames for wings.

Alymere stared up at the monk in horror, but the man seemed... at peace.

That was it, he realised. The monk was content. He could feel it from where he stood. No, not merely content, the monk welcomed the fire as it would bring him one step closer to his Lord. Alymere didn't know how he knew, but he knew. The monk simply stood at the window, drinking in the last sights of his life.

And what sights they were.

In the centre of the courtyard another of the brothers was locked in a fight to the death with two grim-faced reivers, somehow holding them at bay with nothing more than a wooden staff.

The Scots were weary; their claymore blades dragged on the dirt as they circled their quarry. Both were big men. Both were breathing hard. Despite the cold, sweat dripped down their faces.

Alymere couldn't begin to imagine how long the three men had been locked in their fight. Surely, though, it had to be for as long as the fires had raged?

The dirt at their feet was worn smooth, no trace of any snow left, unlike much of the rest of the courtyard, which was still white where the heat hadn't melted the snow to slush.

The smaller of the two northerners, a red-head with a ruddy complexion and braided beard, licked his lips before dropping to one knee as though in exhaustion, but brought his huge blade scything round in a vicious arc, looking to cut the monk off at the knees.

The monk planted the quarterstaff in the dirt, jumped over the wild swing, landed and turned the sword aside with the staff. The impact echoed throughout the cloister gardens. He parried three more blows in quick succession as the reivers found fresh reserves of strength, and then broke away from the fight, retreating three steps and planting the staff once more in the ground between his feet.

Grateful for the brief respite, the warriors did not close the gap between them immediately. The taller of the two turned, seeing the armoured knight racing towards him, and for a moment was torn between fight and flight.

The fire effectively damned him, but that didn't stop him calling out, "This isn't your fight, laddy. Don't make me kill you."

The knight let out a short bark of a laugh. "I'm not the one who's going to die here, northerner. Throw down your sword and I might be merciful."

"Hadaway with yerself before I lose my patience and decide to feed yer your own bollocks for supper."

"You talk too much," Lowick said. "If you thought you could win this fight you'd shut up and fight me. You're trying to buy yourself a few seconds. Well, I will give them to you, as I am a just man. Mark my words for they are the last you shall hear.

There are no second chances in my world. You killed people under my protection, good people. Innocent people. Women and children. That crime is upon your head, and for that crime I shall make your death every bit as ugly as your crime. You shall crawl to your heaven a ruined spirit. I shall cut your hands off, and your feet, and your manhood. But I am merciful; I shall take your head first to save myself from your screams. That is my judgement. Are you ready to die?"

Alymere saw something in his uncle's expression that he had never seen before, and in it, recognized all of the things Baptiste had claimed.

"Come and die then, you bastard," the reiver spat. He brought his claymore up to defend himself, but, exhausted as he was, he was no match for the skill of the knight.

He blocked Sir Lowick's first few blows, the sound of steel ringing out. The Scot rolled with the knight's ferocious swings, but each successive blow weakened his arms, and needing both hands to wield the cumbersome sword, it became harder and harder to defend himself.

Sir Lowick was brutal, ruthless and efficient. The broadsword in his hand became an extension of his body.

It lasted less than a minute.

The knight's thrust slipped inside the big warrior's guard, driving deep into his shoulder. The reiver wore furs in place of mail, but all the fur in the world couldn't have protected him from the knight's next blow. He twisted the hilt before pulling the blade free, opening the wound wide, then spun on his heel and, with all of his weight behind the blow, swept the broadsword through a savage arc that only ended when the edge of the blade embedded itself in the bones of the dead man's neck.

There was so much blood.

Alymere had seen men die, but not like this.

The raider's head fell against his chest, nothing supporting it, while blood gushed out of the gaping wound. For a few seconds it looked as though the dead man intended to go on fighting, and then he stumbled and went down.

The knight's sword was the only thing preventing him from collapsing at his feet. Sir Lowick planted his foot on his foe's chest and freed his sword, turning to face his next victim.

"If you have any hopes of seeing the sunrise you'll throw down your weapon," the knight said. He could have been talking to his own mother, so lightly did he speak.

Alymere crossed himself. The monk merely watched from under his cowl.

"I'm not as easy to kill as Douglas," the Scot hawked and spat onto the dirt at his feet. "So let's have at you."

Sir Lowick shrugged, equally happy to dispense justice twice as once.

They came together in a clash of swords.

The reiver had not lied – he was considerably more accomplished with his own weapon, and stronger despite his smaller build. His arms were powerful, each forearm as thick as a ham hock and his thighs like tree trunks. He planted his feet in the dirt and met the knight's charge head on.

Swords clashed, but otherwise the cloister was eerily silent.

The knight rained down three savage blows in quick succession, arcing the blade down from above, and looking to cleave the reiver's skull in two. The attack left him wide open, but the warrior was too busy protecting himself to exploit it.

Gasping, they broke apart again.

The heat from the burning buildings had sweat glistening on the knight's brow. Rivulets of perspiration ran down to sting his eyes. He blinked them back without once taking his eye off the reiver.

Now they circled each other warily, respectfully. The pair were evenly matched. Four more times they came together, trading blows without working an opening. Neither one pushed the other onto the back foot for more than a couple of blows before they parted again, breathing harder each time.

Alymere stood rooted to the spot. He might as well have been another one of the garden's dead trees. He couldn't look away from the two men as they danced. That was what it looked like to him; every movement carefully orchestrated, every feint and parry, every leap, thrust and counter.

Finally the Scot launched himself, hoping to overcome the knight with sheer strength. Their weapons came together, the momentum of the northerner's swing driving Lowick back a step before his heel dug in. He gritted his teeth as, instead of breaking away, the reiver pressed on with the blow. It took every ounce of strength the knight had to keep the claymore's razor-sharp edge from his throat.

There was neither nobility nor honour in what happened next.

The knight's arm trembled violently with the strain of holding his opponent's sword at bay. The pair remained locked like that for what seemed like forever, and then Lowick's sword arm appeared to buckle, suddenly offering no resistance.

The northerner lost his balance and pitched forward.

As he stumbled Sir Lowick abandoned all pretence of fighting fair and drove his forehead into the middle of the Scot's face.

The sound of cracking bone was sickening. Blood exploded from the reiver's broken nose, spraying both men.

He staggered back, shaking his head and trying to wipe the blood from his eyes, but the effort was pointless. Lowick's blade plunged deep into his gut, opening him up. The shock barely had time to register on the dying man's face.

"You'd do this..." he looked down at the sword still buried in his stomach and at his guts unravelling around it, "for that demon?" The reiver spat blood.

"No," the knight rammed the sword deeper, the bloody tip pushing out through the man's back. "I'm doing it for every man, woman and child you murdered on your way here."

He pulled his sword clear, but not cleanly, slicing through the man's belly as he withdrew. The northerner slumped to his knees, dropped his own blade and clutched at his stomach, as though trying to feed his guts back into the hole in his body. Sir Lowick's face was impassive. "I wouldn't bother," he said, again in that frighteningly casual tone. He wiped his sword on the fallen man's clothes contemptuously and sheathed it. "I've seen plenty of wounds like that before. There's nothing that can be done.

You're a dead man. It won't be a quick or clean death. It will take an hour, two at the very most. You can feel it, can't you? You can feel death stealing into your bones already and making itself comfortable. Nothing can save you. But your passage from this life into the next could be eased, if you were to beg for mercy."

The reiver looked his death in the eye, and rasped bitterly, "I am Cullum McDougal of the clan McDougal. I will not beg any man, never mind a *sasunnach* whoreson." He winced, biting back a fresh wave of pain. The blood leaked out between his fingers. His face was already deathly pale and the colour had begun to leave his eyes.

"Oh, I think you will. I think you'll beg for me to kill you soon enough," the knight taunted. "The pain isn't going to lessen."

"You want me to absolve your guilt?"

"Not particularly. I'd much rather you suffered for all the suffering you have caused my people. If you die, your pain dies with you. Where's the satisfaction in that?"

"Kill me and be done with it."

"No."

He turned his back on the dying man.

Alymere could not believe it.

The injustice of it stuck in his craw. How could his uncle allow this vile man to breathe even one more breath? He saw again what these men had done, the misshapen corpse of the burned child lying in the snow, and remembered with horror the mother dying in his arms. Something inside him snapped.

Alymere moved without thinking.

His first step, he almost stumbled, but by his tenth he was running flat out. He held his sword out in front of him and, shrieking, drove the blade through the man's back. He wrenched the blade free only to plunge it in again and again, and then froze, soaked in blood, staring down at what he had done.

Then he began to shake.

He could not stop.

TWENTY

Alymere dropped his sword.

Sir Lowick looked at him, aghast. For all his coldness, he was a pure man. He held to the tenets of the knighthood. He had sworn an oath of chivalry. An unknighted boy acting in anger, taking the life of an unarmed man – a defenceless man – from behind like that was tantamount to cowardice. "God have mercy... What have you done?"

Alymere didn't have the words, so offered his bloody hands in answer. He couldn't think. Nothing inside him made anything approaching sense. The spark of hatred had gone. In its place there was nothing – a void where hate had, so briefly, burned so brightly. Now he was empty. He strove to find the words to explain what had just happened to him, why he had just run the Scot through, but all he could think was: *he deserved to die.*

The knight ignored his young ward and turned to the monk, pulling his gauntlets off slowly. His expression was grim as he said, "This stays between us."

He expected some sort of objection from the pious man, but the monk merely cocked his head slightly, listening all the more intently to his voice. Lowick saw that his knuckles whitened around the quarterstaff. The knight was an astute reader of men and their intentions. It came with the territory. The monk was tensed to defend himself, not to attack.

And for a moment, as the pair faced each other, Sir Lowick

could have sworn he squared up to a demon across the cloister garden. At least that was how it seemed to him as he gazed upon the monk's disfigured face, back-lit by hellish flames.

The man was battered and bruised and bloody, but none of those newer injuries accounted for his demonic aspect. No. These wounds were much older, and deeper.

He had no eyes.

They had been gouged out, and not recently.

The maiming was almost as old as the man; certainly he had borne the scars since childhood. They were white and thick, crosshatched like veins of bone. The skin of the monk's eyelids had been stretched taut and stitched together crudely to seal the hollows.

The knight could not look away.

He couldn't understand how, being blind, the monk could possibly have held the northerners at bay. It was miracle enough that a man armed only with a stick could beat back the bloodthirsty raiders for more than a few minutes, never mind hours, but that the man was blind was impossible to fathom.

He took a single step toward the monk, who spun on his heel and brought the quarterstaff to bear in one fluid movement.

"Peace," Sir Lowick cried, instinctively holding out his hands to show he meant no harm. "We are friends."

Despite his blindness, there was nothing ungainly about the man. He rocked back on his heels again, turning the wooden staff over quickly in his hands until the movement became a blur, and finally rolling it over his wrist and planting it back in the dirt at his feet. "Speak, then. Let the Good Lord judge the honesty of your words. If you are deemed a liar, you do not leave this place."

The knight looked around him. A dozen fires and more had broken out all across the cloister garden and the surrounding buildings. The chances of any of them walking away from the inferno were slim and growing slimmer by the moment as more of the monastery became food for the fire.

"I am Sir Lowick, Knight of the Round Table, sworn protector of these lands, and this is my ward, Alymere, son of Roth. You may have known his father, my brother."

"The old lord was known to us," the monk said. And that was all he said. He seemed undisturbed by the fire raging through his home, or the dead men at his feet. He turned, as though to look up at the window where Lowick saw one of his brother monks gazing out over the cloister garden despite the fire behind him. Of course, there was no way the blind monk could have seen his brother up there. It was impossible. And yet the knight had to wonder if they could not somehow feel each other, because he was left with the distinct impression that something passed silently between the two men.

But how could it be?

He had heard curious things about God blessing men, robbed of one sense, with extraordinary gifts where the others were concerned, but had always considered them stories to appease the maimed. He could understand men becoming more aware of their environment, perhaps hearing the chirp of the lark and appreciating its beauty come dawn instead of cursing their lost sleep. But that was different. And that couldn't explain the monks passing silent messages between themselves. One was rational, the other anything but.

"You must leave this place, Lowick of the Round Table. Leave now, while you still can."

Lowick felt it then; all of the sadness and suffering Medcaut had seen, all of the painful memories trapped within its stones. It was overwhelming. Such suffering. Such bittersweet sorrow, bursting to be free. To be remembered. He felt the tears come to his eyes, then run down his cheeks unchecked. He didn't know how, and he had still less idea why, but he was sure that the monks had chosen to reveal the secrets of this place to him. He was sure of it in a way that he had never been sure of anything in his life. That was the meaning of the look the blind men shared; they had chosen him to experience the truth of Medcaut. And again, he didn't know how he knew – could it truly be from the stones themselves? What witchcraft were these blind men working between them? – but he was sure that the second monk bore the same ritual blinding as the first. Lowick took a step toward the fire, and then another, needing its heat to break the hold the tortured memories had on him.

He stared at the flames rising higher. Higher.

He heard voices in the flames.

The longer he stared at them the more insistent the voices became, but they were speaking in tongues he had never heard. Tongues, he felt sure, no mortal mouth had ever uttered.

"The Devil abides here, still," Lowick gasped, suddenly understanding the Scot's cryptic warning. It was too late for it to make a blind bit of difference. The knight made the sign of the cross over his chest. It would take more than faith to ward off the evils resident in this place. He licked his parched lips with an even drier tongue and wiped the sweat from his brow with the back of his hand.

With the buildings around the cloister garden ablaze, it was hard to imagine anything holy about the world right then. The fire was unquenchable. After all, fire and flame were the hallmarks of demons and the damned, not angels and the righteous.

Fear had taken root in his gut.

Strangeness gathered all around him.

There was more at work here than his understanding of the world allowed for.

Something darted across his line of sight, skimming the very tops of the flames. It took him a moment to realise it was a crow – a huge crow, more than twice the wingspan of a natural bird. It didn't settle, but flew from left to right, dangerously close to the fire as it skirted the perimeter wall. The bird banked and completed the circle again, and a third time whilst the knight just stared at it. As he watched, time seemed to stretch, sliding away from him until it came to a stop, and then as the crow broke from the third circle and climbed high into the sky, it came snapping back into place and everything began to move too quickly.

Everything changed then.

Sir Lowick felt the overwhelming need to fill the silence between himself and the monk, to bark orders and take charge of the situation, to banish the lethargy that had settled over him in the last few minutes.

He turned to face the monk.

"Two men could not be responsible for this."

"You are right, Sir Knight. Two men did not do this."

"Then where are the others?"

The blind man inclined his head once more, as though listening to the wind and fires. "They sought to flee," he said after a moment. "You will find them on the other side of the island, down by the water bailing out their coracle. If we are done, I would tend to the animals." It was as though the man had no concept of the conflagration raging all around him, nor the danger he was in. It had burned well beyond containment. In a few hours, Medcaut would be reduced to a shell. And in a few years that shell would weather and crumble and there would be no trace of the brotherhood or their monastery on the holy island. That was the way of the world; it purged the past.

But some horrors could not simply be washed away.

Would the memories of the stones always haunt this promontory?

Perhaps.

Lowick shook his head. "No. No. You must leave this place. It is not safe here. Follow the causeway to the mainland. I will find your brothers. How many reside here?"

"We are few in number."

"That is not an answer, monk. Tell me how many of your brotherhood reside here?"

"We number thirteen. Though I fear some of my brothers have fallen."

"If they live, we will find them. You have my word."

"And if they don't, will you bury them?"

The knight bit back on an angry retort. There was nothing to be gained from fighting with the monk, only time to be lost. "We have to get you out of here," Lowick said, hawking and spitting a wad of phlegm into the dirt between them.

"I cannot leave this place."

"It isn't up for debate, monk. You must."

"You do not understand. I *cannot* leave this place."

TWENTY-ONE

ALYMERE FOUND CONTROL of his limbs returning slowly, but his senses still reeled.

He had killed a man.

He moved away from his sword. Just a couple of paces, but enough for a shadow of something, doubt, hesitation, to creep in. It wasn't grief or remorse. It wasn't any feeling he understood.

He caught himself staring at the weapon, though at that precise moment it looked less like a sword and more like some bizarre two-headed monster – one head murderous and vile, covered in blood, and the other bright beautiful and innocent, trapped by the nature of its twin – lying there in the melt.

His breathing came fast and shallow.

He had just killed a man.

It wasn't the sword that had committed murder. *He* was the monster. *He* was the one who had driven it into the man's back, ending his life.

There was no dichotomy. He was the murderous head, his hands were covered in blood, and the sword was trapped by his nature.

And even as he came to that realisation, he knew that he would kill with it again. It was inevitable.

Perhaps he really was a monster?

No. He had a purpose. Guilt would come, and grief and remorse and all of those human weaknesses, but whilst there were deaths that still demanded an accounting he would remain cold.

He stooped to retrieve the blade.

It felt lifeless in his hands, though why should he have expected anything else? It was not as if the weapon were sentient and blood-thirsty. It was cold steel, nothing more. It did not crave blood, nor demand that he feed it.

There was one thing that he yearned to do, he realised, and that was return to that glade in the Summervale and lie side by side with Blodyweth once more.

He looked up at the blood-red sky, then back at the high windows across the cloister garden and the flames reflected there. The shadowy figure was gone, moved away from the window – and there was no way of knowing if the monk were still alive. Given the fires raging inside the old building it was almost certain that he was not, but that did not change the nature of Alymere's first rational thought since killing the unarmed man: atonement.

He had consigned one soul to the flames, it was only right that he drag one from them. A life for a life.

He started to walk toward the chapter house, his gaze locked on the empty window. The fire had reached the gables and seemed to have found its way through cracks in the masonry. The flames reached higher. There was no end to them.

His walk became a run.

The heat was furious. Thirty feet from the chapter house door it was intense enough to burn his face. Twenty feet away it was so fierce it could have cooked the meat on his bones, given time. Ten feet away the pain was beyond feeling. And still he found the will to go closer and climb the four low stone stairs to the huge oak doors.

The sacristy, the chancel, the infirmary, and the night stair, all of them burned. His entire world writhed beneath the agony of fire. Everywhere he looked, as far and as high as the eye could see, there was fire.

Without knowing the layout of the chapter house, there was no realistic chance of him finding the man from the window. Not with all of the smoke and the flames raging. He'd be effectively blind and deaf in there, and unlike the burning hovel, he wouldn't be able to smash his way through a wattle wall if he got into trouble. He needed to think. Were their roles reversed, where would he take refuge from the fire? He dismissed a dozen possibilities in as many seconds. Of all the answers that presented themselves, only one seemed reasonable; he would make for the roof in the hope of escaping the flames. He could only hope that the monk's mind would work the same way.

He knew he had to find the staircase.

Anything beyond that was in the hands of God.

His uncle did not see him mount the chapter house stairs. Lowick was locked in an argument with the blind monk – the words came back to him unbidden, *find the blind monk whose skin is impervious to blades and steal the Devil's book from his hands.*

Alymere turned on the threshold, half in and half out of Hell, to look back at the monk.

The man stood between Alymere and Lowick, with his back to him. His tonsure reflected the flames, but contrary to the Crow Maiden's prediction the only thing he had in his hands was that wicked-looking quarterstaff.

He turned, as though sensing Alymere's scrutiny.

If the monk didn't have the book on his person – and why would he? – it had to be inside the chapter house; but whether it was hidden away in the scriptorium or in the privacy of his cell, depended entirely upon whether it was something the brotherhood were charged with protecting as a whole, or if the task fell to one man.

The scriptorium was the logical place to start looking for a book. Where better to hide one than amidst a multitude of others?

He forced himself to walk up those last three steps to the huge oaken double doors.

They were closed.

Alymere reached for the metal handle, but stopped himself barely inches short, realising the black iron bands would sear the meat from his hands if he grasped them. Instead, he used the tip of the bloody sword to work the latch, and kicked the door in with the flat of his boot.

An incredible wave of heat threw Alymere back down the stone steps onto the wet mud at the bottom. The coastal winds battered the island, fanning the flames.

He sank to his knees and dropped his head, letting the heat wash over him in waves.

Deep inside the building something crackled and roared.

Instinctively, Alymere threw himself to the side, scrambling in the mud in his haste to get away from the door.

He slipped, sprawling flat on his face, which saved his life.

A moment later the backdraught of a huge fireball roared out through the open doorway. The tongue of flame writhed and roiled, rolling in on itself even as it lashed out across the cloister garden. And then, as it was sucked back inside the vast old building, the fireball set about consuming itself.

The monk didn't flinch as the flames coiled around him in what ought to have been a lethal embrace. They retreated, leaving him untouched.

Sir Lowick, on the other hand, scuttled back gracelessly to avoid them, and landed flat on his backside for his troubles. As the fire receded he scrambled back to his feet.

Alymere crawled toward the doorway. He moved cautiously, fearful that at any second another huge fireball could burst from the stone arch. There were no sounds beyond the fire now; no ominous crackles or pops deep in the belly of the old building. Whatever had caused the fireball had burned itself out in that one powerful explosion.

Licking his lips, he pushed himself to his feet and walked cautiously toward the open door.

The heat was every bit as fierce as it had been, but as he climbed the steps again his body became inured to it. He refused to be cowed by it, no matter how painful each successive step was to take.

This was his atonement. This moment. Here. Now. He had committed murder, now he would perform a single act of salvation.

That the Devil's book lay inside the burning building – the

relic the Crow Maiden had claimed so dangerous to the entire kingdom, to Arthur, to Camelot, and to everything he loved along with them – was about to be lost to the fire ought to have offered some sort of blessed relief, but he couldn't help but think if there was one element any possession of the Devil ought to be immune to, surely it was fire?

Meaning it would survive the inferno.

The threat would not simply burn away.

He was not thinking rationally, he knew that. He knew that it was impossible for parchment and leather binding to survive contact with fire, no matter what otherworldly properties were ascribed to it. A book was a book.

But that wouldn't stop the doubt from gnawing at his gut.

What if the book could somehow survive and they left it alone in the ashes of the monastery for anyone to find? What if it were being taken by the reivers at this very moment?

Could he live with the risk?

Unless the monk clutched the book in his hands he was going to have to.

Save the man or save the book?

There was only one answer: retrieving the book had become a compunction he could not resist.

Do not fail me, or the Devil take your soul...

Hell's fire waited for him to take a single step forward into its infernal belly.

Just one step.

He turned, caught in a moment of indecision.

Do this one thing for me... Promise me...

Nothing good could come of setting foot within the burning building. It was not so much a fool's errand as it was a suicide pact he had unwittingly made with Blodyweth. And yet... and yet... he was helpless to do anything but walk through the doorway and into the flames.

Steeling himself, Alymere cast one last lingering look back toward his uncle.

The knight was on his feet again, but too far away to stop him from doing what he was about to do. He saw the horror register in his uncle's eyes as he realised his intentions, and that, this once, he couldn't save him from himself. Sir Lowick took a step forward and began to call out, one word, "No!" demanding he stop, demanding he drop the sword, demanding he climb down from the steps, but Alymere was deaf to him. From somewhere deep within the building, he heard an entirely different cry: a man was screaming.

He couldn't ignore it. He turned his back on the knight.

Clutching the sword and thinking only of atonement, Alymere focused on the voice and plunged into the burning building.

Perhaps, if he ever emerged from it again he would be able to live with himself. Perhaps the fire would cleanse his soul?

But more likely it would blacken his bones.

TWENTY-TWO

THERE WAS NO air.

He was prepared this time – to an extent at least. The fire was different. It formed a tunnel around him, having spread up to and across the stone ceiling. Unlike the wattle hovel it wasn't eating through the thick stone walls, but was contained by them, transforming the passageways into tunnels of fire. He moved deeper into the building. Everywhere he looked the fire had taken hold; the same corridors of fire branched out left to the refectory and right to the chapel, whilst straight ahead of him, and continuing deeper into the warren of narrow corridors and monastic cells, another tunnel of fire formed a burning cross. He stood at the centre of the cross. Fire chased up the walls around him. The scriptorium would be down one of those flaming passages. *And the Devil's Bible...* he could almost hear Blodyweth's voice urging him to walk into the fire. It was so seductive, so tempting. He felt himself wanting to please the woman even though she wasn't there.

He turned and turned about, but there was no sight of the staircase. His world was reduced to fire and smoke.

The fire burned at its purest here, but somehow didn't touch him.

Alymere tried to recall the exterior of the chapter house and guess where he would find the stair, but with the flames pressing in it was almost impossible to think.

The screaming came again. It didn't sound any closer than it had from outside.

The man's screams were the purest sound of human suffering he had ever heard.

He made his choice then. He had to find the man and save him. A single life had to be worth more than any book – no matter how holy or unholy – didn't it?

Alymere followed the screams.

The walls might have been thick enough to withstand the heat, but the monastic trappings of the chapter house were not so resilient. The fire claimed the oak furniture and the tapestries, the tall dressers and the chests, the high-backed chairs and the long tables of the refectory, the benches of the chapel and even the lectern beside the altar itself. All of them fed the fire. Anything that could burn was burning.

Alymere found the screaming man at the foot of a great winding staircase.

It was not one of the brothers, though, but a reiver. It was too late to save him, even if he had wanted to. The northerner's body was broken from the fall. His limbs sprawled out at impossible angles from him. His screams had nothing to do with his terrible injuries, but from the fire that had found him. His furs burned, fusing to his skin, and the leather of his boots and sword sheath bubbled and shrivelled, tearing the meat away from the bone as it did. It was an ugly death, but the man deserved no better.

Alymere could not get close to the body, and at length the screaming stopped.

At the top of the staircase Alymere saw the shadow-man watching him impassively, utterly unconcerned by the fire around him. The shadows cast by the flames danced in the sunken hollows where his eyes should have been. Had every brother in Medcaut put out his own eyes? Was the mutilation part of their benediction? How could being blind serve to bring them closer to God? Or was their blindness some form of protection? Were they blinding themselves to the sins of the flesh and the evils of their world?

Alymere's reflection was cut short when he saw that the blind monk clutched a small book in his hands.

He couldn't help but feel a pang of disappointment at the

mundanity of the so-called Devil's Bible. It looked like no more than a prayer book. But that was the nature of evil, wasn't it; to wear the face of something normal, something banal and harmless, to mask its true intent?

"I have been expecting you," the monk said over the sound of the flames.

Behind the monk's shoulder, the huge window succumbed finally to the heat and shattered, showering shards of glass out across the cloister garden below.

"Give me the book," Alymere said, climbing the first step.

"You are making a grave mistake, knight."

"I don't think so," Alymere said, reaching the fifth step. "In fact I've never felt so sure of anything in my life."

The words came almost like an incantation; there was a hypnotic rhythm to them. "That is the book, not you. Leave this place. Run. Run and don't ever look back. Forget you ever heard mention of the Devil's Bible. Do not let it get inside your head. It is not too late. Run."

"Give me the book," Alymere repeated. "I have no desire to hurt you."

"But you will," the monk said with certainty.

"It doesn't have to be this way. Leave here with me."

"I cannot leave here."

"You cannot stay. Come dawn there will be nothing left of the monastery."

"And yet we shall abide. It is you that must leave. Believe me."

Alymere reached the tenth step. There were only three between them now.

Close to, the mutilation to the monk's face was even more severe than that of his brother outside. The scars had that same hard-white quality of age, but these were not restricted to his eyes. They spread all across his face, carving out his cheeks and opening his nose so his nostrils appeared to be nothing more than ragged holes in the centre of his face. The scars continued down his neck before disappearing beneath the collar of his habit. He saw them emerge again from the cuffs and continue from his wrists across the back of his hands and again from the hem of his skirts, criss-crossing his ankles and every inch of flesh not covered by his sandals.

Alymere was in no doubt that the man bore the savage scars all over his body.

The blind monk whose skin is impervious to blades...

"I will only ask one more time, monk. Give me the book."

"And so it comes to this. Kill me if you will, knight. I shall not surrender the Devil's book to you willingly."

"I have no intention of killing you," Alymere said, the lie catching in his throat. The thought had occurred to him five steps below. If the monk would not surrender the bible willingly, how else could he uphold his promise to Blodyweth? He was horrified by the thought that the monk, even without eyes, could read his intentions so clearly.

"Let's pretend that is true, shall we? You can use the last few steps to make peace with yourself before you strike me down," the monk said.

"Silence," Alymere barked. His fist clenched around the hilt of his sword. It felt heavy in his hand. How heavy was human life? The weight of the blade that claimed it? The weight of the corpse it left behind? Or the weight of all of those lives it could never touch again, combined?

"The truth is barbed, is it not? My murder weighs heavy on you already, does it not?"

"I said silence!"

"So that you may cut me down without my words pricking your conscience? No," the monk said, tilting his head slightly as though listening to the voices of the fire. "You are already too far gone for that, aren't you? The book already owns you."

"No-one owns me. I am a free man!" Alymere's denial was fierce but his words sounded hollow in his own ears.

There were forces at play here that he could not understand. He was merely a play-thing to them. He shook his head, trying to clear the fog that shrouded his thoughts.

"Have you not wondered why the flames do not touch you?"

Alymere's only answer was to lash out with his sword.

TWENTY-THREE

THE WALL OF heat was impenetrable.

Sir Lowick couldn't follow his young charge into the chapter house.

"He is lost to you," the monk said, as Lowick threw himself once more at the flames.

"I refuse to believe that," he spat stubbornly.

"Why, when it is the truth?"

"It isn't the truth. It is just words."

"And like words, it is written. The tragedies of this day have long been known to us."

"You expect me to swallow that? What sorcery is this? Futures written? Do you huddle over a scrying mirror, or perhaps read the entrails of sacrificial lambs? You are supposed to be pious men. Christian men!" the knight spat.

"There is no sorcery here. We are merely entering the final act of an-age old ballad. We knew this day would come. We did not know when. Likewise we did not know who would deliver our damnation. We thought, perhaps, it would be the reivers when they came, but their part was merely to lead death here, not to deliver it."

"There will be no more dying here today," the knight said.

"It would be nice were that true, but there is yet dying to be done. Breathe in the air, smell it. It is heavy with violence to come. It reeks of it, especially around you. But then, you still have a part to play in the killing."

"Do I now?" The knight said sceptically. "And I am to believe you knew we were coming and that this is all some ancient prophecy unfolding, or some such folly? I will kill because the stars are in alignment, perhaps? Or did some soothsayer predict the sharpness of my blade and foulness of my mood?"

"Who is to say that you will be the one doing the killing?" The monk offered. His expression was unreadable.

The knight shuddered.

Above them, the streaked glass in the huge window shattered. Dagger-sharp shards of glass rained down.

"You cannot help him," the monk said, as though reading his mind. "Your future lies down a different path," he pointed toward an archway between the granary and the kitchens. "Follow the path to the misericord, and on through the rose garden to the infirmary. Behind it you will find a door in the sea wall, and through it a narrow stair that leads down to the wharf. Death waits on you there."

TWENTY-FOUR

THE MONK THREW up his hands to protect himself as the edge of Alymere's sword bit deep, slicing clean through his cassock.

The impact caught Alymere unprepared; part of him had truly expected the blind man to possess some sort of mystical aura that would turn aside his blow. It didn't. The sword drew blood, cutting deep into the soft meat of the monk's forearm.

He screamed, but the sound was lost in the insanity of the encroaching flames.

Alymere swung again. He'd lost all reason. The Devil was in him.

Again and again, raging.

And each blow bit, opening another deep cut.

The blood ran freely down his forearms as the gashes widened.

"Don't do this," the monk pleaded, the agony of each fresh cut echoed in his voice. "Please."

But in the fury-haze, Alymere didn't hear him. Instead he heard the Crow Maiden urging him not to fail her, and with each breath of smoke he inhaled her heady musk, taking it into his lungs and letting it fill him.

The entire chapter house was creaking now, the stones groaning and grinding as the fire worked away at the mortar binding them. It was a dead house, filled with twisted and smoking detritus.

He launched more brutal swings, each wilder than the last. There was no grace to the attack, and any half-adequate swordsman would have taken Alymere apart. But the monk made no move to defend himself. It was as though he was content to be cut down.

Alymere didn't see the thick white scar forming over the first cut, the second and the third. As quickly as he delivered a new wound two of the older ones began to heal, leaving more of those thick white veins across the surface of his body.

And through it all the monk clung onto the book as though it were the only thing keeping him alive.

The notion made a sudden, sick, sort of sense to Alymere.

How else could he be immune to the flames?

Alymere realised then that the only way he was walking out of this place alive was with the Devil's Bible in his hands to serve as his shield.

"Give me the book," Alymere demanded, seething and raging like a man possessed. There was a sickness in his soul. "Or I won't be responsible... just give me the damned book."

"This isn't you."

"I don't want to kill you. I came in here to save you."

"This isn't what you want."

Instead of trading more words, he pressed the advantage, four lightning-quick blows hacking away brutally at the man in front of him, all sense of self abandoning him, but the monk stubbornly refused to fall.

Alymere stepped in close, and rammed the blade into the monk's gut, forcing it in all the way to the hilt. "Give. Me. The. Book."

The monk stiffened, the skin around his empty eyes stretching as he straightened. His one free hand closed around Alymere's, both of them clutching the hilt of the sword, as a gasp escaped his clenched teeth. His lips parted and he sighed. It wasn't a gentle sigh. Alymere tasted the sour bile of death at the back of his throat. They stood, locked together, on the stone staircase as the fire rose around them. The intensity of it changed, the flames quickening. The speed with which it spread now was unnatural; as though whatever force had held it at bay was dying with the monk.

"The book!" Alymere yelled, his face twisting with fear. Suddenly he was the blind man. The fire moved quickly now, licks of it darting across the stone stairs trying to find his feet.

"I forgive you, knight," the monk managed, blood bubbling up through his lips. He slumped toward Alymere, causing his sword arm to take the sudden weight.

He could barely hold him. Every muscle in his body was spent. All he wanted to do was take the book and lie down and let the fire rage over him whilst he waited for it to burn itself out, safe in the arms of the Devil.

He shuddered then, repulsed by the notion.

Alymere staggered back a step, relinquishing his hold on the sword.

He looked down at the hilt protruding from the monk's stomach and said, "Oh God, what have I done?"

The monk had no answer for him. His legs gave out beneath him and he fell forward into Alymere's arms.

The fire coiled around the wooden balustrade, and leapt onto Alymere's cloak as he brushed against it. It only took a few seconds for it to spread from the woollen cloak to his hair and across to the man he held in his arms.

Together they burned.

Alymere made a desperate grab for the book, trying to wrest it from the monk's hands, but even down to his last few breaths the damned man refused to give it up.

The fire reached Alymere's face.

Its caress, more intimate than even the most demented lover, was pure agony. The flames spread like tender fingers across his cheek, but in their wake came only intense burning pain.

Shrieking, a terrible banshee wail of a cry, Alymere threw himself at the monk. His momentum drove the dying man back, the pair of them still inextricably locked together in their fiery embrace, toward the broken window – and then kicking and screaming through it.

TWENTY-FIVE

Sir Lowick found the door and the hidden stairs. He had to stoop to walk through them, as though entering some secret garden. Immediately on the other side of the door the sea breeze turned blustery, picking at and buffeting him as he negotiated the narrow steps. Hand-carved into the volcanic rock, the steps were rough and irregular despite the constant battering of the elements and shuffle of cautious feet as the monks made the daily journey down to the water. He picked his way down the cramped steps on his heels, and the further he descended, the slicker they became with sea spray, and the more treacherous.

A blood-curdling scream tore at the night behind him.

Lowick froze, half-turning, prepared to run back the way he had come, and almost lost his footing on the wet stair. He reached out for the wall to brace himself. He was more than fifty feet beneath the wall, still another hundred or more down to the water. He steadied himself, and then looked back the way he had come.

All he could see were the crenellations of the wall, the top of the bell tower and the thick black smoke rising around it.

There was nothing he could do back there, and the blind monk's words gnawed away at him. His path took him to the wharf – where death awaited him. Try as he might he couldn't shake a sense of creeping dread, and that dread was a killer every bit as ruthless as any reiver's sword. But Sir Lowick had no intention of dying today, nor any other day. Like most men of the sword, he was arrogant enough to suppose he might just live forever, if the Lord willed it.

Looking down at the churning whitecaps and the four brutish men wrestling with a pair of coracles, the knight believed for the first time that there was a chance he really might die on the pebble beach below.

Instinctively, he made the sign of the cross to ward off ill-fate and cursed the monk.

"This is not how I die," he said to the seagulls and the wind and the world and whoever else, deity or devil, might be listening. "Do you hear me? This is not how I die!"

The tremors in his sword arm belied his words. At this rate, if he couldn't rein the dread in, by the time he reached the bottom step his death would be a foregone conclusion.

Sir Lowick started down, moving faster than was safe on the treacherous stairs. He clutched his sword in his right hand while the fingertips of his left brushed against the damp rock of the cliff face. He saw the black crow – he was sure it was the same bird he had seen skimming the tops of the flames – perched on an outcropping above his head, watching him intently with its beady yellow eyes. The bird gave him the creeps. Every warrior had heard talk of the deathbirds; the carrion eaters who knew when death was imminent and came to shepherd souls toward the light of heaven.

The knight brayed a raucous caw of his own, startling the bird into flight.

It was the worst thing he could have done.

The bird erupted into the sky in a flurry of feathers and caws so loud the men below turned to see the knight as he came down the last few stairs.

They were there to meet him at the bottom, and the battle was joined.

The size of the northerners' two-handed blades kept them from fighting side-by-side. There just wasn't room for them to swing on the narrow pebbled strip of beach. The knight had no such problems, and coming off the steps his reach countered the length of their blades.

Breathing deeply of the salt air Lowick felt good about life. He felt alive.

"We have no fight with you," the Scot rasped in his thick brogue. Lowick could barely understand him. His eyes were wide and wild and his muscles were corded so tensely that his entire body quivered. "All we're after is getting off this cursed rock, and putting the damned sea between us and these demons. If you had half a mind, you'd do likewise."

"As far as I can see there are only four demons here, lads," he inclined his head at each in turn, "one – two – three – four. Repent and I might absolve your sins[7] before you move on to your next life. But know this," the knight said, gravely. "You will not leave this place alive. That much I promise you."

"So be it."

One of the reivers broke ranks, plunging into the sea and wading toward him, forcing Lowick to defend himself on two fronts. The northerner was hip-deep in the water, but the knight was forced to divide his concentration, which could prove fatal.

Lowick took the first wild overhead swing from the grim-faced raider on the flat of his broadsword. The entire sword shivered from *foible* to *forte*. The sheer ferocity of the blow had the Scot's blade slide along the length of his broadsword and slam into the cross-guard. The knight heaved his wrist around, disengaging. His heel butted up against the back of the step. He grunted, another eerily bestial sound. The warrior backed off, allowing the man in the sea to swing. His was a more controlled two-handed thrust; a manoeuvre his cumbersome sword was not best suited for, but that didn't make it any less lethal should the point find its mark in the knight's sweetmeats.

Lowick whipped his sword around barely in time, an almost dismissive flick of the wrist sending the thrust wide and very nearly wrenching the claymore out of the big northerner's meaty hands. It was only the man's brute strength that prevented the sword from ending up on the seabed.

---

[7] In Malory's Arthurian world, knights are holy people in their own right, and it is not unknown for them to perform spiritual duties.

The knight countered with a clubbing left hook square into his opponent's face. The man staggered back, rocked by the blow. The cartilage of his bulbous nose ruptured, spewing blood and mucus. He spat one of his front teeth out. The other sat crooked, giving him a gap-toothed cemetery smile as he came back for more. Blood dribbled down through the stubble on his chin.

Sir Lowick blocked two more savage thrusts as they came in from his flank. The big Scot had planted his feet as best he could, but the shifting stones and roiling sea betrayed him. His huge, broad shoulders didn't help him. Desperately trying to maintain his balance, the reiver only succeeded in announcing his intentions a moment before he could deliver the blow. The knight read him, turning both strokes aside.

The killing stroke itself seemed almost an after-thought, a left-over from the parry. Sir Lowick rolled his wrist with the momentum of the thrust, letting the raider's own strength lend itself to the blow that killed him. He locked his elbow and bought the broadsword up in a wicked arc that slashed down through the reiver's torso, opening a gaping wound from his throat to his balls before ending in the water in a bloody splash.

The northerner dropped his claymore and clutched at his throat, and the knight turned his back on him; any potential threat he represented was extinguished. In a moment or two he would sink to his knees and go under.

"Do you regret your crimes?" The knight asked the three men in front of him.

"The only thing I regret is setting foot on this damned island. If that is regret enough for you, then aye, I regret."

"And the families you destroyed on your way here? What of them? Do you not regret what you did to those poor people?"

"They were weak! Just like you. You want me to fall on my knees, weep and beg for mercy? Well you can kiss my hairy crack, laddy. Now come down here if yer in such a hurry t'die!"

The reiver stepped back, inviting Sir Lowick to come down onto the shifting pebbles, and brought his claymore up to kiss the flat of the blade.

The two other men fanned out across the stone beach to take up position beside him.

"It matters not to me where you die," Sir Lowick said, stepping onto the stones. "I can kill you just as well here."

"You talk a lot for a dead man."

"It's a curse," the knight said grimly, bringing his own blade to bear. "So, shall we dance, boys?"

They came at him, three at once, bellowing their hideous ululating war cry as they rushed across the unsteady ground at him.

Sir Lowick braced himself, regretting the lack of his shield, which he had left back with the horses in his haste. There was nothing he could do about it now. Gritting his teeth, he met the first blows head on.

The clash of steel was lost beneath the crash of the waves and the roar of the surf.

The knight's sword moved seemingly of its own accord, so perfectly attuned were the man's body and mind that nothing separated thought from action. Every breath he took was in perfect concert with the cut and thrust of the fight. It was a long, brutal, and bloody slaughter, but as he had promised them, the reivers did not leave the beach alive.

Spent, the sweat of survival thick on his skin, Sir Lowick raised his hands and bloody sword to the heavens and cried, "I'm still alive!"

TWENTY-SIX

ALYMERE FELL IN a ball of fire.

The agony was incredible. The right side of his face was burning, but it was nothing compared to the pain that came with hitting the ground. The only thing that saved his life was the monk taking the brunt of the fall, cushioning him from the impact.

He tried desperately to roll away from the dead man, but could not move. His body refused to obey him.

He stared into the monk's crudely stitched eye sockets. He couldn't feel the man's breath on his cheek.

Alymere tried to get his hands underneath himself and ease away from the monk but even that little victory was beyond him. His entire right side was wracked with convulsions. As his vision misted over, he was sure he had killed himself.

He felt someone stand over him, rather than saw them; felt them tear the cloak from his shoulders and slap at his head, dousing the flames. They dragged him off the monk and rolled him onto his back. The sky was fiery red. He tried to focus on the stars; to hold them in his mind, knowing somehow that to lose them, to let go, would be to die.

His skin felt too tight for his body. He tried to open his mouth, to breathe, to speak, but he couldn't work his jaw. The pain was blinding. The entire right side of his face felt like it had been dipped into Hell's pit and pulled out barely a fraction of a second before the flames scorched the meat from the bones of his skull.

It went beyond any concept of pain he had ever known, or even imagined, and into a whole new territory of suffering.

"Hush, now," the man said, though his words lacked any real substance. He felt his hands gentle over his wounds, and then, alarmingly, the pain subsided, as his body went into shock. "Rest easy, son. Don't try to move."

He couldn't even if he had wanted to.

Black veins threaded through the sky, thickening as they spread to slowly block out the stars.

He felt his grip on consciousness slipping.

He tried to call her name. For a moment, as all colour fled his world, he thought he felt the press of her lips on his, their souls mingling as she breathed life into him in that shared kiss, making him immortal. And then he tasted the rancid breath in the back of his throat and all fantasies of Blodyweth were banished.

He opened his eyes and saw the crudely stitched eye sockets of a blind monk just inches from his face.

At that moment, it was the most beautiful face he had ever seen.

TWENTY-SEVEN

Sir Lowick found the monk hunched over Alymere's body.

Seeing him lying there, lain out on the muddy grass all broken and ravaged by the fire, it seemed impossible that he could still be alive.

All the pride he felt at cheating death swept from his body in a wave of grief; the stupid fool of a boy had gotten himself killed.

He raced across the cloister garden to his side, the sorrow caught in his throat.

The blind man's fingers were in Alymere's mouth.

Was he trying to choke the last bit of life out of him?

The man seemed to be trying to pull the tongue out of his throat with his filthy fingers.

The knight roared, grasping the hilt of his broadsword with two hands and raising it high above his head as he charged across the muddy grass, ready to do murder.

And then he saw his chest heave.

And everything changed. He dropped his sword and sank to his knees beside his nephew. "What have you done to him?"

"The boy lives," the monk said, trying to calm the knight, "but whether it remains that way is in the hands of the Lord, Knight. His wounds are most grievous indeed. His skin was ablaze as he plunged from up there," he pointed up at the shattered window with unerring accuracy. For a moment it was impossible for Sir Lowick to comprehend the fact that the man was truly blind; he spoke with such certainty, yet all of his understanding came from sounds and smells and touch, not from what Lowick thought of as the most basic and trustworthy of all the senses, sight. "And but for my brother's body beneath him, the fall alone would surely have killed him. Yet, for all his fortune, without aid far beyond my limited skill I fear he will not live to see morning. Once, perhaps, we had the medicinal herbs here on Medcaut, and the physician's gift, but now, now our home is burnt barren. Who knows what is left in the herbarium worth scavenging? And I fear that after this night nothing will grow. As much as it saddens me to say so, there can be no healing for Alymere here." The knight could not recall having used the boy's name in front of the monk. That he seemed so familiar with it placed a chill in Lowick's heart. "You need to take him to the mainland."

Tenderly, he rolled his nephew away from the body beneath him and onto his side, seeing the raw pink flesh where the fire had burned away the features down the right side of his face. His cloak had burnt onto his neck. The knight teased the blackened wool away from the sores, whispering wordlessly over and over. He had no unguents or salves and no way of lessening the fire beneath Alymere's skin. All he could do was pray, and pray that words uttered in this holiest of places found their way to the Lord all the more quickly.

He saw the book clenched in Alymere's hands. Its leather binding was burned beyond recognition, but as far as he could tell the pages within were merely scorched along the edges. The skin from Alymere's palm had burned off on the front of the book, leaving a black and bloody handprint in the middle of the binding. He tried to ease it out of his nephew's hands, but Alymere's grip on the book was rigor-tight. And try though he might, Sir Lowick could not pry the damned book from his hands. He left it be, and instead cradled his nephew in his arms.

Until dawn it was as though the burning monastery, the blind monk, all of the dead men and the raging sea ceased to exist.

The world was reduced to the boy in his arms. Everything beyond that was gone.

Sir Lowick did not see the blind monk kneel over his fallen brother, nor hear the low mumble of his prayers, the rhythm of his words matching the ebb and flow of the tide, and so he missed the one true miracle that would ever occur in his presence, as the blind monk wrapped both of his hands around the hilt of Alymere's sword, drew the blade from his brother's chest, and cast it aside.

The dead man drew in a sudden sharp breath and shuddered back to agonizing life. The cackling of the fire masked his moans.

Neither did Sir Lowick see the wound in the hitherto dead man's stomach begin to heal as the skin puckered around thick scar tissue and drew together to form yet another long white gash in the mesh of old wounds that marred his abdomen.

Nor did Sir Lowick witness the dead man rise like Lazarus and walk away with his brother toward the shadow-figures that stood waiting at the monastery gates. Had he looked up he could have counted the silhouettes and realised that not a single monk had fallen to the raiders' claymores.

The Brothers of Medcaut left him alone with his grief, merging with fire and flame until only their shadows remained, and as the fires died down those too departed.

Come dawn the fires had burned themselves out completely, leaving only scorched earth and a few walls of the blackened shell that had been Medcaut's holy monastery intact. The stones still smouldered. Atop their highest point the black bird watched intently with yellow eyes. When finally content that Alymere would live, it took flight, banking in the clear blue morning and flying back toward the mainland and the forest that was its home.

Their horses had long since gone, driven away by the raging fire. No doubt they had bolted as soon as the tide allowed.

The knight gathered Alymere into his arms and walked the miles back along the causeway to the mainland. Grief cut through the soot on his cheeks and the tears flowed freely. His nephew was near weightless in his arms; like a scarecrow, he was no burden at all.

The tide lapped around his ankles as he walked, his gaze fixed on the horizon.

He never stopped praying, beseeching the Lord to show mercy, to save his flesh and blood, and making promise after promise of what he would do in return for a moment's grace, as though he were in a position to bargain with the Almighty.

Twice more he saw the crow in the periphery of his vision, shadowing him as he walked toward the stretch of beach and the dunes and thick maram grass beyond them, but every time he tried to watch it for more than a few moments the bird banked sharply and flew away. He would never have seen it save that it was the only bird in the sky.

TWENTY-EIGHT

THE HEALING PROCESS was arduously slow; days bled into weeks, weeks crawled into months, the seasons turning, before Alymere could bear the agony of standing on his own two feet, and even then his uncle kept looking glasses out of his reach for fear of what they would reveal. The knight did not want him to have to bear the ruination of his once handsome features. And with good reason; the fire had remade the shape of Alymere's face. It had recast him as a monstrous thing. The entire right side of his head, from the burned stubble of roots at his hairline down to the lumpish deformity of his jawline, had melted into a single smooth plane of flesh. There was no ridge of cheekbone, no declivity of eye socket, and when he spoke – when he smiled, when he sobbed against the pain – no crease in the corner of his lips, no dimple in the middle of his cheek, no cleft in the middle of his chin. And his right eye, burned out, was a milky white orb in that featureless flesh.

The fire had robbed the young man of half of his being; even a simple smile was beyond him. It was as though his own flesh was telling him he was not permitted to smile, not in this house of death.

And that was what he thought it was: he imagined he could still see things through his ruined eye – shadow shapes, ghosts. And for a while, in the agony of the long dark nights, he would open his ruined eye, seeking the dead, for surely his dead eye could see dead souls? And for a while he believed he could hear them all around him, could hear their agonies in the draughts of the old manor house, but as he retreated further and further from the veil and returned to the land of the living, those voices became nothing more sinister than the creaks and sighs of the old walls. In other words, the ghosts of his fever became the foundation of his world when he awoke. They became real. Honest. Was it the Book doing this? Or merely his fever? He could not shake the feeling that the dead watched him. That they were drawn to him. And once a day, when he first closed his eyes, he would hear them all, every one of them, screaming. Those screams would last until his heart threatened to rupture, so fast was it beating, and it was all he could do to will his body not to burst into flames. And then they left him. The dead, it seemed, could only torment him once a day.

And through it all he refused to let the book, the Devil's Bible, out of his sight.

Strange things had begun to happen from the very moment his hand had come into contact with the curious leather binding, and they had only turned stranger once his palm print fused with it. Somehow, in that moment, the damned book had become a part of him, and in return he had become a part of it, though how that was possible he could not begin to say.

At first it had only been sounds, like the dead voices, but though these were obviously alive and full of concern and compassion, he could not recognise who was talking to him through the haze of pain.

In fact the only time the pain seemed to ebb was when his hand rested upon the book.

He tried to read it once, opening the cover and running his finger over the first few words there: *being an account of the entire wisdom of Man as transcribed by Harmon Reclusus*. He turned the page, but beyond that he could not read. The language of the verse, which appeared to be a prayer, was unknown to him. Baptiste had taught him his letters, and his uncle had schooled him in the language of the Church, but this curious curling script was unlike any he had ever seen. It seemed almost serpentine as it crawled across the page. Why should it be that the title, promising the entire sum of human knowledge, should be in one language while the rest of the book was in another? Alymere turned page after page, but each was as indecipherable as the last, until he came upon a painting toward the back of the book: a colourful cloven-hoofed devil playing pipes. There was something almost whimsical about the image. It was childish in its simplicity and not at all sinister, and yet, the closer he regarded it, the more precise he realised the ink strokes were and the more detailed the supposed simplicity. It was a work of art. A perverse, brilliant painting as well rendered as any he had ever seen. But it had no place being in there amid the monk's painstaking work. Alymere could not begin to imagine how many years it must have taken a single man to illuminate such a text, and he was in no doubt that it had been created by a single man, the monk Harmon, by hand: the shaping of the letters and the pressure of the quill upon the page was even across the hundreds of bound sheets. It was quite possibly the man's life's work.

He closed the book and set it down reverently upon the small table beside his cot, drawing the blanket up over his bare chest.

He could smell the sickness in the airless room.

His mind raced with thoughts he could barely follow through the delirium sweats.

Why was this book so precious to Blodyweth?

Why would the monk refuse to surrender it, to the point of it costing his life?

Why should the fate of kingdoms rest upon it when only the most learned could hope to read more than a single line of its supposed wisdom?

That posed another question: was it in fact a grimoire? Were those words he could not read in truth incantations scribed in the secret tongue of witchcraft?

As Alymere felt fresh beads of perspiration trickle down the too-smooth side of his face, he made a vow: if he had not learned its secrets before his two years and a day of servitude with Sir Lowick were at an end, he would bring the book with him to Camelot and present it to the king's mage, Merlin, along with the story of the maiden, the Summervale in the heart of the winter forest, the burning monastery and its blind guardians. If the book contained even a trace of magic, for good or ill, surely Merlin would know.

But until that day he would devote himself to learning its secrets. If nothing else, it would give him something to live for.

That night, in the depths of his fever dreams, he heard a haunting melody calling to him, and found himself dreaming of trees and the hunt, chasing a cloven-hoofed piper deeper and deeper into the darkness.

And whilst he tossed and turned in the grip of the dream, the black crow perched upon his windowsill, watching over him.

TWENTY-NINE

ALYMERE DRIFTED IN and out of consciousness. His dreams were the worst of it, for in them he wore the face of a monster. His imagination defined him. He ceased to be the young aspirant and became the beast; the cloven-hoofed piper with wild hair and mischievous eyes. He tossed and turned, fever-sweats soaking his outline into the mattress and sheets beneath him. Light played tricks on his mind. There was a single mullioned window in his sick room, and as the sun moved across the sky it conjured the shadowy bars of a gaol all around him.

He was in no doubt that he ought to have died. As it was, he was far from assured of surviving his injuries. The first few weeks were excruciating, but he welcomed the pain, as it proved he was still alive. These bed-bound days were his transformation, the raw pink scar tissue his cocoon. When this agonising gestation was over, when the fevers finally broke and the pain subsided, he would be born into a second life. And, in the madness of delirium, he swore it would be glorious. He welcomed that rebirth, knowing he would be stronger for it, more vital, for he had walked into the very pit of Hell and emerged bearing the Devil's scars, marked but not beaten.

Mildew grew in the corner of his room, masking the smell of his sickness.

His uncle visited daily, sometimes hourly, during the worst of it, but he was not Alymere's only visitor. The woman, Gwen, came to him often, mopping his brow with a wet rag as she tried to take the sting out of the fever. He did not recognise her at first, thinking her an angel. As she took on a more earthly form, plainer and yet more divine for the hard-won creases of life worn into her face, he found himself remembering fragments, splinters of the days leading up to the fire. He saw himself emerging from the burning hovel and his nurse taking the babe from his arms. She was no great beauty, neither was she some reckless girl. She was his saviour. And he tried to tell her so, but the words wouldn't come. His voice cracked, so easily betraying him that it was easier to stay silent.

And always, when she finished pressing the cold wet rag against his brow she brushed his hair away from his eyes and leant down to tenderly kiss the smooth skin between his left eyebrow and the denuded arch where his right had been.

He could not feel it.

That was the bitterest crime of his new body; it robbed him of even the simplest pleasures.

Still, he closed his eyes, as though savouring this one moment of compassion. He closed his eyes not through any rush of feelings, but rather through fear that he might see his own ruined face reflected back at him in her eyes.

And so it went on, day and night, with no sign of his fever breaking or his strength returning.

What came was hunger; deep, gnawing, stabbing, spearing hunger pains. He could not bear to eat, and what he took in he could not hold down. So every mouthful of food, every morsel Alymere tried to digest, caused his stomach to cramp and shooting pains to twist his gut until he vomited it back up. The woman tried broth, but it was no better. The strings of meat and lumps of potato were too much for him. So, in the depths of his delirium she fed him not food, but water. As he shivered and convulsed beneath the piss-stinking blankets, she dripped water from the rag she mopped his brow with onto his tongue, knowing that even a mouthful would send his body into rebellion. Just a few drops at a time, never enough to quench his thirst, but enough, she prayed, to keep him alive.

When he was alone he turned again to the book, clutching it to his bare chest so that his sweat might seep into the skin that bound it, finding another way to bring them closer together. He felt the ridge of its spine against his left side, resting on his ribs. He felt nothing on his right. As he breathed he felt his breaths echoed in the book, as though it breathed with him, augmenting his strength with its own.

But he could still not read more than that first line.

At the height of the sickness, when surely his body was too frail to make it through until dawn, Gwen slipped naked beneath the blanket and pressed up against him. He could not feel her there at first, pressed up against his burned side, but as she moved against him she sighed and he felt her breath on the unburned skin of his neck. She raised her leg over his so that they touched from hip to toe. "Is this what you want?" she whispered in his ear. He turned, moving in to her. She was so cold against his hideous heat. In the near-dark he saw for the first time that she had flecks of yellow in her eyes. It made it seem as though a fire burned within her, too.

He reached out to touch her with his right hand, but felt nothing as his palm rested on her cheek; the skin dead where it had been torn away and fused with the infernal book. The fever tormented his mind. Through his one good eye he saw not Gwen, with her well-worn face and her sad smile, but Blodyweth in all of her radiant beauty. He gave himself to her, welcoming her like death, sure in the knowledge that this night was to be his last and that all of his pains would end here, in this bed, in the arms of the maiden who haunted his dreams. If this was love, he welcomed it. If it was not, he would cherish it still, for he had felt nothing like it in his short life.

On the window ledge the watching crow unfurled its wings and cawed raucously. The silver moon threw the shadow of its wings across the wall behind the bed, and as she straddled him, taking what should have been the last of his life into her, the four of them joined – Alymere the Burned, the beautiful maiden of the Summervale, the woman who now wore her face, and the crow – and when release came, so too did rebirth.

His fever broke within their communion and as he fell back, spent, her fingernails digging deep into the scars of his chest, she knew he would live, inside her and out.

She lay down beside him, her head on his chest, breathing in his sweat and listening to the shallow rise and fall of his breathing. She whispered words of love like an incantation, but Alymere was beyond hearing them. He drifted into dream, once more transformed into the cloven-hoofed piper, though now he led Blodyweth on a merry dance through the very glade where they had first made love. She did not catch him, and her laughter rose above the melody of his pipes, filling his head and his heart while he slept on. Ahead of him, through the trees, he saw a man he knew better than he knew himself – though as he neared the mask melted, shrivelling until all that remained was bone and a death's head grin. His father turned and bolted, disappearing into the trees. The piper gave chase. Every time the dead man glanced back over his shoulder Alymere saw he wore a different mask, and the last mask before he woke, sweating and screaming, was that of his uncle, Sir Lowick.

Long after the bird had flown, his bed-mate still wore the shadows of its wings.

Come morning she was gone.

THIRTY

ALYMERE AWOKE WITH a raging thirst.

He pushed himself out of the low bed and walked unsteadily toward the window. Even those five steps were enough to exhaust him. He leaned heavy on the windowsill. Beads of sweat ran down his brow, but this was the honest sweat of toil, not the sickly sweat of fever. His head pounded and his mouth was drier than a witch's withered teat, but these things only reminded him that he was alive. And today was a good day to be alive.

Shades of green were the first thing he saw of the new world beyond the window. The snow had gone. Spring owned the land. Pollen blew on the wind and the sky was a ceaseless cobalt blue. Alymere threw the window open, eager to breathe in the fresh air.

This was his father's house. This was the room he had grown up in as a child. Once, so much of his life had been lived in these four walls, though they seemed so much smaller now. Here he had rescued fair maidens, slain dragons and quested for lost treasures. Here he had bent his knee before the great kings of the land and fought side-by-side with the grail knights for the honour of Camelot. Here he had loved and lost and won the hands of the fairest, worn their favours and been welcomed to the Round Table a hero. Here he had been a child.

He had so many memories of this place, not all of them good.

Behind him, the chamber door opened. He didn't turn.

"It's good to see you up and about, my lord," Gwen said. He saw her reflected in the glass. Her hair was pinned up and she looked a good ten years older than the last time he had seen her. She hesitated by the edge of the bed. Her coyness was touching, but given what they had shared, seemed misplaced. He turned away from the window and walked towards her, managing three unsteady steps before he stumbled forward into her arms. She caught him easily and Alymere leaned in, his lips only inches from her ear, and whispered, "Thank you." They were the first words he had spoken, and they came in a voice that wasn't his own. The smoke had damaged his throat every bit as much as the flames had damaged his face.

He held her a moment longer than was necessary, then leaned back so that he might look at her properly. She did not pull away from him, but neither did she seem entirely comfortable with his scrutiny. Was he so ugly that even a dried-up old maid couldn't bear the sight of him? The thought burned. He felt his anger well up then, and imagined for a moment lashing out to strike the woman across the face. The intensity of feeling shocked him. He swallowed it down, though at his side his hand trembled as though with palsy. She had saved his life and in repayment he imagined striking her? She had been nothing but kind. It didn't matter if she only cared for him out of guilt or honour, because he had saved the child – her child, now. She had been at his bedside day and night when others had left him alone to live or die.

He stepped out of the embrace and turned away, unable to bear the shame of his own thoughts. She watched him through the streaked glass of the window. It was not so easy to hide in such close confines and he wasn't strong enough to walk away from her. How could his mind sink so low? How could he fail to see the good in a simple act of kindness? She had brought him back to himself the only way she knew how. There was no devilry in it. Shame burned in him as hot as any lingering damage from the flames. He looked away.

"I should leave," Gwen said. She sounded unsure, frightened, as though she sensed his inner turmoil and just how close he had come to lashing out. But she didn't move. She was waiting to be dismissed.

"No, please," Alymere said. "I am sorry. Stay."

"If you wish, my lord."

"I do. I owe you my thanks," he said, sinking down onto the bed.

"You do not owe me anything, my lord. It is I who owe you, for the gift you gave me. You saved the lives of two people that day." He thought for a moment she meant the mother, but he remembered too well the look in her dead eyes and the funeral pyre. "With my John gone, and so many of my friends, you gave me something to live for in that little girl. I would not be here without her."

"And I wouldn't be here without you, of that I am in no doubt. You saved my life."

She sat down beside him. There was no intimacy in it, no gentle brush of thigh against thigh, nothing to suggest that they had been lovers. But at least the fear seemed to have left her, and for that he was grateful. If she did not fear him, perhaps he should not fear himself?

He began to doubt his memories.

Had their bodies really joined in communion or was that another fragment of delirium? Some dream-image conjured by his feverish mind as it sought to find a way back from the brink? Why would she have crawled into bed beside him? She was old enough to be his mother. He looked her in the eye but saw nothing beyond gratitude there. He made a decision, then. He chose to believe it did not happen.

"Tell me about the little girl and your new life," he said, kindly. "What did you call her?"

"Alma," she said.

"And do you feed her soul as she does yours?[8] Is she happy, Gwen?"

"Yes, my lord, I believe she is."

[8] A medieval pun. *Alma* means "nourishing" in Latin, but "soul" in medieval Italian. Hence, "nourishment for the soul."

"That is good. I am not sure we can ask for more, can we? Children should be happy. They should not have to know about death," he was talking about himself then, about his father and this place. "Gwen, do you ever think you see ghosts?"

She thought about it for a moment, although she couldn't know why he had asked. "No, my lord."

"Nor I. More's the pity, for I should dearly like to see my father one last time. To say goodbye. I was born here, do you know? In this house. I lived so much of my life here, and then my father died and everything changed."

"I am sorry."

"There's nothing for you to be sorry about. This is my life; I have long since made my peace with it. But that does not mean that every now and then I do not think about what it would be like to speak to my father man-to-man. It is one thing for a boy to say I love you, it is unconditional, but it is quite another for a grown man to share such a bond, I think."

"Perhaps it is so, my lord, but who is to say that unconditional bond ever changes? Who is to say that a son's love isn't always unthinkingly given? Would it even make a difference?"

"I never got to say goodbye," and there it was, the one regret of his life expressed in six simple words. He didn't need to see ghosts, not when there were so many memories alive in everything around him. "Help me, Gwen. I would get out of this house. It only makes me maudlin."

"Is that wise, my lord?"

"Perhaps not, but when is anything I do considered wise? I am still allowed to hide behind the folly of youth for a few more days yet." He held out his hand.

She helped him to rise, taking much of his weight on her outstretched arm. Alymere wasn't ashamed to lean on her. Together they walked slowly to the door. The pain of it was evident on his face, and even before they reached the threshold she questioned again the wisdom of over-exerting himself. Alymere shook off her concern with a brusque shake of the head, which he immediately regretted but refused to admit. "I would feel the spring air on my face and remember how it feels to be alive and well, not sick."

That day they made it as far as the hundred-year-old apple tree in the centre of the lawn. They sat in the shade of it while Alymere gathered his strength for the short walk back. The main treeline of the forest was still hundreds of yards distant. It seemed like forever away. Every muscle burned.

"What of my uncle?" he asked, plucking a yellow buttercup from the grass and stripping its petals one by one.

"He carried you all the way from the sea in his arms. It was truly a miracle. He carried you for three days before he collapsed, finally, in sight of the house. Even then he would not rest. He summoned healers and watched over you day and night when first you returned, my lord, worrying as a man would for his own son. But when it became clear that there would be no quick healing and there was little these men could do for you, he had no choice but to ride south to Camelot and report the attack on Medcaut and the slaughter of our villages to the king. Not that he has confided in me, but I believe he plans to urge the king to raise arms against the North. His only instruction was that we tend the fields as usual, for no matter what, we would all need to eat."

"Ever practical," Alymere agreed, especially if there were to be more mouths to feed. His blood ran cold at the thought of what such an act of war would mean. Blodyweth had promised so ominously that if the Devil's book were to fall into the wrong hands it would mean the end of Albion as they knew it, but how could civil war against the northmen be any less devastating? "When did he ride out?"

"When the weather broke, my lord. He has been gone near two weeks."

Two weeks. More than long enough to ride to the Seat of Albion and back alone, if you flogged the horse, but not with a war party. Supply lines would slow them down greatly. He had to assume this meant war was coming to his home. It was impossible to believe, looking up at the endless blue sky and hearing the music of the grasshoppers' wings and the birdsong.

They walked together back to the house, and within minutes Alymere succumbed to exhausted sleep.

The walk became a ritual, with Alymere gaining strength every day. The exercise was cautious at first, no more challenging than climbing the staircase unaided, though even that had him reliant upon the wall more than once for support. Before the week was out they made it as far as the treeline and back without rest.

Still his uncle had not returned.

Seven more days and Gwen was sitting in the shade of the old apple tree watching him run, first no more than a gentle loping stride, the distance more important than the speed with which it was covered, and then pumping his arms and legs furiously as he gave every ounce of strength he possessed to the sprint. Frequently his body buckled beneath the exertion and his legs betrayed him, but sheer determination always had Alymere back on his feet before she could come to his aid.

Afternoons, he stripped off to the waist and gave himself to physical labour. His body tanned with the sun, or part of it did. The scar tissue left by the burns whitened where the old skin browned, making him appear even more like a man of two aspects, two souls.

Gwen never left him. She urged him on as he split logs, working his upper body until some semblance of power returned to his frame. His muscles slowly returned as he hefted the axe over and over, slamming it down into the logs.

When the heat became too much, he would descend to the cellar and spend an hour or more moving casks of wine and mead, and hulking sacks of grain over his shoulder to carry them from one side of the cellar to the other, back and forth, back and forth until his legs refused to carry him.

He forced his body through more and more gruelling exercises, bringing the casks up from below to load up a broken cart – which leant precariously on its splintered axel – so that he might press greater and greater weights, building the muscle in his shoulders and lower back, and before long he surpassed his previous physique.

He was born again, body and soul.

And still his uncle had not returned.

A curious relationship formed between Gwen and Alymere during his rehabilitation. There was a tenderness there, and pride, friendship even, but it was completely maternal. He welcomed it. Of all the servants in his father's house, she was the only one who could bear to look him in the eye. Not once did they speak of their fevered coupling, so he became more and more certain that it had never happened, although that only left disquiet in his bones.

It was a month before he realised what it was that so disturbed him: during all of their time together he never once saw her with the child, Alma.

THIRTY-ONE

Alymere read the words again, his index finger running over each of them slowly as he sounded the syllables inside his head: *being an account of the entire wisdom of Man as transcribed by Harmon Reclusus.*

Those fifteen words promised so much; the entire wisdom of Man. That he couldn't read more than those fifteen words was a torment beyond reason. He had stared at them for hours, lost in their shapes, imagining he could hear them come alive inside his head without ever knowing what they meant. Why had the monk chosen to record such precious words in a language few could read?

For protection, of course, to safeguard that wisdom from those unworthy of it, or unready for it, from those who would corrupt it or use it to do harm. Like the sword, wisdom was itself merely a tool, it was how it was wielded that made all the difference.

He turned the page, breathing in the musty smell of those old sheets as he thumbed through them. The fragrance he thought of as the smell of knowledge filled his senses.

Alymere studied the shape of what he assumed to be a prayer as it was laid out on the page, tapering to a point. His finger traced the ragged shape of the stanza, resting upon the two words, alone at the bottom of the page, and he realised he could read them: *Black Chalice.*

He read them over and over again, but there could be no mistaking what they said. "Black Chalice," he said aloud, barely breathing the words. It was enough to send a thrill through his entire being. He felt it in that intangible place men call the soul. And it was electrifying.

How could he have missed them?

The entire body of text pointed towards those two words as though they were the focal point of the stanza itself.

How could he have been so blind as to not see them?

Did that mean there were other words in the book he had somehow failed to recognise? Heart racing, he turned page after page, quickly, eyes hungrily scanning the rows of indecipherable text for anything, even a single word, that made sense.

He found the same two words repeated several times within the book: *Black Chalice.*

He could only wonder how, in all of his poring over the book, he had missed them.

He set the book aside.

This time when he dreamed it was of a hanged man and a cup. As the man twisted and turned against the bite of the rope a shadowy figure – a woman, he thought – used a silver dagger to open the artery at his ankle and bleed him, catching the slow drip, drip, drip of his death in a black cup. She raised it to her lips and drank the blood of Iscariot, the traitor, and Alymere sat bolt upright in bed, sweating and screaming, the taste of blood on his lips where he had bitten through his cheek.

He did not see the crow cross the moon.

THIRTY-TWO

MORE THAN A month had passed with no-one tending to the law of the land, but that did not mean that the disputes of the people under Sir Lowick's protection ceased, merely that they simmered, slowly building to the boil.

Without the knight there to dispense justice and keep the peace, neighbours grew fractious: conversations which would normally have been civil took on an undercurrent of spite, and arguments came to blows. It was not some dark magic that gripped the people. It was nothing more mysterious than fear. Word of the raids had spread. While they might not know of the fall of Medcaut, they each knew or claimed to know someone who had lost family to the reivers that winter. They were not cowards. They were as brave as the next man. All any of them wanted was to feel safe in their own homes.

It was Gwen who suggested he should preside over the Assizes.

Despite his misgivings, she convinced him that the people needed to see that they hadn't been abandoned. In his uncle's absence it was his responsibility to see to their needs. His father, she said, would have expected no less of him. They had been his people not so long ago. Alymere could not argue with her reasoning and so took the seat in the great hall and listened to the endless procession of petitions from frightened people. He could remember watching his father in the same seat, dispensing justice. Firm but fair, his father had always maintained. They came to the knight's seat looking for justice – if they left having discovered fairness then it was a day in which Albion itself triumphed.

He did not feel comfortable sitting in judgment.

As he had said not so long ago to Gwen, it was not yet his lot in life to be wise, but when he had said that he had no way of knowing just how few of his foolish days were left to him. In those five long days that the Assizes ran, listening to petition after petition deep into the hours of darkness, he learned something of the nature of people – good people in the main – that he would never have thought true: it didn't matter how rich, how poor, how humble or ugly or beautiful or bitter, how clever or cunning, how hardworking, how venal or base or scheming, how dishonest or desperate, how noble, how proud, people were all inherently the same, and that similarity boiled down to simple self-interest. It turned his stomach. Just once he wanted to hear of a man bringing claim for the betterment of his neighbours, not to redress some perceived loss to himself or his property. Was it so hard to find a man who cared more for the wellbeing of those around him than he did for himself? It was all just so... petty.

Alymere kept the realisation to himself. It was, he decided, just one of the many things that separated a true man from a common one.

He shifted in the seat. The muscles of his lower back ached and no amount of fidgeting seemed to lessen the pain.

He rested his sword across his thighs, as though the blade might lend some gravitas to his decisions.

"Speak," he said, looking down at the woman and the two men on their knees before him. None of them would look at him as they spoke. It was hard to make out some of their mumbling over the whispers of the onlookers and other petitioners crowded into the house's great hall.

Justice had become a spectacle. He fingered the hilt of the sword.

"My lord," said the first of the men, a balding, overweight wretch with the grease of more than one meal marring the front of his shirt. He coughed, and somehow even that little sound succeeded in sounding obsequious. "This man, Isaiah, who I used to call my *friend*, has wronged me gravely and I come before the court seeking redress. Only what is right, nothing more."

"Now there's a surprise," Alymere said wearily. "How, pray tell, were you wronged by your *friend*, and why should it warrant my intervention? What is it? Money? Land? Crops? Did he steal from you or, no, I see a woman between you, perhaps he cuckolded you? Is that the crime for which you would have him punished? Enlighten me as to why two grown men need me to sort out their differences."

"We had a deal, my lord. A bargain struck in good faith. I delivered upon my side, but when it came time for him to honour his word, he broke faith. I am an honest man. A decent man. I do not understand why it should have to come to this, but there is no reasoning with him. I only want what is rightfully mine. As I said, nothing more."

"All well and good. What was the nature of this bargain of yours? Would either one of you care to explain?"

The woman looked up then. There was a look of weariness in her eyes that spoke of fear so blunted it had faded into resignation. She was not pretty, but neither was she ugly. Her face possessed an almost masculine strength, with a sharp jawbone, narrow cheeks and aquiline nose, but it was her eyes that fascinated Alymere. They were where the woman lived.

She did not say a word.

Beside her, the second man stood. Where his accuser was both corpulent and slovenly, he was a spindle of a man, all slack leathery skin and protruding bone. His clothes were threadbare with wear and patched in several places. Alymere could see a thousand wrinkles in the wattle of his neck and found himself thinking that if it were possible to age a tree by the rings of its trunk it ought likewise be possible to age a man by the wrinkles of his neck. "Master," he said, his voice as thin and reedy as his frame, "Craven speaks true in that he paid a fair price for my daughter's hand, I can't dispute that, but I have offered every coin back and more. He simply refuses to take it."

"Because I want what's mine, Isaiah. I want the girl."

"Ah," Alymere said, understanding. "You traded away the hand of your daughter, the price was paid, and now you seek to change the terms of your arrangement? Is that it?"

"No, my lord, I would simply give my friend back his coin and let my daughter be free of my foolishness. I am an old man, I let fear rule my heart instead of love."

"What does love have to do with business, Isaiah? I met your price and you were happy enough to take my pigs, were you not?" The fat man interrupted.

"You sold your daughter for pigs?" Alymere asked, barely able to keep the smirk from his face.

"Aye, and goats too. A dozen sows, three nannies. Plus coin. More than a fair price," the fat man said.

"I am sure it is," Alymere agreed. "So why the change of heart?"

"My daughter came to me and begged me to free her of the deal."

"She has you wrapped around her finger, you old fool. I will give her a good home. She will want for nothing. And I say again, a deal is a deal."

"But will she be loved?" The thin man challenged.

"What has love got to do with anything? You get enough pigs and goats to keep you fed into your dotage and I get a brood mare for fine healthy sons to take over the farm when I'm done," the fat man said, shaking his head in disgust. "That was the bargain and well you know it."

"Let me think on this," Alymere said, raising his hand to forestall any more outbursts. Both men lowered their heads, but the woman looked at him. He found himself unable to think as he met her gaze. "There is a moral root to the petition as well as a fiscal one. A man should be held to a bargain he has made. If a man can break a pledge, what then is the value of his word? Where is the honour in such a man?"

"Exactly," the fat man muttered.

"Silence!" Alymere bellowed, pushing himself up out of his chair. "I have little love for you, fat man. One more word and I shall have your tongue cut out so I don't have to listen to any more of your bleating. Understood?"

The fat man's bloated face had gone a sickly shade of white. He said nothing.

"Good." His outburst over, Alymere sank back into his seat. He felt the blood pounding in his temples. He ran a hand across the rough stubble of his beard. "On the other hand, he has offered full recompense, returning the animals and the coin so that neither party is worse off than when the bargain was struck, and surely there are other brood mares out there that can bear you children, because, as you so rightly advocated, love has nothing to do with it, after all. She does not need to be comely, only fertile. When you open your mouth I find that I am of a mind to throw out your petition, Craven, and tell you to go back to your farmstead with your pigs and your goats, but, and this is the only thing that may save your case, when I think of a world in which a man's word is worth naught my blood curdles. Are you familiar with the Oath to which knights swear?" he did not wait for the man to answer. "A true man must never do outrage, nor murder. There has been no murder here, at least. A true man must flee treasons of all kind, making no room for treachery in his heart. Treachery? Could the breaking of faith be considered treacherous? Perhaps. One could certainly argue so.

"A true man must by no means be cruel but rather give mercy unto him who begs it. If a daughter goes to her father and begs mercy, should he not give it if it is his to give? Again one would think so. But as his chattel a man is free to sell his daughter for pigs should he think it is a good trade. That is the law of the land whether I like it or not, and more pertinently, whether you like it or not.

"A true man must always give ladies, gentlewomen and widows succour, and never must he force himself upon them. And whilst Craven has bought this woman it is no different to the bartering of station and binding of families that goes on all over Albion. He has offered a good match, promising that the daughter of Isaiah will want for nothing. He has fulfilled his obligations in good faith. So how can she refuse his offer without bringing dishonour upon her father?

"A true man must never take up arms in wrongful quarrels for love or worldly goods. Both of you, I suspect, should be commended for bringing this fight to me rather than killing each other.

"And for my part, never will a true man stand by idly and watch such evils perpetrated by others upon the innocent, for a true man stands as last bastion for all that is just. A true man is the last hope of the good and innocent. A true man must hold fast to the Oath above all things. Only then might a true man do honour to Albion and stand as a true knight.

"The question is, should a commoner be held accountable in the same manner that a knight would? I think it is unfair to assume so, or all men would be knights, would they not? Still, this is no easy decision. Before I make it, I think I should like to hear from the girl, as she is the prize in this dispute."

She met his gaze full on.

Already he had become used to people looking away from his scars, but she did not. The challenge in her eyes brought a smile to his ruined lips.

"I should be most curious to hear a single good reason why you should not be wed, assuming you have a tongue?"

"Aye, my lord," she said. "I have a tongue,"

"Excellent. Then let us hear from you on this matter. This court is nothing if not fair, so speak. One good reason is all I ask, and let's have no talk of love. As has been argued already it has no place here."

"Very well, my lord," she said, rising to her feet. "But if I am to level accusations against the character of Craven, I would do so in private, not with the gawpers looking on." She gestured towards the ranks of onlookers crowded into the chamber. "I would not needlessly destroy a man's good name by turning his life into gossip for his neighbours."

"I think you've already done that, madam," Alymere said.

"Then I would not cause undue damage beyond what has been done. I beg your indulgence, my lord. Just a few moments' privacy, then I will heed whatever decision you see fit to make."

Alymere rose from his chair and stepped down from the dais.

"Come then, miss."

He led her behind a sun-faded tapestry that hid an alcove and afforded some little privacy.

"Speak your piece."

They were close, uncomfortably so. He could feel her breath against his neck. There was nowhere to hide from the intensity of her eyes. The dark around them made it seem as though they had no whites. He had been wrong on two counts. She was beautiful, he realised, and her fear had not faded into resignation. She was resigned, yes, but that did not blunt the fear one iota. It was only then that he recognised the spectre lurking behind them for what it was: death.

"My lord, it is simply this: I have heard tell that Craven's first wife, six years in the ground, was helped there by her husband's hand."

Her words had the ring of sincerity to them, but that did not mean for a minute that they were true, only that she believed them. "A serious accusation indeed," Alymere said, thoughtfully. "I can see why you would not want to say this before all and sundry. You told your father this, and obviously it was enough for him to break off the betrothal. I understand now. What father would knowingly send his daughter into the bed of a killer? But that in itself would make this a perfect lie for someone looking to escape her fate without destroying an old man's honour, wouldn't it? After all, who is going to punish a father for protecting his child? So, you are either a very cunning creature or a very desperate one. Tell me, which is it?"

"I am not a liar, my lord. I believe Craven murdered his first wife, Elspeth, because she was barren."

"Then do you have any evidence to substantiate such wild accusations?"

"None, save that when I look into his eyes I see the truth of it."

He found it difficult to think with her so close. He could smell her hair and found his eyes drifting down to the nape of her neck, where the smallest trace of sweat had begun to gather. He felt his body stir and loathed himself for such human frailty. He wanted to touch her.

"So you would have me spare you the same fate based upon

some flight of fancy? An imagined evil behind the eyes? With evidence I would have no hesitation. Hellfire, I would rain righteous vengeance down upon his head, believe me. The fat man's screams would be heard all the way to France. But without it, my hands are tied. I do not know what else I can say."

She reached up and placed her palm over his heart. "Then do not say anything. Look into his eyes, my lord. The soul cannot be hidden. You will know the truth. That is all I ask. Look into his eyes and ask him about Elspeth."

He drew back the curtain and returned to his seat to offer judgement, although what that judgement might be he still did not know.

Every eye was on him. Expectancy hung in the air. The two men watched him, each desperate for the verdict to go their way. Craven was sweating. It clung to the front of his shirt, leaving a dark stain beneath his pits and across his belt.

"I have one question for you, Craven, answer it and I shall offer my decision."

"Ask anything, my lord. I have no secrets."

"Good. Then my question is this: is this to be your first union?"

"No, my lord. I was married once before, to my beloved Elspeth. She was taken by the sickness some six years gone and there isn't a day I do not think of her. There is not a night that I do not lie awake and mourn her loss, and wish that I had some small part of her to live on, a son to labour side by side with me on the farm, a daughter to welcome us home after a hard day's graft. I loved her with all of my body, which is why I will not marry for love again. I could not bear the loss."

The words were smooth, but they were not glib. He had not rehearsed them, so perhaps they came from the heart? Whatever the truth, Alymere could not see the lie in Craven's eyes. So for all the woman's protestations there was no glimpse of the man's blackened soul to make the decision for him. And, as he looked down at her on her knees before him, the surge of lust he felt all but made his mind up for him. A true man must be pure of heart and free of earthly desires, and that meant unpicking the knot of these temptations and teasing out the lies, the suspicions, the falsehoods and misdirections and getting to the core of it.

He lowered his head, trying to imagine what his father would have done in his stead. Roth would no doubt tell him he could not damn a man for what he *might* do, and lacking any evidence of what he *had* done, his only choice was to enforce the betrothal.

When he raised his head again, he saw a line of crows had gathered upon the window ledges high above the benches, adding their beady eyes to the gawping crowd. He counted two dozen of them, but only one of them held his gaze for more than a second. It had a streak of white in its feathers, and neither preened nor primped but merely watched. He thought of the red hart he had chased into the forest and how he had taken it as a sign. Could this too be a sign?

"I have weighed the evidence presented by both parties and find no compelling reason to dismiss the man Craven's claim, as much as I might want to, and so with heavy heart I must find in his favour. I take no joy from this decision, save that it is a fair one." He turned his attention to the fat man, whose delight was evident on his ruddy features. "I would urge you not to wed merely to sire sons but risk your heart once more, for that is the great triumph of man, our ability to love again and again. The old wounds hurt, but new loves can heal them better than any unguent. But if your mind is set on this course, then so be it. It is not for me to change it. If you cannot love, then at least you can fulfil your husbandly duties and provide for this woman so that she does not want, and in that be the best husband you can be to her. This is my verdict. Do you agree to abide by it?"

"Aye, my lord," Craven said. "Thank you."

"Do not thank me. A life without love is no life worth living, as far as I can tell." He turned to Isaiah. "And what of you? Do you swear to abide by the judgement of this court?"

"Yes, my lord," the tall man said. Where he had seemed like a spindle as he first shuffled towards the chair, now he seemed like reed broken in the wind. His back bowed, the strength gone from his spine. There could be no doubting the fact that he truly believed his daughter's claims and took Alymere's judgement to mean she had just been condemned to death. Maybe not today, maybe not tomorrow, but the when of it was not important. It took what little strength remained to him to walk away from the seat without having to lean upon the bailiffs for support. He maintained that much dignity, at least, though he could no longer look at his daughter.

The woman spared no such thoughts for dignity. She cried out: "No!" struggling against the hands that reached for her. And he realised he did not even know her name. Like the two men she stood between he had treated her as nothing more than a chattel to be traded. The realisation made him sick. To her he said, "You do not deserve this, and I feel that I have failed you. For that I am truly sorry. I can only hope that you find happiness." And to the men, "I do not want to see either of you before me again. The pair of you sicken me to my stomach. Think on what has happened here. Do right by each other, I implore you." To the galleries, he called, "The court is ended. I need to scrub the taint of this decision from my skin."

As one, the four and twenty birds took flight, the flurry of their wings against the glass turning every head. Only the white-streaked crow remained. It did not fly away until Alymere left his seat and the Assizes came to a close for the day.

THIRTY-THREE

WORD CAME TO the house less than a week later that the woman had died by her own hand the first night she was to have slept with the fat man, Craven. That alone was enough to wrench his heart from his chest and trample on it, but it was not the end to her tragic story. Her father, Isaiah, learning of her suicide, and believing he had failed the girl when she needed him most, broke into the house of his former friend, and cut the fat man's throat, bleeding him like one of his own pigs before turning the knife on himself. The three deaths weighed heavy upon Alymere's shoulders.

He sat beneath the old apple tree, his back pressed up against the rough bark. He had not spoken since news of the deaths reached him.

He had based his decision upon what he felt was right, but it had killed them all, so how could it possibly have been right? He had failed all three of them.

Had he just had the courage to believe the girl – her name was Josephina, he now knew – they might all be alive now. Had he not placed such ridiculously high value upon a man's word that man would not now be consigned to the flames of hell as a murderer. He thought nothing good of the man, Craven, save that he did not deserve to die.

His breath burned hot in his lungs. Alymere reached up and snapped off a sour apple from a low hanging branch. He did not bite into it – the fruit was not good to eat – but simply toyed with the stem, thinking of the people he had killed with his judgement.

That was his burden to bear. He felt himself wanting to be free of his mind, to drift away somewhere he did not exist, where he could not feel and he could not be hurt – nor hurt others. He wanted to fall away from himself; to become no-one.

But he could not.

These were his dead as surely as if he had killed them with his own hand and he had no choice but to own them.

He looked up and saw Gwen walking towards him across the lawn. The sun shone through the diaphanous material of her gown, bringing her shape alive beneath it. Again he was struck by her faded beauty, and found a deep-seated loathing within himself for thinking his lustful thoughts. She had been nothing but kind to him, and all he could think of was how the cloth sashayed around her legs and rode her hips as she walked. She deserved better from him, but then, so did everybody. It was self-pity, he knew, but knowing was not enough to quell it.

She sat beside him.

"You did not give her the knife, neither did you hold it to Craven's throat," she said. "These were the deeds of others, sweet man. You cannot be responsible for them."

He looked at her, then. The leafy shadows mottled her cheeks. "If I had decided the other way she would not have taken her life. My decision brought about her death."

"Perhaps, but who is to say that by denying Craven his new wife, he would not have sought some other recompense? It is not hard to imagine a man like him taking her life as punishment for her father breaking faith, is it? There was no love there, he freely admitted so himself. This was a dispute over property. He came before you a wronged man. Had you ruled against him he would have left the manor house both wronged and humiliated, a dangerous combination in a man like Craven, I think. The only truth here is that we cannot know the minds of others, my lord. It is torture to think that we can. It could be that her death was writ on the very day she was born, or that God sealed it the day He took Craven's first wife up to Heaven. Ours is not to question Him, only to abide here before we are worthy of His paradise."

He tossed the apple away. "She is but one soul in the grand scheme of things, true, but how could such evil come from good intention? That is what I find hardest to bear. I truly believed he would give her a good life, even if not the one she would have chosen for herself."

"The fires of Hell are fuelled by good intentions, my lord."

"True." Alymere snapped off another apple, and despite knowing full well the fruit was sour, bit into it. He chewed and swallowed three bites before tossing the core away. "Tell me of Alma. I would hear something good on this wretched day."

"She is an angel, my lord. I bless the day you brought her into my life and every day thereafter."

THIRTY-FOUR

AT NIGHT, ALONE, the voice came.

Still, he could not make out a word it said.

He didn't need to.

The words formed impressions inside his head and those impressions came alive inside him.

He lay in his bed, his entire body hollowed out, so that when the voice came, it filled him. It swelled to reach every corner of his being. The shapeless sounds repeated the same sibilance of syllables, chanting them over and over and over again:

chalicechalicechalicechalicechalicechalicechalicechalice...

And for once he did not feel alone in the great manor house.

THIRTY-FIVE

HE COULD NOT say what instinct caused him to open the Devil's Bible the next morning – having left it untouched for days – but even as he opened his eyes to the morning he found himself reaching for it.

It felt so familiar to his touch; cold and marble-smooth, like the skin of a dead man.

As Alymere turned the first page and saw those familiar words – *being an account of the entire wisdom of Man as transcribed by Harmon Reclusus* – he knew that more secrets of the book were going to reveal themselves to him.

He looked at the words, at the shape of them as they bled across the page, and found his still sleep-addled mind imagining them running together. The letters moved, twisting and sliding into and away from one another, forming new nonsense words and old familiar ones, although never settling for more than a heartbeat in any shape that allowed him to read them. As he rested his fingertips flat on the page he saw the ink stain them, the words climbing from the page to stain his skin. They curled around his fingers, sharing secrets with his flesh that he could not know, rising up the soft smooth expanse of the meat of his forearm, each line becoming a vein and artery, feeding the life of him as completely as might blood. He rubbed at his eyes, knowing it was impossible for words to rewrite themselves once writ and that they could not move of their own accord, nor tattoo his body, and in the back of his mind heard the soft sibilant whisper of the word *Chalice* again, though this time he was awake and in full charge of his faculties. There could be no pretending the voice was the work of ghosts.

The spell broken, the words fell back onto the page – although in truth they had never left it – and Alymere pushed himself up in bed. He leaned on an elbow, and called, "Who is there?"

No-one answered, not that he expected them to.

"Father?" he asked, not daring to believe it possible and feeling stupid for thinking it. "Is that you?"

Again there was no answer.

When he looked down at the book this time there were more words that he recognised – incomplete phrases that alone made no sense, though in the centre of the poem, above the words *Black Chalice* he could now read seven more words: *The White Crow and the Devil's Tree.*

He recalled the white-streaked feathers of the crow that watched him preside over the Assizes, the last of its kin to take flight. Before he could check to see if any more of the words within the book had made themselves known, a floorboard creaked outside his room.

Someone was out there. There could be no mistaking it this time.

He closed the book, and as the pages came together again the word *chalice* slipped into the back of his mind, repeating itself, *chalicechalicechalice*, in a woman's voice this time. No, he realised – not a woman's, a boy's.

That he had imagined the word spoken by three different voices ought to have steered his mind toward the truth, or at least some revelation of his own madness. Instead, ignoring the implications, he called out, almost shouting, "What trickery is this?"

Again, the deliberate sigh of a floorboard beneath someone's foot, and then silence.

"Who goes there?"

This time, his question was answered by a soft knock on the chamber door.

The iron handle twisted and the door opened a crack, and he could see a sliver of shadow sneak into the room.

He sprung from the bed, casting about for something to defend himself with.

As the door opened wider he saw that it was the woman, Gwen. She wore a simple white shift, her face like ash as she stepped into the room.

The tension ebbed from his body, leaving him standing naked in the middle of the floor. He laughed at his own unease, and pulled the blanket from the bed to cover his nakedness.

"What is it?" Alymere asked, and realising that she could not answer him, abandoned any pretence of modesty and grasped her with both hands, forcing her to meet his gaze. "What is wrong?"

"It is your uncle."

Alymere felt a dread chill blossom in his heart. "He is here?"

The woman nodded. "They brought him in on a stretcher. He is grievously wounded, my lord. They fear he may not make it through the night."

"What happened to him?"

"I do not know, and did not think it my place to ask."

"No. Of course. Thank you, Gwen."

Alymere grabbed his shirt, discarded the night before with the rest of his clothes in a heap, and buttoned it with trembling hands. Three times he missed the eyelet and the button slipped through his fingers. He pulled on his hose and tied the leather thong tight, before running barefoot out of the room, his feet slapping on the hardwood floor.

The entire house was in a commotion. He could hear people calling out, barking orders. There was none of the laughter he had come to associate with his home.

He stopped dead on the landing, clutching the balustrade, caught between looking down the great staircase to the reception room where servants and soldiers gathered, and what had been the door to his parent's chamber along the landing. The white hart painted onto the heavy oak had faded, but it was still visible in the morning gloom.

They would have taken Sir Lowick to his room so that he might die in his own bed, he knew, though the bitter little voice at the back of his head insisted on reminding Alymere, it wasn't his uncle's bed at all, and that already one of two brothers had died in it.

He forced himself to walk down the passageway to the door, and knocked once, his knuckles striking the belly of the white hart.

Pushing open the door without waiting to be summoned, and seeing the dying man sprawled out upon the sheets, his skin already the texture and tone of the dead, Alymere could not help but see the grotesque symmetry in the fates of the brothers Lowick and Roth.

He was not alone in the room. A giant of a man knelt at his bedside, head bowed in prayer. He did not look up until he had offered his final words to the Lord, beseeching the Almighty to make his friend's final journey a peaceful one.

Alymere could not see his face, but he did not need to. The voice was unmistakable, as were the wild black curls that spilled over his clasped hands, and the sheer bulk of the man. It could only have been Sir Bors de Ganis at the bedside.

When finally the big knight raised his head, all mirth and wildness had gone from his eyes. He appeared tortured; haunted by the things he had seen and by the things he had done since last they met.

"Tis a good thing you were not a pretty boy to start with, lad," he said, pushing himself to his feet. "For the fire has done you no favours. Still, no doubt some doxy will want to kiss it all better."

Alymere felt like he was a child again, tiptoeing into his parents room to sit beside his dying father. There were too many dark memories in this room. Stripped down like this, the two of them – the memory and the man – looked so similar it rocked him to the very foundation of his being. He recalled the vow he had made when his uncle first claimed the manor house – that he would never set foot in this room again – and yet here he was, fate making a liar out of him as he watched another man slowly die.

Alymere made a new vow then: no one else would die in this room. He would have it walled up when he became the man of house.

He looked at Bors, seeing for the first time the tears streaking the knight's face, and every certainty he had ever had failed him. He threw himself into Bors' arms, and for a moment they hugged fiercely, bonded by grief. "What happened?" Alymere asked, extricating himself from the big man's grip. "I see no dressings, no wounds. Is it sickness?"

"No, lad. Poison. Tis a dark day when a faithless whoreson can bring down a good man thus." He shook his head.

"Poison?" Alymere's mind raced.

"Aye. The poor bastard's dying from the inside out, lad. His body has been failing him ever since he swallowed that damned water from the chalice." That word again. Alymere felt his blood run cold as it coiled like a serpent through his brain: *chalicechalicechalicechalicechalice...*

"Every hour another part of him loses its grip on life. Never thought he'd last this long, but the old man's always been one stubborn cur, so why should that change just because he's dying?"

Alymere had no answer for that.

"All he would say was that he wanted to die here, that he wanted to be buried beside his brother. The poison ate away at him 'til he couldn't stand on his own two feet, 'til his eyes lost their focus and his body turned gaunt because he couldn't keep a damned thing down. It's only ever been a matter of time, as much as we wanted to deny it. No medicine touched his fever, no herbs quieted the pain in his head or settled his stomach. In truth it would have been a mercy had he died days ago, lad, but he's hung on stubbornly, wanting to come home. No doubt to finally make his peace with you."

"We made our peace a long time ago, Bors. There are no secrets between us."

"Then perhaps he just wanted to see you one last time."

"I don't understand how this could happen," Alymere said. "I thought he came to Camelot to urge Arthur to dispatch knights north to help secure the border? Was he poisoned there?"

"No lad. We rode out weeks ago. It's been a bitter spring,

make no bones about it. Those faithless northerners are hard: they paint themselves up and fight like demons, they'd sacrifice their own grandmothers if they thought it'd give them the upper hand, and no matter how hard you beat them, they just don't know when they should lie down. Bitter weather and treacherous conditions only added to the hell of it. I've lost too many friends these last weeks, but in many ways this is the worst of it. It's one thing for a man to die with his sword in his hand, fighting for what he believes in, it's another for him to toast supposed peace with his killers and drink in their bloody poison."

Alymere began to put together a vague picture of events. The how: poison; the where: at a parlay brokering peace between the northmen and the knights; the who: well, the victim was laid out of the bed before him, and the killer, as far as he knew, was still out there fighting; the when: more than a few days ago, less than a week, meaning right around the time he was pronouncing his ill-fated judgement on Craven's suit; but the why of it, that he could not divine from either his uncle's body or Sir Bors' brief description of what had transpired.

He was not even sure it mattered.

"Come here, boy," Sir Lowick's voice was empty of strength, like wood charcoaled in a spent fire. It was so quiet it barely registered as a sound at all. Alymere could scarcely believe it had come from his uncle's mouth.

Lowick had raised a hand. His eyes were open, but his stare was glassy.

"Go to him," Bors said, steering Alymere gently toward the bedside and backing away. Alymere knelt and took his uncle's hand. It felt like the fragile body of a bird nestled between his fingers; so thin, and the skin so slack around it, that Alymere feared simply squeezing too tightly would shatter his uncle's hand.

He brought it to his lips and kissed it, then lowered his head, pressing the delicate bones against the scarred tissue of his forehead. He didn't move until he felt the warm wet track of tears on his cheek. Alymere breathed in deeply, willing himself to be strong.

"I will leave you alone," Bors said softly, and closed the heavy door behind him.

"I can't see you, boy."

"I am here, uncle," Alymere said, soothing him. "You should rest. I will be here when you wake."

"No, I'll rest soon enough." Lowick's eyes roved wildly, unable to focus on anything. The veins at his throat fluttered weakly. "First, I need to make my peace with my maker. There are things I need to unburden from my soul before I meet Him. And then, God willing, I need to make my peace with you. I owe you that much. After that, I can go." His grip tightened feebly, and a hacking cough wracked his body, leaving blood flecks on his lips. He lacked the strength to wipe them away, so Alymere tended to him, cleaning away the blood with the cuff of his shirt. "I need you to do something for me, boy," the knight said at last. "I need you to bring the priest here. Will you do that for me? Can I count on you?"

"Of course, uncle," Alymere said at once, immediately hating himself for the sense of relief the request sent flooding through his system. It wasn't until he reached the door, his hand on the iron handle, that he felt anything other than relief that he would be spared the bedside vigil for however many hours more.

"Twice in these last months I have watched over you, thinking you not long for this world, and here it's me that leaves it first. That, at least, is how it should be."

He turned to look back at his uncle, and in that moment was overcome by almost childish resentment that this man he had come to love was leaving him, and rather than spend the last few hours he had in this life with his nephew, Lowick had sent him away.

Why should he want to make his peace with some unknowable God before he made peace with his own flesh and blood?

He wanted desperately not to think ill of the dying man, but it hurt.

Alymere made the sign of the cross over his chest.

"You were always a good boy, Alymere. I am proud of you," Sir Lowick said, but Alymere had already closed the door.

Bors leaned against the balustrade, face grave. He looked as though he needed to hit something. Alymere could identify with the feeling. "What did he say?"

"Nothing," Alymere said, biting down the bitterness in his voice. He couldn't help himself. "Save that he wanted me to fetch him a priest so that he might confess his sins, I suppose. So much for hanging on to see me one last time; he was only worried about his soul."

"Do not be too harsh on him, lad. Dying is never easy, no matter how laboured its step as it creeps towards us. It is understandable that he would seek to put his house in order."

"Then why leave me to last?"

"Whatever needs be said, I have absolute faith will be said. Lowick is one man who will not go to his rest until he is good and ready, and on his own terms, that much I know," but it wasn't what Alymere wanted or needed to hear.

Alymere pushed away from the big man and half-walked, half-ran back to his room, his bare feet slapping too loudly in the silence. Bors let him go.

Gwen had gone. He was glad of that. He didn't think he could have taken her sympathy, no matter how well intended it was.

He wasn't dressed for a long ride. He couldn't think straight. He cast about the room, looking at the sum of his life, pitiful as it was, before gathering his travelling cloak, boots, and a woollen over-shirt, and dressing properly. Then, at the last moment, Alymere stopped beside the bed and stooped, reaching under the wooden frame until he found the familiar skin binding of the Devil's Bible beneath his fingers.

He stuffed it inside his shirt, keeping it close to his chest, and left the room.

Sir Bors de Ganis stood at the head of the stairs like a giant guarding the threshold. "Take Marchante, lad. There isn't a faster horse in your uncle's stable, and no matter my confidence he will live long enough, why make it harder on him?"

"Thank you," Alymere said, clasping his hand. "Truly. Your kindness... You have always been so kind and I always sound like a spoilt child. Who would have thought this day even possible when we first met, eh? I was so filled with childish anger and blamed him for everything, for my father's death, my mother's, our exile, and it was only ever fed by Baptiste. It took two years and the wisdom of a king who didn't know me from Adam to show me he was a good man, and now, now that I know it... he's being taken from me. It just... brings back memories and I'm feeling sorry for myself..."

"Understandable, lad. Don't ever apologise for your feelings. They are what will make you a great knight one day. You are so very like your father in that regard. Now go, ride like the flaming wind. I will watch over Lowick 'til you return."

THIRTY-SIX

ALYMERE GAVE MARCHANTE his head. The sheer power of the great warhorse was incredible; he felt every corded muscle bunch, tense and release beneath him. There was both grace and majesty in the beast's body. Hooves drummed on hard ground so quickly they seemed to become a single incessant sound. The wind whipped at his face and tugged through his hair. For the first time in weeks he felt alive. It was elemental, raw.

He spurred Marchante on. The animal's mane streamed back like the snakes of a gorgon's hair, and still Alymere dug his heels in.

There was a chapel within the grounds of the manor house, but it had been years since a priest resided there; Sir Lowick had served as spiritual leader for his tenants in the priest's absence. The nearest church lay a little over thirty miles due south as the crow flies, where a single holy man tended to the souls of many of the smaller settlements within walking distance. There was nothing to say that Alymere would find him at the church – he was known to walk hundreds of miles a month to share the word of God with farmers and labourers, and others who otherwise would have lived beyond the reach of the Lord. The church stood as a fulcrum of faith in the area; there were four monasteries, one each to the north, south, east and west of it, but each was more than a day's ride. Although, with Medcaut burned, there were only three now, Alymere realised.

The terrain was far from flat, though, so despite the road

being good, the journey to the church and back would take well over six hours, even if he ran the horse into the ground – and assuming he could find the holy man in the first place, never mind make his case vehemently enough to convince him to drop everything and ride out with him there and then.

It would be well after sundown before he returned. He could only pray his uncle would last that long.

Alymere gripped the reins tight in his hands and rode with his head down low, close to the horse's neck, urging him on faster and faster, as he raced towards the road.

A dart of black and white in the sky above him caught his eye, and he looked up to see the crow with its streak of white feathers. It flew straight and true, skimming low across the treetops. The fact that the last time he had ridden this stretch of the Stanegate Road, the Maiden Way, another animal had changed his life forever, did not escape him. The bird's flight appeared to mirror the road below, so for miles into the forest, Alymere let himself be led on by the crow.

And the deeper the road took him into the forest, the more aware he became of the Devil's Bible pressing up against his stomach.

The White Crow and the Devil's Tree...

The Black Chalice...

You are my champion.

Do this one thing for me...

Do not fail me, or all of this will be lost.

Promise me now, make this the one promise you keep.

The damned book pulsed against his skin, breathing. Alive. All of these words, snatches of phrases and portents pounded through his mind, matching the relentless drumming of Marchante's hooves on the road and the pulsing of the Devil's book against his chest.

Or the Devil take your soul...

Up ahead of him, the Stanegate Road divided around a lightning-struck tree the locals called Hangman's Oak, because of the way one of the branches had been split away from the trunk by the lightning strike to form a gallows arm. Some called it the Devil's Tree.

Alymere slowed Marchante, pulling up on the warhorse's reins until he slowed to a canter.

The crow perched on the furthermost tip of the gallows arm, the white feathers clearly visible as it stared at him intently, but it was not the bird that caused him to stop, but rather the crook-backed figure of an old woman resting in its shadow.

She raised her head and a long gnarled finger, which she levelled at him. He saw something then, in her eyes, that frightened him bone deep. She moved forward two shuffling steps. The shadows cast by Hangman's Oak on her pallid skin came alive beneath that slight movement, stretching and writhing as they were pulled out of shape. He didn't care about the shadows; they could not hurt him.

"What do you want from me, witch?" he called, hating the way his new voice sounded in his own ears still. It was as though a stranger spoke through his mouth. But why should it be any different when a stranger wore his face?

"Alymere, Destroyer of Kingdoms. Alymere, Killer of Kings. Alymere, Champion of the Wretched. Alymere, Saviour of the Sick. Alymere, son of Albion? Which is it? Which do you choose, now and forever; who shall you be?" He had heard these names once before, when Blodyweth, the Crow Maiden, first greeted him. To hear them again now, so close to where he had stumbled upon the Summervale, caused him to doubt more than just his ears. The woman before him was no maiden. It was impossible to imagine her as ever having been young, and harder still to imagine her having been beautiful. But then beauty was a transient thing. He touched his own ruined cheek. Who was he to judge now?

The old woman pointed first to the right of the Devil's Tree, "The path of the righteous," she said. And then to the left, "Or the sinister path? Which is it to be? For the day of Alymere the Undecided is at an end. Life is not a single continuous thing," she said, mirroring his own thoughts of days before. Could she somehow tap into his mind? "It is made up of lots of smaller lives. Your old life is at an end, Champion. You are born again. So tell me, who are you?"

The church lay to the left, the nearest settlement to the right. It was possible the priest was to be found at the end of either road, or nowhere at all.

"Who am I?" he asked, as though the old hag might offer answers. He drew himself up in the saddle. "I am my father's son," he said simply. A smile split half of his face.

The crone cackled at that. "That you are," she said. "That you are. I was there at your birth, young warrior, and I will be there at your death," she told him. "And that is the one truth you will utter in all those days in between."

"What is that supposed to mean, woman?"

"There are many lies around you, warrior. Even the face you present to the world is not your own. Some lies are yours, many are not, but that does not change the fact that they are woven around you like the cloak you wear. So, I ask again, who are you, warrior?"

Beneath his clothes he felt the words of the book crawl across his skin, bleeding into him. In his mind he heard the echoes of the same phrases over and over again:

The Black Chalice...

You are my champion.

Do this one thing for me...

Or the Devil take your soul...

"I am Alymere. No more and no less than that. You can speak your riddles, they mean nothing to me. I am not your plaything. Now move out of my way. I will ride you down if I must." He did not wait for her to scurry out of his path. He spurred Marchante forward. The warhorse reared onto its powerful hind legs and kicked at the air. When they came down the horse set off running.

Alymere took the left hand path as the crone had always known he would.

THIRTY-SEVEN

HE STOOD AT the door of the church, but could not bring himself to cross the threshold. He hadn't noticed it before, but carved into the transom, in the block of wood above the doorway, there was a goblet – a chalice – and the constant abuse of the weather had turned it black.

There was nothing untoward about a church bearing the mark of the grail.

He and his uncle had sought the grail once, as had most of Arthur's court at one time or another; so much had happened since they had ridden out together across marsh and field in the rising fogs to find the Chapel of the Fallen Brother, where the first clue to the whereabouts of the grail was carved in stone. It had begun as a great adventure and ended in bitter frustration and disappointment. But that wasn't what Alymere was remembering. The recollection came to him with unerring clarity and for a moment it was as though memory were layered over reality, both doors before him. There had been a single carving etched into the keystone of the chapel's entrance, a chalice.

Could this humble church be part of the grail quest?

Was that what the carving meant?

There was no mistaking the image – it was the cup that had caught the blood of Christ. What more holy symbol could there be?

But for it to have turned black...

He could not shake the feeling that it was an ill omen.

His mind raced, making leaps of logic that churned his stomach: the Devil's book, the Black Chalice, both, surely were the antithesis of these most holy relics, God's Book and the Holy Grail? It made a sickening kind of sense, and explained why Blodyweth feared the book falling into the wrong hands. If the grail were the ultimate prize of good, then surely the black grail must stand as its counterpart on the scales of balance, the ultimate prize of evil?

Instinctively, Alymere made the sign of the cross over his chest, and then winced as the sudden movement caused the book tucked beneath his shirt to dig into his ribs.

He hammered on the door with his clenched fist and waited.

The words of the crone still haunted him all these hours later.

What did she mean, his life was wrapped in lies?

What, if anything, did these lies have to do with the Devil's cup?

Before he could answer the questions – not that he ever could – the door groaned open and a pinch-faced priest peered out through the gathered shadows. His complexion, sallow skin and tired eyes, set into waxy dark circles beneath his heavy brow, bespoke years of austerity and hardship. But for all of the exhaustion there, there was strength too: the strength of faith, the certainty that he was walking the path his God had lain before him, and that every step was a step taken towards Him. Alymere had no such faith. It had been a long time since he had. He could name the day, all those years ago when he became Alymere the Poor Knight instead of Alymere son of Roth. So, for that unwavering confidence, he envied the priest.

In that moment, before he recognised Alymere, the old man's face betrayed his fear.

Then recognition came and he was no longer facing a ghost.

Reflexively, the priest made the sign of the cross, mimicking the gesture Alymere had made only moments before.

"Do I look so bad?" Alymere said, barely masking the bitterness in his ruined voice. He touched his face self-consciously.

The priest stepped back, the door opening another six inches. The moonlight carved a swathe from neck to waist through the man's vestments. "No, my lord. No. Forgive me. I did not mean offence. For just a moment I could have sworn it was your father standing in your place." He shook his head as though trying to rid himself of the last lingering trace of the ghost in his mind. "The similarity between you is striking to say the least."

"And then you saw my scars and thought what, that hell's fire had burned the poor soul as he clawed his way out of the pit?"

"You do me wrong, my lord. More, you do your father wrong. He was the best of men. There is not a day goes by that I do not mourn his absence from this world. Believe me, it is a lesser place without him. He does not reside with the Devil."

"I am sorry," Alymere said, and found that he meant it. "My mood is foul. Fears press on my mind. You don't deserve the lash of my tongue simply for observing what so many others have. All of my life it has been the same: *you look like your father, the apple did not fall far from the tree, the blood ties are strong.* There are days when I hate being my father's ghost and days when it makes the living easier, if that makes sense?"

"It does, my lord. Family is the strongest bond of all, forged for us; *despite* us, oftentimes. You have no need to beg my forgiveness, my lord."

"Thank you, but I suspect you might change your mind once you learn why I have arrived on your doorstep in the dead of night looking for help."

Alymere took a step towards the door, his eyes flicking upwards to look once more at the weathered chalice carved into its wooden frame, then checked himself. He couldn't explain rationally why he didn't want to set foot inside the church, because there was no rational explanation. The priest saw his hesitation and took it as a sign of courtesy.

"Come in, come in," he said, opening the door wider.

Alymere closed his eyes and crossed the threshold. He did not know what he expected – his skin to blister and blacken as his soul burned, his eyes to melt and run down his cheeks, his sins to boil up from inside him and ooze out in the form of corruption and putrescence. Or perhaps the book pressed so close to his skin would ignite when exposed to the air of the sanctuary, scorching through him to the bone in the process?

His skin did not blister, neither did his soul burn.

He opened his eyes, and was three steps inside the church. He had to stifle the urge to laugh. The church was of plain Norman design, a sturdy construction with little in the way of decoration. The one concession to aesthetics was the stained glass window behind the stone altar. In it, Christ was surrounded by every kind of animal the artist could imagine. Each creature was beautifully rendered. During the day every colour of the rainbow must have been scattered across the inside of the church.

It was the first time Alymere had set foot within the place. He had long since ceased praying and had little time for a God who had failed him so consistently, but still the little church was humbling. For the first time in as long as he could remember Alymere felt as though he were in the presence of the divine. Habit, long ingrained, had him genuflect before the altar.

"What can I do for you, my son?" The priest asked, breaking the silence. He had moved silently to stand beside him. "You did not ride all this way without purpose, I am sure."

"A small mercy, father. An act of kindness, and not for me but rather for my uncle. I have come to beg you ride with me, through the night, to the manor. I fear there is little time. We may already be too late."

"Too late?"

"He is dying and would make his peace with God before he goes."

"Oh, sweet Lord," the priest clutched the crucifix at his throat. "How? How could such a thing happen?"

"It is a family curse," Alymere said darkly. His face twisted, on the side still able to betray emotion. "We die young."

The priest shook his head. He looked uneasy; frightened that even in a house of God Alymere would so tempt the fates. "Do not say such things; do not tempt Lucifer's mischievous hand, even in jest, even in this place. The Devil's ears are sharp and stone walls are no protection from his black humour."

If only you knew what I have brought with me into your sanctuary, Alymere thought bleakly, *then you would have reason to be afraid*. He did not give voice to the thought, but apologised. "Sorry father, but it is difficult sometimes to think of us as anything other than cursed. Perhaps it is a blessing that my ill-fated line will come to an end with me."

The priest was not so easily pacified. "You are maudlin, my son, which is understandable given how this life has treated those you love and hold dear, but look at the people you serve: the farmers, the fishwives, the boys born into a life of scrimmaging and struggling for every mouthful of bread and tell me you are truly cursed, my son. Every day I see true hardships and true heroism side-by-side and thank the Lord for His gifts. And like it or not, to those people, *you* are one of those gifts."

"There are more ways of suffering than privation, father," Alymere said, and something in his tone struck a chord with the priest, who bowed his head in acquiescence. "If any man should know that, I would have thought it would be you."

"I do not mean to diminish your suffering. Sometimes I forgot how young you are, my lord. I see the knightly garb and the proud jaw and forget the trials you have faced in your short life. My apologies."

"There's no need to apologise. In many ways you are more than right; I have lived a life of privilege, and for most of it have not wanted for anything; not love, not food, nor a roof over my head. No matter my personal hardships, I should thank the stars for my good fortune. All I can say is that it is too easy to be consumed by one's woes. I think too much of the things that I have lost, instead of remembering the things that I have. Despite my best efforts, I am alive, I have my health, my looks," he chuckled a little self-deprecatingly at that, his fingers instinctively moving to touch his ruined cheek, "and in but a few hours the fates will conspire to make me master of the house I was born in, and all that I lost will be mine once more. But, and here is the God's honest truth, priest: I would gladly give up my inheritance if it meant my uncle, my mother, my father

– anyone I have ever loved, for that matter – if any one of them were restored to me." He shrugged. "But if wishes were fishes I too could feed five thousand. Debating the relative merits of one sadness over another serves no-one, so rather than grow ever more maudlin, let us ride out if you are willing?"

"Of course, of course. Let me collect a few things and we can leave."

The priest bustled around, snuffing candles and dousing oil burners before beginning to gather the objects of his faith: a small wooden cross from the stone altar, a stoppered vial of blessed water from the font, and his battered Bible from the lectern. He moved with familiarity through the richer darkness once the candles and burners were out, collecting a rough hessian sack. He emptied out the few remaining root vegetables that filled it, and then refilled it with the things he had collected. He slung the sack over his shoulder and stopped as the realisation hit him. "Ah, I have no horse, my lord, only my feet." He looked distraught. "No matter how fast I walk, I fear we won't make it in time; it is days to the manor from here," his voice trailed off helplessly.

"Fear not, father, there is room on my horse for two, and Marchante is more than capable of bearing us both. If we leave now we will be back at the house for dawn."

"Then we must not tarry a minute longer than necessary. With God's speed, let us away."

The priest took a few moments to close up the church, and then, as Alymere untied Marchante's reins from the tree he had tethered him to, mounted up. Alymere swung up, joining the priest in the saddle. Desperately uncomfortable on the horse's back, the priest wrapped his arms around Alymere's stomach and buried his face in the folds of his cloak, clinging to him for grim life as Alymere spurred the great warhorse on.

If the priest felt the Devil's Bible beneath Alymere's shirt, he gave no indication.

Alymere, however, was painfully aware of its presence. He felt the leather binding prickle hotly against his skin as the words churned through his mind. This time the voice was recognisably Blodyweth's.

Do this one thing for me...

Promise me now, make this the one promise you keep. Or the Devil take your soul...

When they reached the Devil's Tree there was no sign of either the crow or the leather-faced crone. The moon was obscured by low lying cloud, but a sliver of it shone through, turning the road silver.

Alymere spurred Marchante on, willing Sir Lowick to hold on for just a few hours more.

THIRTY-EIGHT

THEY REACHED THE manor an hour before dawn.

Early morning dew weighed down the tips of the grass. Together with the moonlight it looked as though thousands of gemstones had been scattered across the lawn. Marchante cantered out of the trees, trailing branches pulling at them, and the priest stirred.

"The house is awake," Alymere said, seeing the lamps burning in the upstairs windows.

They rode to the door.

Two servants were there to meet them before they could dismount. The grief was fierce in both of them. No-one spoke; one of the servants took Marchante's reins and led the warhorse around to the stables to see him fed and watered, while the other offered the priest his hand and guided him up the short steps to the house. Horse and priest alike visibly steamed in the pre-dawn chill. He tugged at his vestments uncomfortably, trying to adjust them after the long ride before giving up and following the servant inside.

Alymere raced up the steps behind him and through the door.

He tried to read the house, to prepare himself. Sir Lowick had drummed the necessity of thought into him. Logic and reasoning were the greatest gifts of God, according to the old knight. He believed it was possible to know far more about what you were walking into if only you used your eyes and your mind together. So that was what Alymere did now.

There was an air of mourning about the house. It was obvious despite the lamps in the upstairs windows. Much of the ground floor was draped in shadow.

Bors came down the stairs wearily. The wooden boards sighed beneath his weight. Each step appeared to lessen him until by the time he reached the bottom he was no longer the invincible giant Alymere had met outside of Camelot, but a normal man stretched to the point of breaking. He had never loved the big knight more. There was no doubting the toll the long night had taken on him, both mentally and physically. He looked as though he had not slept for days – which, Alymere realised, was probably the case; he had almost certainly ridden through the one night to bring Sir Lowick home to die, and had then sat his bedside vigil through another – but the worst of it was in his eyes. Alymere recognised the spectre that haunted them for what it was: the ghost of his own mortality.

Bors was a man whose strength defined him; strength of body, strength of mind, of faith, conviction, character. It gave him courage, and in a curious way, cloaked him in immortality; the kind of immortality every knight needed to charge recklessly into battle time and again with only his sword and shield between him and death.

And now his friend was dying an ugly death, robbed of his own strength, and it had hit him hard. Not only that he was dying, but the manner with which death had claimed him. No amount of martial skill, no thickness of armour or swiftness of sword could have saved him from a poisoned cup.

It was no surprise that it would haunt a man like Sir Bors de Ganis. He could just as easily have been the one to drink from the parlay chalice.

"He is still with us," Bors said, seeing the dread in Alymere's face. "But we are talking minutes rather than hours, lad."

They climbed the stairs side-by-side, silently.

Draughts caused the flames to flicker erratically and the shadows to stretch and twist on the walls. The doorway at the far end of the passage was closed, and for the time it took for

Alymere to reach it he wished it could stay that way forever. He had no wish to open it and watch someone he loved die, not when, like Bors, he was helpless to change things.

He closed his eyes and opened the door.

His uncle lay on the tangled sheets, fever sweats ringing his weakened body. He looked ten times worse that he had just a few hours before; his breathing came shallow and erratic, each new breath successively more difficult to take. Alymere stood in the doorway, unwilling to enter the death room. The priest rushed to Sir Lowick's bedside and dropped to his knees, then shrugged the sack off his shoulder and began to remove the few things he had brought from the church: first the cross, then the vial of blessed water and finally the Bible. He offered a short prayer from the book. Alymere understood only a little of the Latin, but knew the passage well: the third chapter of Ecclesiastes, speaking of the timeliness of the seasons of a man's life, whether in birth or death, in silence or speech, in peace or in war.

The knight stirred, opening his eyes. He reached out with an emaciated hand, resting it upon the priest's cross. There was no strength to be gained there. He coughed; it came out like a death rattle. There was no recognition in his eyes when he saw Alymere in the doorway and said quietly, "You can leave us now, my son." Alymere didn't correct his uncle. He stepped out of the room and closed the door behind him, affording Sir Lowick a few minutes alone with his God to unburden his soul.

He paced the passage outside the door, walking back and forth, back and forth. He couldn't sit or stand still for more than a few seconds before he needed to be off again, pacing. Bors left him alone to work his way through the conflicting emotions that ate away at him. His body was tired – beyond tired – but his mind was wide awake, and his mind always won out of the two.

Eventually the door opened and the ashen-faced priest emerged.

He looked at Alymere, but couldn't look him in the eye.

"He would see you now. He is very weak, and his mind is gone, I fear; little of what he says makes sense outside his own mind.

The poison is robbing him of his clarity, but there are things he needs to tell you, if you are willing to hear them. It is not my place, my lord, but I think it is important you hear what he has to say. For yourself if not for him. I am sorry for your loss."

"He's not dead yet, priest," Alymere said, more harshly than he intended.

He left the holy man stumbling over an apology and closed the door behind him. He settled into the room's only chair and, steeling himself, said, "I am here, uncle."

THIRTY-NINE

THE DEATHBED CONFESSION took everything he believed about his life and made a lie of it.

"You were always a good boy," Sir Lowick said. "But I could not be prouder of the man you have become." Even those few words took their toll on him. He sank deeper into the sweat-stained bolster and closed his eyes. His lips moved, and for a moment no words came. His breathing became shallow and erratic as he struggled to master it; he was determined to say his piece. "I remember well the day I went to the king and petitioned for the right to finish your training." He managed a smile. "How could I forget the hot-headed boy I found waiting for me in Camelot? You were so determined to believe I intended to kill you..." He chuckled at that. It was a brittle sound. "But why would I kill my own flesh and blood? My own..." he trailed away into thoughtful silence. For a moment Alymere thought he had died, whatever he so needed to say still unsaid, but he opened his eyes again and said, "If only you had known the truth of who you were to me..."

"Uncle," Alymere said, softly. The word barely carried from his lips, and if Sir Lowick heard it, he gave no sign. He was somewhere else, lost inside his confession. Alymere let him talk.

"But why should you know my shame? Five people kept our secret, three of them have been dead for many years now, and the fourth is about to join them. By rights that ought to mean it is a secret easier to keep. The priest knows now, but he will never tell, and I should let it go to the grave with me, lad... but I can't. Won't. You deserve to know." He broke off, his entire body convulsing with each violent cough. By the time the hacking subsided he was too weak to wipe away the spittle from his lips. "Damn this body of mine. I am not ready. Not yet." He reached out, grasping Alymere's hand with surprising strength. It was the final rally; he would be gone soon. "Boy, I have one last lesson. Take from it what you will. All I ask is that you believe me, because you won't want to. Please remember I have nothing to gain from lies, not now... I have lied for too long. We all have."

"I promise," Alymere said, making another promise with his heart he couldn't keep with his head.

"I can't remember the first time I realised I was in love with Corynn. Your mother was special, lad, a brilliant, beautiful woman. It was certainly before she was married to my brother, though. Long before. Three friends growing up together in this place, it was always going to become two men in love with the same woman. It was impossible for it to be any other way when that woman was your mother, believe me. She was... incandescent."

"I don't need to hear this," Alymere said, but Lowick's grip only tightened and he found fresh resolve. Now was the time; his story would be told.

"I did love her, son, with all of my heart. Did you never wonder why I never took a wife? My heart was already given to another. I tried to stifle it, to kill it, but she was the world to me, and without her my world was nothing more than a broken land. There could be no healing. I didn't mean to do it. I didn't. You have to believe me, son. I didn't mean to do it."

"Do what?" Alymere asked, his heart already sinking. He didn't want to hear the dying man's confession. He didn't want to know. It would change everything. Everything.

"It was the worst moment of my life..." His voice trailed off, barely a whisper now as the last of his strength seemed to ebb out of it. The next few words were lost beneath the rasp-rattle of the dying man's breathing. If not for the fact his lips moved,

Alymere wouldn't have known he was trying to speak.

"What are you trying to tell me, uncle?" He leaned in so close he could feel the knight's lips brush against his ear as they moved.

"You are my ghost."

"I don't understand."

"My ghost. You remind me. Whenever I look at you, I see her. See what I did. And remember my weakness. I am sorry, son. I am so sorry. You look like your father," and for a moment that was all he said. Alymere thought he was gone, and felt the sadness of grief well up within him, but before the tears came the knight whispered, "It is my one great regret that you never knew... that you never looked at me and..." another bout of coughing stole his words away. "I loved your mother. I loved my brother. I was weak. He was gone. At war. We were alone. She wouldn't... It should never have happened... I betrayed... myself. It was a mistake... but when I look at you I don't understand how such evil could create such a perfect thing... God forgive me."

And Alymere understood. How could he not?

But he didn't want to. He wanted to live in ignorance. He wanted to be a child again. This was the truth of his happy family; of why his mother would not live in the manor and died scratching about in poverty; of why Baptiste, his father's man, filled his head with so much hate for Lowick; of why the knight had turned up at Camelot two years ago to claim his stewardship; of all of it. He was his uncle's son. His uncle – this man he had come to admire and adore in equal parts – had forced himself upon his mother.

And now, having watched his father die once before, he was going to have to witness it all over again.

He backed away from the bed.

His mind raced.

It was such a gross betrayal... how could Lowick have lived with himself for so long...? How could... and suddenly an idea struck him. He didn't want to believe it. Couldn't. Wouldn't. But once the thought had taken root it was impossible to dig it out.

But it was idiocy. He'd seen his father die, that slow collapse of the self. It hadn't been self-inflicted. It had been cruel fate. Hadn't it? Could he have poisoned himself? No. Alymere shook his head. He was jumping at shadows now. He couldn't let his imagination run away with things. Roth hadn't committed suicide, but so many things made sense now. Making sense didn't make them better, though.

He pressed his fingers to his temples, feeling the coarseness of the burned skin beneath his fingertips. He turned away. He found himself staring at the door and wishing he could just walk back through it, out into the hallway with its creaks and groans and sighs and pretend his uncle had never made his confession.

His *father...*

If only he could step back a few moments in time. Just two, three; to the moment before the knight unburdened himself.

He could have lived out his life without ever knowing why his mother had refused to live in the same house as the knight.

It didn't help him to know why she had chosen to live in the filth and squalor of the village hovels and scraped and scrimped for food. It didn't make the humiliation of it all any more bearable. They had lived off the charity of others for years instead of in their rightful home.

He ran his hands down his face, stretching his features like dough.

It was too much.

He knew it would help one day, but not yet. It was all too raw. Too much, too soon. For now, the only person this unburdening of the soul helped was dying and had chosen to pass the knowledge on to him like some insidious canker. It soothed the knight's conscience. Alymere understood that, but he still couldn't bear to look at the man on the bed.

He paced the room, frustration welling up inside him – and beneath it, anger. The intensity of it surprised him. His breathing came harsher and faster, each breath shallower than the last, until he had to reach out to steady himself before he swooned. His vision swam. He clenched his fist, squeezing it so tightly his dirty fingernails dug into his palm and drew blood. It trickled between his fingers and down the back of his hand as he raised his fist. Alymere couldn't feel a thing. He looked down at the blood numbly, walked across to the window and braced himself on the sill. The world outside was unchanged. How could it be so? How could it be that everything inside this room had turned the world upon its head, and yet outside nothing looked in the least bit different?

He desperately wanted to lash out and hit something, to let the rage vent out of him.

He imagined driving his fist through the streaked glass.

Words raged within his mind. So many accusations, so much hatred. He slumped forward, his forehead resting against the cold glass.

Had Alymere been in his right mind he would have recognised the source of the voice – and its bleak nature. It was the same insidious voice the book used to goad him. But he was far from his right mind.

"I have to know," he said, staring out at the world through the window, "did she... were you... was it love... or... did you?" he danced around the word, unable to bring himself say it. Alymere drew in a deep breath and forced himself to ask, "Was I conceived in violence?"

"I am sorry, son."

Alymere closed his eyes. He felt his anger thickening. He dug his fingernails into the wooden sill, not feeling the splinters.

Do it.

He heard it plainly.

Kill him. End his life in violence. Take the pillows from behind his head and smother him. He's too weak to fight you. Do it. Make his death the mirror of your birth. In violence the son is begat, in violence the father is slain.

Alymere felt every bone and fibre in his body sing to the black anger coursing through it. The voice of the book was more than merely seductive, it was empowering. It spoke to his soul in a way that only another creature born out of violence could. They were aspects of the same hate. It went beyond a disembodied whisper, becoming in that moment a distinct voice within him – not *of* him, but *in* him. It didn't stroke his fragile ego or stoke his disgust at his own origin, it merely suggested:

Offer his death as a gift to your mother's shade. Let her spectre know vengeance. Let her rest, content that the bastard who raped her is burning in Hell for his sins. You owe her that much.

And it sounded so reasonable.

FORTY

ALYMERE STOOD OVER his father.

It was true, the familial resemblance was strong. Stronger than it had a right to be, he thought.

"Why?" he asked. He could have been asking so many questions, but what he really wanted to know was why the dying man had chosen to burden him with his crime?

"Love," the old man said. "I loved her."

The voice of the Devil's Bible crooned inside his skull:

The sins of the father shall be visited upon the son a thousand times.

"No," he said, though whether denying the knight or his own fate he neither knew nor cared. "Don't say that. Don't lie. Not now. Don't lie to me."

Fathers shall not be put to death for their children, nor children put to death for their fathers; each is to die for his own sin.

"I want to hear the truth. If you are going to burden me with your guilt I want the whole truth. I don't want you painting yourself as a tortured hero unable to resist the maiden's charms, none of that. I want the truth."

The soul who sins is the one who will die. The son will not share the guilt of the father, nor will the father share the guilt of the son. The righteousness of the righteous man will be credited to him, and the wickedness of the wicked will be charged against him.

Kill him. Do it. Take the pillow from beneath his head and put an end to his lies.

For every living soul belongs to me, the father as well as the son – both alike belong to me. The soul who sins is the one who will die.

Tell me he did not sin, tell me he did not betray the greatest trust of all, and in that act forfeit his right to life. Tell me. No; show me.

"I loved her. Every day of my life."

"Not good enough," Alymere said, not recognising the voice that came out of his own mouth. He reached down and tugged the bolster from beneath the knight's head. He held it between them for a moment, staring down with nothing but hatred and disgust for the man in the bed. Something passed between them, unsaid. Lowick understanding what was about to happen, accepting it, even. Alymere leaned forward and pressed the bolster down over the old man's face, holding it firm as the knight's heels kicked at the mattress. His face twisted as Lowick reached up with frail hands to scratch and claw at him. He felt one of Lowick's fingernails break off in the back of his hand. The scratch wasn't deep. He watched with grim fascination as a single drop of blood broke and ran across the back of his hand and fell, staining the perfect white of the bolster. Alymere didn't stop pressing down until Sir Lowick stopped kicking and clawing at his hands and went still.

And then, with grim economy, he placed the pillow beneath the dead man's head, arranging his body so that it looked as though he had passed peacefully, closed his accusing eyes, and left the room.

It was an illusion. There was no peace in the death mask Sir Lowick wore – he looked as though he had just come face-to-face with the Devil himself. The horror of it was wrought plain upon his face for all to see.

And beside his head, that single spot of blood on the white pillow could so easily betray his murderer if any of the household thought to question it.

Alymere met Sir Bors upon the landing. The big man saw his expression.

"He is gone," Alymere said.

"I should pay my respects. Will you be here when I return?"

"I need air."

"That is understandable. I will find you when I am done. Then we must make arrangements for his burial."

Alymere shook his head. "No. It was his wish that he should burn."

FORTY-ONE

HE GRABBED A flagon of mead from the dresser in the kitchen, ignoring the protestations of the cook, and uncorked it with his teeth. He took a deep swallow, smacking his lips as the honeyed drink hit the back of his throat and he felt the burn of the alcohol. He took a second and third swallow, swatting the woman away as he drained the bottle dry. Alymere looked around for a second flagon and snatched it up, pulling the cork out of its neck and throwing it at the guttering fire. He turned around and stumbled out of the kitchen, down the long passageway and out into the fresh air.

It hit him hard.

Taking another huge swig of mead from the bottle, Alymere ran toward the old sour apple tree where he had sat so many times with Gwen over the last few months, thinking to drink and lose himself there. His head was spinning, less from the drink than from what he had just done. A few steps from the apple tree's shadow he turned away. He didn't want to contaminate the place with the blackness of his soul. It was the only happy place left to him in this house of lies. Instead, he walked toward the graves of his parents on the outskirts of the estate. Lime trees interspersed with elm formed a long passage that led from the furthest edge of the lawn to the stone mausoleum on the hill. He drained the second flagon before he was halfway down the leafy tunnel, tossing it aside. The alcohol spread through his blood, thinning it and affecting his balance.

The air felt so much colder up here, and the drink offered little in the way of fortification. He looked up at the sky, thinking it really ought to have been raining. He wanted the world to be in mourning, as he was. He shivered again and wished he had thought to grab his cloak as well as the mead on the way out of the house. His throat burned and his eyes itched; he felt the mead churning around in his stomach. But it couldn't soak up the sudden surge of guilt he felt at what he had just done. He tried to justify it by reminding himself that Sir Lowick would have died in a few hours anyway, but that didn't matter. He had snuffed out his life, and in that single act had become a murderer and betrayed every promise he had ever made. He thought of the Oath the king had made him swear, and for the first time in his life couldn't remember all the tenets of it.

He was crying.

He left the tears to stain his cheeks, wearing them like his shame, and walked unsteadily toward the mausoleum. His head felt cloudy, his thoughts muggy. Snot ran from his nose and he smeared it across his face.

"Why?" he shouted at the sky.

The heavens had no answers for him.

The dead house was overgrown with vines, where nature had begun the slow process of claiming it. In a decade or more it would be invisible against the landscape, but for now it was a sinister blend of stone and vegetation. He walked slowly toward the door, not really certain what he intended to do. He could hardly push his way inside and rail at the coffins lined up within, could he?

Alymere leaned against the door and closed his eyes.

His mother and father were on the other side of the door – or so he had thought for years now, but the man buried there wasn't his father.

He pushed at the door, more out of frustration than any hope of it swinging open.

It was locked, of course, but he wasn't about to let that prevent him. He put his shoulder to it, thinking suddenly to batter it down, and rocked back on his heels, steeling himself, but at the last moment thought better of it. He had other options. The lock wasn't complex. It didn't need to be, no-one would rob the dead. Not here. They respected his family too much; they were every bit a part of the land as the mountains or the trees.

Alymere crouched and put his eye to the mechanism. He felt a wave of nausea swell up inside his throat and swallowed it down. He ran his fingers across the seam where the door met the stone wall. There was a thin gap between them, barely wide enough for him to slip the blade of his dagger into. The tip scraped across the wood at first, as he fumbled with it, but, grating against the stone and cutting free splinters from the edge of the door, he managed to work it into the gap. He worried the metal against the lock's latch, trying to pry it free again and again, until, exasperated with his lack of success, Alymere slammed his shoulder against the door, screaming out his frustration, and the metal latch gave way.

The door swung open and he tumbled inside, cursing as he sprawled across the floor. It was a drunkard's entry, lacking subtlety or grace, but he was inside. Alymere pushed himself to his feet and slowly dusted himself off. He looked around the mouldering tomb. It was too dark to see anything but the vaguest outlines of the stone sarcophagi inside. The air smelled dead. He reached out to steady himself on the lid of his mother's sarcophagus, and then recoiled as though he had just laid his hand on her cold dead face.

A thin line of light cut like a sword through the centre of the dead house. Alymere stepped into the light.

"Mother!" he shouted, surely loud enough to wake the dead. He gritted his teeth, turning in circles and listening for the slightest sound, the tiniest indication that she had heard him and was going to answer.

The dead slept on.

"How could you lie to me for so long?" This time there was no strength behind his words. He turned again, facing the stone box where his father's bones mouldered. "How could you pretend like that? How could you look at me and call me son when you knew?" And the question he really wanted to ask, "How could you not hate me?"

The wind called forlornly across the hillside, whispering around the mausoleum's door. It didn't cry his name. There was no answer. No satisfaction.

"Or did you hate me? Did you look at me and see his crime over and over again? Did you see him in my face? Is that why you gave up? Is that why you let yourself die? Was I your shame?" His voice spiralled out of control at the end. He was drunk. He was crying. He felt stupid and he felt angry. He wanted to break something. But even as he said it he realised that was his greatest fear; he couldn't bear to think that he had been a constant source of grief for the man he had idolised. "Father..." he said. Birth had nothing to do with it; Lowick wasn't his father, he never had been. He'd given up every right to fatherhood by his betrayal. Roth was his father and always would be. "I'm sorry." It sounded woefully inadequate once he said it, but it was honest.

He was a child of violence. The hatred of his very conception had imprinted on his soul. He touched the hard skin of the scars on his cheek, recalling the rage he felt trying to wrest the book from the blind monk, and worse, the thrill, the enjoyment that came with it. He was broken in some essential way and always had been, all the way back from before he was born.

He wasn't going to have some sort of revelation here. There wasn't going to be an epiphany where suddenly what had happened was understandable or excusable. And he wasn't going to find forgiveness. Instead of looking for any of that he stumbled over to his mother's tomb and knelt, pressing his forehead against the cold stone. "Sleep well, Mother. Rest easy in the knowledge that after all these years, reckoning has finally been had. He went to meet the Devil full of fear," he breathed deeply, again reliving that moment, recalling how it felt to choke the life out of Lowick. "And now he's burning."

Burning, the voice of the book echoed in his drunken mind. *Burning, burning bright,* it cackled. There was something manic, almost childish about its delight.

He stayed on his knees for long minutes before finally pushing himself to his feet. He lowered his head again, unable to look at the stone sarcophagi.

"You are avenged," he said, finally, realising why it had been important for him to come here. They needed to know, even if they couldn't hear him. He had to believe that somehow their bones would carry his words to their ears, wherever they were. Finally they had their justice. They could rest now. The lies were unravelled, justice delivered.

And yet he felt hollow inside.

Something in him was broken and no words were going to fix it. Words were empty. All they had ever done for Alymere was hide the truth.

He kicked out at his mother's tomb, spinning clumsily around. His arms windmilled as his balance betrayed him and he pitched backward, stumbling into the wall. He grunted and slumped, sliding down the cold stone until he sat propped up and staring at the two tombs. "I curse you," he muttered. "I curse ever knowing you. I curse ever knowing what brought me into this damned world. I wish... I wish... I..." but what did he wish for? He couldn't very well wish that they were dead, though neither did he wish that they were alive. Could he wish that they hadn't turned him into a murderer with their lies? Well, he could wish, but that wouldn't change the fact that, less than an hour ago, he had betrayed everything he believed in, because his beliefs had been ripped out from under him. It was all just words and excuses and he was tired of both of them.

His own words haunted him: *A true man must never do outrage, nor murder... never will a true man stand by idly and watch such evils perpetrated by others upon the innocent, for a true man stands as last bastion for all that is just.* He was caught in the contradiction of his own vow. Lowick's evil had been done against his own mother. How could he sit by idly? The man would never have gone to trial, and so would have avoided mortal justice.

You did the only thing you could, the voice of the book whispered in his head. There was something different about it; it wasn't so much seductive as satisfied. *You had to open yourself up. You had to feel the rage. And in the end, you had to kill him. That was justice. It was right. You became a man. A true man.* But the way the Devil's book said the words "true man" left him in no doubt, it didn't mean them in the way the knights of Albion intended them. Hearing them now, they spoke of man's base nature, not his nobility.

"Leave me alone," he said.

Never. We are one and the same. You cannot live without me. I have made you what you are, forged in the furnace of life. Shaped by the hammer of death. I have made you whole. And without you I would be nothing. We need each other. We are each other.

And yet he had never been more alone in his life.

He saw her face then, plain but not unappealing; pretty in some ways. But more than that, Gwen was the only person in this world he considered a friend.

Gwen.

He pushed himself up to his feet, needing the wall to stop him from falling. His mind reeled, the ground shifting beneath him. He needed to find her. He needed to... to what? Be loved? No. That wasn't it. Alymere shuffled forward an unsteady step, screwing his face up against the light that speared through the heart of the dead house. She didn't know what had happened today. She didn't know who he was – *what* he was. And she didn't care. She wouldn't judge him. She was his friend. The more he thought about it, the more it made sense to his drunken mind. He wasn't damaged in her eyes, at least not beyond the surface scarring. And not once had she shied away from looking at him. Not once had he seen revulsion in her eyes for the monster he had become. She only saw her friend when she looked at him. Nothing went deeper than that.

He touched his cheek. The scars burned beneath his fingers.

He needed to find Gwen.

He turned his back on the sarcophagi, and stumbled out into

the daylight. He raised a hand to shield his eyes from the bright light, but still it stung them. He screwed up his face, looking down at his feet. It was only when he lowered his hand and raised his head that he saw the crude wooden crosses planted in the earth a dozen paces away.

FORTY-TWO

THE MAUSOLEUM, THE crude crosses planted in the dirt, and all the trappings of death that went along with them weren't there to honour the dead, he thought, seeing them. He walked unsteadily towards them. Just as the funeral rites themselves had nothing to do with the needs of the corpses left behind. They were there to prolong the grief of the living. The crosses were nothing more than spars of wound, bound together crudely with twine.

He sank to his knees in the freshly turned dirt, dusting away the soil that covered the base of the first cross to uncover the name engraved into the wood: Alma. He had heard that name before, but couldn't place it. The dirt had worked its way into the pulp of the wood, staining it black. He shuffled across to the second cross and scrabbled at the base of it desperately, knowing without really understanding why he knew the name that he uncovered: Gwen. Alma and Gwen. He closed his eyes, a low keening moan escaping him. There was nothing to indicate how they had died, but all he could think was that he'd never seen his friend with the baby girl after he had rescued her from the burning house, and that he had never seen Gwen in the company of others since his return.

He pushed himself to his feet.

He stared at the dirt on his hands, desperately wanting not to believe... and struggling to remember a single time where he had seen Gwen with other people around, just a single instance where he had seen her interact with another soul, but he couldn't. He felt a thrill of fear.

"Oh, my God," he breathed, backing away from the graves.

His feet left deep imprints in the dirt, dragged like scars across the freshly turned soil.

He couldn't bear to look at the graves; didn't know what they meant.

He was losing his mind. That was all he could think. He was losing his mind, root and branch. It was spinning away from him. Nothing made sense, from the world he thought he believed in to the mad depths of the underworld he found himself living in, so much deeper and closer to Hell than he had any right to travel. And every step he took seemed to take him further down. Alymere tore at his hair, tugging the roots from his temples, and screamed. It was a long harrowing cry that swelled out over all the land – or so it felt to him. For it to do justice to the agony in his soul it would have had to carry from coast to coast, and even then it couldn't match the pain inside. They deserved that much from him.

When he opened himself up to it, the grief was overwhelming.

He rubbed at his face. He was numb; hollow. Nothing made any sense to him.

The silence around Alymere was suddenly split by a single raucous caw. He spun around, scanning the trees for the crow, knowing even before he saw it that it would be the white-streaked bird that had been haunting him. He felt the bird's cry reverberate through his bones.

Each breath came fast and shallow. He looked up at the sky, the first fat drops of rain hitting his face. He opened his mouth, tasting the rain on his tongue. For a moment that was all that existed. This dark country that he found himself trapped in was reduced to the taste of the rain on the back of his throat. He felt his grip on the world unravelling. He wanted to cry out, to beg for help, but he was frightened what might answer him. What monsters would come to the aid of a murderer? None that he was prepared to face.

He felt the sudden chill in the air. It was more than just the rain. He wasn't alone.

Alymere forced himself to open his eyes.

He saw her standing, watching him, baby Alma in her arms. The child was crying silently. She looked so very sad standing there in the shadow of the lime tree that Alymere wanted to run to her, to hold her and thank God that it was all a huge mistake, that his mind had run away with itself, but there was something about the way the light didn't strike her and the rain didn't soak her that stopped him. He stared at her, realising that the sunlight filtering through the leaves left no shadow in her wake.

She beckoned for him, but he couldn't walk over to her, no matter how much he wanted to.

He felt betrayed once more, not grasping until long after she was gone and he was alone that she had saved him. Gwen's shade had denied itself the peace of the grave to repay him for everything he had done; saving Alma, giving her friends a home, avenging the men they had lost to the reivers; every good deed he had done had kept her here while he needed her. And without Gwen he would have been lost, there was no denying that. It didn't matter that he was blind to her sacrifice as he stood by her graveside in the pouring rain, that he had no comprehension of the pain it must have caused her to linger. So acute was his self-pity that all he could see was another abandonment. Someone else that he couldn't trust, someone else who wasn't they seemed.

And so, despite everything they had shared, the intimacy that went beyond simple friendship into spiritual healing, he turned his back on her.

He felt her pain then, but in denying Gwen, he effectively banished her shade, consigning her finally to the grave. Why should she linger if he had neither want nor need of her?

When he turned back to the avenue of lime trees leading to the house, she was gone. He stayed by her graveside for a while, and the rain washed away his guilt.

He looked around until he saw what he was looking for: a cluster of daffodils, their trumpets heavy with pollen. He snapped them off at the stem and laid them on Gwen's grave without a word. It was the closest he would ever come to admitting he had done wrong by her.

Alymere walked away from the dead house and the paupers' graves, the rain matting his hair flat to his scalp and soaking through his shirt. It clung coldly to his skin. Spirits whispered through the dragging branches of the lime trees as he passed beneath them, the leaves rustling in their wake. Somewhere between the mausoleum and the manor the Devil's book spoke to him, promising: *I am your friend. I won't leave you. I won't fail you or lie to you. I am you and you are me. We are bound. Together we are mighty. Together we are Alymere. They will hear our name and know fear. Now come, I have such secrets to share with you.*

And as that voice took hold, he was truly lost.

FALLEN SON

FORTY-THREE

For the first time Alymere could read the book in its entirety.

There were no more secrets, no hidden words in the writhing script teasing him, staying just out of reach. Everything it had to say was laid bare in a language he could understand.

He trembled as he laid the old book out on the bed, cracking it open and turning page after page quickly, drinking in the words without focusing on what they said. They spun through him, creating web after web of connections, joining thoughts he had never imagined, and, at the centre of the web, one single image, the Black Chalice. It was there at the heart of all of it, the one great truth of the Devil's Bible. The word *chalice chalice chalice* blurred into a single sound inside his mind. It began as a low insistent echo, like the distant sound of thunder rolling over the hills, and it grew louder, as though nearing, and becoming more demanding with each repetition. The word caused him to wince as it drummed over and over again through his head, *chalicechalicechalice* repeating itself so many times it lost all shape and form, sacrificing its own identity to become something entirely new, like a snake coming alive in the darkness at the back of his skull. And as its tongue lashed around the hissing sibilants, the word stopped making any sense. But it was no less demanding for that insanity. Far from it, it was all the more demanding.

Alymere let his fingers rest on the indentations of the actual words and the shapes they made within the page, feeling out where the scribe's nib had dug into the paper. And as he did so, more and more of the words came alive inside him, starting with the very first line, *being an account of the entire wisdom of Man as transcribed by Harmon Reclusus,* and he knew beyond any doubting that all of the secrets of the book were going to reveal themselves to him.

For all that promise, the only thing he was interested in learning about was the Black Chalice.

He drank it all in hungrily, all the dark knowledge that the Devil's Bible contained, beginning with the confession that the book owed its creation not to Harmon's pen and ink, but rather to the pact the monk had made with the Devil himself. Harmon, if his confession were to be believed, was, at the time of writing, a prisoner of his own kind, locked away in the spire of Medcaut for his human frailties – his perversions, as he called them – without food or water. The only things his brothers would allow him, in order to record his confession, were a quill, inks, and parchment pages. But rather than baring his soul and recording his sins, the monk had chosen to embark upon a far more noble – and impossible – task: to record everything he had ever learned in a single volume. It was nothing short of hubris to declare it the sum of human wisdom, of course, but that was only one of his many sins. Harmon Reclusus had been working on the illuminated manuscript for years, but there was no way he could possibly hope to complete his life's work. Not now. His body was in the final stages of the greatest betrayal imaginable.

He was dying.

He could not keep food down. It had been days since he had had even a cup of water, let alone a meal, and as he felt himself weakening to the point of unconsciousness and the inevitability of death, but tormented by the thought of failure, of going without finishing his masterpiece, Harmon had fallen on his knees and made a prayer.

This prayer was not offered to God, who had forsaken him in his hour of need, but to the Devil himself.

It was a desperate plea.

And Satan had answered, granting him a single night of feverish consciousness throughout which he would do more than just finish his book, he would channel the entire knowledge of the divine and demonic, far beyond the understanding of mere man, into the pages of his manuscript, thus transforming it from the wisdom of a single man into something far more dangerous: the Devil's Bible. By sunrise, Satan told him, he would be spent, gone, burned out in a blaze of black wisdom – and the cost of this bargain? The book completed in return for his immortal soul.

Harmon had sealed the pact with his blood, drawn to the promise of forbidden knowledge.

How could he have resisted, wondered Alymere? After years of isolation and study, giving everything of his life to the completion of one great work, the penitent had succumbed not to earthly temptations, not to the sins of the flesh, but to the simple promise of finishing what he had started. It was not about knowing everything, for he would hold that knowledge for less than a single night. And so what if the cost of it was something he himself neither had use for nor believed in? God had abandoned him. That only made the deal all the more appealing to the monk. Harmon got what he wanted, he finished his life's work, and the Devil was just as happy with the price they'd agreed.

Alymere knew all of this in seconds, opening himself up to the book, and understanding even as he did who the voice inside his head belonged to.

I am glad we understand each other, the voice preened inside his mind. Oh yes, he was well aware what – or who – had taken up residence within him. And rather than repulsing him, Alymere found himself embracing the invader. As he had promised, together they would become everything it was possible for him to become. Together they would be Alymere, Destroyer of Kingdoms. They would be Alymere, Killer of Kings. They would be Alymere, Champion of the Wretched. They would be Alymere, Saviour of the Sick and Alymere, Son of Albion. They would be all of the things the Crow Maiden had foreseen for them. Together they would be all of these and more.

I can feel the hunger burning inside you... It is unquenchable. It roars. It rages. It consumes. There is nothing like it, nothing like the desire for vengeance, against the world that has wronged you, against the people who have betrayed you, against the black veins of sickness that permeate every work of God, from the foundations up. I can feel it. You cannot hide it from me. It nourishes me. In return I will nourish you. I will be the fire in your blood. I will be the righteous fury in your fist. I will be the passion in your loins. I will be the flame that stirs your heart. I will be the ambrosial milk that grants sustenance even as it spills from your lips. I will be the light in the darkness of your soul. I will be you. And you will be me. Do you want that?

"Yes."

How much?

"More than anything."

I want you to do something for me, for us, to bring us closer together, to make us complete. Will you do that for me?

"Yes."

As the image of the Black Chalice swelled to fill his mind, the Devil commanded: *Bring it to me. Bring me the Chalice. Go first to the great Laird's cairn; you will know your way from there.* And, as Alymere closed his eyes, all of the real secrets, the darkest, most thoroughly hidden treasures of the Devil's book made themselves known to him in a dizzying rush. The thrill of them raced from his fingers to his heart, traversing every nerve and fibre, transforming him into a conduit for the book's dark wisdom. He opened himself to it, drinking it in, absorbing every fateful ounce of knowledge from the first sins to the greatest evils, the secrets of creation and the lies of faith and flesh. Every treachery, every deceit and betrayal, every bare-faced lie whispered or told bold as brass, echoed through his head; not the words, but a deeper understanding, of the lies themselves. He not only understood the drive to lie, to cheat, to steal, but revelled in it. The thrill he felt was almost sexual in its nature, a force that owned him body and soul. And it came at no little cost. His entire body trembled, every muscle tensing, and then he began to convulse violently as the arcana took root within him. Beads of sweat broke and ran from his temple and brow over the too-smooth planes of his deformity. He blinked them back as they stung his eyes. He chewed on his lower lip until it bled. His breathing was ragged. Excited. Fearful.

Alymere whispered the words back to the air, repeating what he heard inside his head. As they left his lips, the words began to take on a life all of their own. He fell into a rhythmic chant that matched the pounding of the blood through his temples. The words came faster and faster, growing louder and louder until he was sure he was shouting, yelling, but he couldn't stop himself. And he couldn't pull his hands from the book.

Alymere's eyes rolled up inside his skull, his jaw locked open in a silent scream as the ink chased up from the page, roiling through, over and under his skin, painting him as the illumination fled the book. The symbols chased after each other across the flat plains of scar tissue up to his throat, then up over his chin and across his cheekbones and into his eyes, flooding into him. They began as words, identifiable, legible, but as more and more wisdom bled out of the book into him the ink became a solid blackness that transformed him into something demonic: a creature of ink.

As the last traces of writing fled the page and entered his hands, racing up his forearms, the skin left in its wake returned once more to raw, pink flesh. Stain by stain, his body returned to its natural state, the words of the Devil bleeding into his eyes to stain upon his soul, and then he began screaming again. It was a scream like none that had ever been heard in this house.

Seconds after the screams began the door flung open on its hinges, slamming against the wall.

The huge figure of Sir Bors de Ganis filled the doorway, sword in hand, as Alymere fell forward across the book, utterly spent.

For a moment Bors didn't move. He stood as though trapped in the doorway, staring at Alymere's collapsed body, and then everything exploded into sound and panic as a bird flew at the glass window, cannoning off it in a flurry of feathers as the glass cracked, and whatever spell had bound Bors broke along with it. Seeing Alymere was alone, he dropped his sword and crashed into the room, and bounded forward, arms outstretched as though to catch Alymere, despite the fact that he had already fallen.

The knight gathered Alymere into his arms.

He lifted him and carried him to the cot, where he laid him down, stroking the matted hair away from his brow with curious tenderness. Alymere didn't move; didn't make a sound. It took a moment for Bors to realise he wasn't breathing. He couldn't think. He feared the worst, ready to beat on the boy's chest and try to hammer the life back into him, but as he leaned in close he heard a sound, so quiet he almost missed it: a gasp as the breath caught in Alymere's lungs escaped. It might almost have been a death rattle, but it was followed by a second and a third breath. He felt the warmth of Alymere's breath against his cheek as he began to breathe again.

Bors closed his eyes and said a silent prayer of thanks.

He took the blanket from where it was bundled up at the bottom of the bed and covered Alymere with it.

Seeing the book on the floor, Bors stooped and turned a few of the pages, but could make no sense of the scrawled words. Something about the book, however, the very physical presence of it, repulsed him. It was wrong in a way he couldn't begin to explain. Looking at it, he had the overpowering desire to take it across to the hearth and consign it to the flames.

His skin crawled as he reached down to close the book, and as he did, he broke whatever connection Alymere had to it, but when it came to it he couldn't throw the Devil's Bible into the fire.

It didn't matter. Even with the book closed, Alymere truly was no longer himself. Burning it would not have saved him.

Bors did not see the single white feather that had caught in the broken window. Even if he had, he could not have known what it meant, nor how far his young friend had fallen.

GRAIL KNIGHT

FORTY-FOUR

ALYMERE REGAINED CONSCIOUSNESS some time before dawn. He came
to slowly, still groggy and, while not feverish, sheened with
sweat. He pushed back the blanket. The first thing he did was
reach for the book, but it wasn't where he had left it and wasn't
in its hiding place beneath his bed. A surge of panic rose within
him, and he threw himself out of the low cot and scrabbled
about on the floor, looking around frantically for the Devil's
book. He clawed up the rug and tugged at the corners of several
floorboards to pry them free, but while they creaked and groaned
beneath his weight none of them were loose enough to lift. He
turned, still on his hands and knees, and saw the ash in the
hearth, all that remained of the fire that had burned out during
the night. He crawled across to it, a low, feral moan escaping his
throat as he sifted through the ashes. There was no sign that the
book had been burned. But where was it? He felt as though half
of his soul had been stolen from him. He didn't need the book.
The words were alive inside him. But be that as it may, he *wanted*
the book. It was near, somewhere – he could feel it – just not in
this room.

Who had taken it?

And then, some thing, some trace of his nightmare, crossed his
mind and he saw Bors looming over him in the open doorway.
Bors had taken the book. He must have. He had put Alymere to
bed after he collapsed, and had found the book lying open on the

floor. Had he tried to read it? Had he tried to steal it from him? Had he found it, started to read, and then the book offered up its secrets? No. No. That couldn't have happened. Bors couldn't have read a single word of it, so pure was the knight. The thoughts raced crazily through Alymere's mind, each coming before the previous one had time to fully form. He tried to think, to reason, as his uncle had taught him to; to think through the problem using only the evidence at hand, not chasing flights of fancy. Bors had taken the book. No other explanation made sense. And for his reasoning to work, that meant, surely that the big man had taken it simply to destroy it? But why would he do such a thing? Why would he take the one thing left to Alymere, the last good thing in his life, and crush it?

Because, the voice crooned at the back of his mind, *like everyone else, the knight only cares for himself. That is the extent of his virtue. You are nothing to him. Why should it matter to him if you are whole? Why should he care if you are fulfilled? He treats you like a child. A joke. You are neither. We are neither. Go, find him, take the book from him, and if he tries to stop you, cut him down.*

Alymere stood slowly, looking around the room. "Yes," he said. "It is mine."

The sky outside was bruise-purple and moonless. He padded over to the window, which he saw was broken. He touched the crack in the glass, unable to remember how it had happened. The world beyond it was still deep in sleep.

And as he cut the pad of his index finger on the broken glass, he remembered what the Devil had asked of him:

Bring it to me. Bring me the Chalice. Go first to the great Laird's cairn; you will know your way from there. The words came to him like ghosts. He knew who the great Laird had been; his father had told him stories of Nectan, clan-lord of Tay, and the constant thorn he had been in Alymere's grandfather's side, leading his raiders deep into his protectorate, pillaging, raping and burning. And Alymere knew where the stones had been laid to mark his burial place. North of Dùn Chailleann, high in the mountain ranges of Sìdh Chailleann.[9] His father had called it the Constant Storm, and told stories about how it never stopped raining there, but said that others, more superstitious, called it the Fairy Hill[10] for the uncanny air that clung to it. But it didn't matter what they called it, really. The Caledonian mountain was far over the border, beyond both Rannoch and Tay lochs, and through the deep woods of Coit Celidon into the heart of reiver country, and for Alymere that made the journey suicidal.

But he could no more refuse the Devil than he could save his own soul, book or no book.

His travelling cloak was draped over the back of the room's one chair, his pack bundled into the corner of the room. He fastened his cloak around his neck, ignoring the reek from his clothes. The pack was empty, but he shouldered it anyway. He would need something to carry the Chalice when he found it. And he had no doubt that he would recover it, with the Devil at his back.

And then he saw something he had thought lost: the strip the Crow Maiden had torn from her dress and given to him as a favour. He had not worn it since the fire. She had set him on this course. He remembered his promise to her, how naïve he had been to think love would conquer all. Still, he took the linen and tied it tightly around his forearm. He couldn't have explained why he did it, nor accounted for how important such a little thing would prove to be. It just felt like the right thing to do. He was a grail knight now, albeit a dark one, riding off into peril. It was only right he wear his lady's favour; after all, she was the only one who had never lied to him, he realised bleakly.

He took one last look around the room he had grown up in, feeling that he would never return, and closed the door behind him. It settled in the frame with an air of finality.

He did not look back.

---

[9]In the manuscript, "Dunnkelyd, [Dunkeld] haut in the montaynes of Sheehallyon [Schiehallion]," referring to Dunkeld, Perthshire. I have substituted the Scots Gaelic names, here and over the following pages.

[10]*Sidh Chailleann* literally means "Hill of the *Sidh*," or fairies.

FORTY-FIVE

He found Sir Bors de Ganis in the Great Hall, the book open in his lap. He looked up as Alymere walked toward him. He hadn't slept all night; that much was painfully obvious. His usual jovial demeanour had deserted him. His face was grave, his eyes dark hollows. His skin had a sickly waxen cast to it and his beard, where usually it was well groomed, was unruly and wild. Had he been pressed, Alymere would have said it looked as though the big man had been fighting for his life all night, and fighting hard, but there wasn't a mark on him, and nothing to suggest he had left his seat in hours.

"What is this terrible thing, lad?" Bors asked.

Alymere stopped, still five paces short of Bors' seat.

"It is a book," Alymere said, aware that his words were laced with sarcasm. He did not smile. The old Alymere would have, trying to be affable, looking to please the big man, but no more. He wanted the book back.

"I can see that, but that is not what I mean, and well you know it."

"Then perhaps you should be more precise in your questions, no?"

"I'll let you have that one, but talk to me like that again and –"

"And what? You'll strike me down? I don't think so. You don't have it in you. So, give me the book. It is mine."

"I don't think so, lad. I might be many things, but I am not a fool. Listen to yourself. You're changing. I don't think I should let you anywhere near it. There's something not right about this thing, I can feel it. And I can feel what it is doing to you. No good can come of it, you mark my words."

"You are so sure you know what's best for me, aren't you? So sure that you lied about who my father was, to my face, and now you expect me to honour you? Go to Hell," as Alymere spat the last words out, his face twisted into a sneer.

His words hit their mark. Bors closed the Devil's Bible, dust wafting up from the pages to dance and drift in the first rays of dawn that crept in through the high windows. For a moment, a single heartbeat frozen in time, the knight's face betrayed his true revulsion of the man before him, before he mastered it. "You want it? Take it." He said, without offering it. He didn't move.

Alymere took a single step forward, closing the gap between them to just a few feet. He was still a few steps shy of being able to snatch the book out of the big man's grasp. His eyes flicked from Bors' face to the book in his lap and back again.

"Take it, lad, if it is so damned important to you," Bors repeated. There was no kindness in his voice. "I will not stop you. Take it and be damned right along with it. Who am I to prevent you destroying your life?"

"No-one," Alymere said, taking a second step. "And I owe you nothing. Not anymore. Whatever bond I thought we might have shared, you severed with your secrets and lies. So whatever game you are playing won't work on me. Now, give me the book."

The big man shook his head. "No. Take it. I'll not be party to ruining a good man. I owe your father more than that."

"And which father would that be?"

"You won't goad me into a fight if that is what you are trying to do, lad. If you want the damned book, on your head be it, but you have to take it. You have a choice, lad. Take it, carry it to the fire burning in the hearth, and consign it to the flames, and be free of whatever hold it has on you, or take it and walk out of here. The choice is yours, but if you chose not to burn the damned thing, then I advise you to get as far away from me as you can, because I swear I don't ever want to see your face again. Do you understand me? You're better than that. Stronger. You have the makings of a great man. Don't throw your life away, son."

"The *one* thing I am sure of right now is that I am not your son," Alymere said.

He held out his hands for the book.

Bors did not move. He said nothing.

Alymere covered the last few steps in a rush, snatched the book out of Bors's lap and backed off before the knight's hand could snake out and snag him.

"So what's it going to be, lad? Fire or damnation?"

Alymere didn't answer him, not with words. He turned on his heel and walked out of the room.

Sir Bors de Ganis sank lower in his chair, reduced by the exchange, broken. He had genuinely thought – hoped – that Alymere would do what he couldn't, burn the book. He had gambled everything on it. And lost.

But it wasn't just that he had lost, it was the manner of that loss. It went far beyond a battle of wills. He had put his faith in the lad, not realising just how lost to himself he was.

The dilemma he faced now was a simple one: was he the sort of man who would break his oath in order to save a friend? Or was he stubborn enough to turn his back on one during the time of their greatest need?

Oath-keeper?

True friend?

Couldn't he be both? Why did it have to be one or the other?

FORTY-SIX

ALYMERE FLED THE Great Hall. He clutched the book to his chest, feeling his heart beating wildly against it. And for a moment he could have sworn he felt its corresponding heartbeat pushing back against him. But that was impossible. Wasn't it?

Nothing is impossible, Alymere. Don't you know that already? Can't you feel the possibilities bubbling inside you? Don't you feel the thrill of the stone and the dirt coursing up through you? That is creation. That is power. True power. Magic, if you will. It is the life blood of Albion, of the world. And the world is there for the shaping, for the taking. Together we have it in us to shape destinies and bring kingdoms crashing down. Together, Alymere, you and I. We could raise up armies out of the firmament. We could carve out the future in our own image... with the Chalice, anything is possible. Everything is possible. Bring it to us. Reclaim it. It was ours and it shall be again.

"I already said I would," Alymere snapped, barely recognising his own voice for the malice in it. "I cannot conjure it out of thin air. I am not a witch."

No. You are so much more.

Alymere bustled out of the main house, flinging the door open with his one free hand, and strode out into the rising sun. Dawn had taken the cold edge from the air but it still had that wonderful bite deep in his lungs as he breathed it in. It was going to be a glorious day. Dew sparkled on the grass.

And then he realised what was wrong: there was no dawn chorus. On any other day he would have emerged to incessant bird song, But today, nature was silent. That sent a shiver through Alymere that had nothing to do with the cold. He moved to make the sign of the cross then stopped himself. It didn't feel right to him anymore.

He put his head down and hurried all the way to the stables, clutching the book tight to his chest. "Saddle up my horse," he barked at the stable lad before he had half-stumbled out of the hay where he had been sleeping. The poor boy was reed-thin and looked like he would snap in two at the ferocity of Alymere's tone but that didn't stop him scampering about the stable. Alymere took advantage of the moment to slip the pack from his shoulder and stuff the book inside. "I don't have all day!" Alymere shouted at the lad's back as he struggled with the buckle on the saddle's girths. The boy jumped physically, causing the horse to startle. It took a full minute for him to coax it back under control and finish buckling the saddle firmly into place.

A few minutes later Alymere rode out, ducking beneath the low lintel of the stable door even as he spurred the horse forward. The animal snorted, steam billowing from its nostrils as it reared up and its hooves came down. And then it was off in a burst of speed. As they reached the shadow of the old sour-apple tree, Alymere drove his heels into the horse's ribs again, harder this time, urging the great animal into a gallop.

He guided it toward the road that would take them north, toward the Tay Loch and Dùn Chailleann, through the deep woods of Coit Celidon and up to the mountain ranges of Sìdh Chailleann beyond that.

He did not look back once.

He had no interest in the past, only the future.

FORTY-SEVEN

HE RODE FOR three days and three nights, riding the animal into the ground. He did not stop for rest, did not sleep, did not eat and barely drank. When the horse's legs finally buckled beneath him he was halfway through the forest, surrounded on all sides by shadows, thick leaves and low-dragging branches that crowded him. He still had five miles or more to go before he reached the base of Sìdh Chailleann. The beast pitched forward to the road, shuddering and snorting as it lay there. He watched its chest heave three times, one of its back legs kicking out weakly, and then walked away from it, leaving the horse to die alone.

He walked the last five miles to the mountain, purpled with gorse and heather.

He could not see the summit for clouds.

A fine mist of rain clung to the air and insects flew around his face, in his eyes and mouth. At first he tried to swat them away but it was futile, so he walked on, doing his damnedest to ignore the midges as they got in his mouth and up his nose.

He was dizzy with dehydration and hunger.

Before him, he could barely make out a narrow path worn in the grass at the foot of Sìdh Chailleann. It suggested the clansmen still made regular pilgrimages to their ancestor's cairn. He had not anticipated that, but he should have. He should have thought it through properly. The reivers had come south as far as Medcaut looking for the book, and while they might not have known the true nature of their prize, they must have known the book was little more than a devilish treasure map, meaning they suspected the treasure was buried somewhere in their lands – why else would they have come?

Alymere could only hope the faithless bastards would honour the dead as woefully as they did the living.

He dropped to his knees, studying the worn grass. He was no expert when it came to reading tracks, but this changed things.

Would they have set a watch?

He reached down, resting his hand on the pommel of his sword. It would not matter if they had. He had fought and killed the reivers once, and could do so again.

The wind whipped down the mountainside, whistling mournfully through the gullies and crevices in the ancient rock. He climbed a few hundred feet closer to the clouds and the fog of midges gave way to a permanent wetness in the air that soaked through his clothes in a matter of minutes, even under a clear blue sky. He pulled his sodden cloak tighter and soldiered on, his footsteps leaden, small stones scuffing under the soles of his boots. When he looked up again he saw a bird – the first he had seen in days. For a moment he thought it must have been a falcon or a kestrel, from the way it seemed to hang in the air before sweeping down, but as it flew by him he saw the streak of white feathers mottling the black and knew it was the same damned crow. It could only mean that he was on the right path.

Not that the Devil inside him would confirm that. The book had been strangely silent for days. He found himself missing its voice, something he would never have thought possible.

And then he saw it no more than two hundred feet above him on the slope, the pile of broken stones laid one atop another to form a huge cairn. Even from this far below, it was obvious that the cairn was huge – a fitting monument for a fallen king, he thought. Three, four times his height and vast in circumference.

He saw the shadowy outline of a man standing before the cairn, but as he took a few more steps and the angle of the sun shifted, he seemed to disappear into the stones. There was no-one there. The effect was unnerving. Alymere reached instinctively for the comfort of his sword, not trusting his eyes. Things, in his experience, did not simply disappear. He thought again of what the Scots called this place, the fairy hill, and what that might actually mean. The Picts were superstitious to the point of being primitive, but they were not stupid. Was it possible this place stood between worlds? Was this a gateway to the the land of Annwn?[11] Did Nectan's shade stand as guardian over the Chalice in the dead lands?

All he knew for sure was that Sìdh Chailleann was sacred to the clans, and the Devil had promised him all would be revealed once he reached the cairn of the great laird.

The bird cawed raucously, banking in the air before him, and streaked away toward the cairn. He watched as the crow circled it once, twice, three times, widdershins, only to vanish in an instant from the clear blue sky.

He stopped, staring, refusing to believe his eyes. The crow did not reappear.

"I am here," he said, not daring to look away from the stones in case something slipped through from the other side unseen. The clouds were thicker here, strands of white clinging to the heather behind the cairn like ghosts. The lowering sun filtered through the wraiths of cloud. Mist gathered to transform the hillside into an eerie half-world of light and shadow shapes. His breath misted up in front of his face. It was colder now, and not just a little, he realised. He hadn't felt it happening, but the cold was now biting.

He walked cautiously toward the cairn, not sure what he expected to happen. It dwarfed him.

He found himself mirroring the crow, circling the cairn cautiously. He tried to look everywhere at once; down the mountainside, across the treetops of Coit Celidon and the crystal blue waters of Loch Tay, at the stones themselves stacked one atop another, and

---

[11]Literally, "the Helle of the Scots." I substitute Annwn, the land of the dead from Welsh myth, which is the closest approximation of Hell in Celtic myth to survive in modern writings.

the deep shadows between them. He tried to watch the sky for the crow, in case it might suddenly reappear in a burst of caws and falling feathers. He tried to take in the rest of the path as it rose toward the peak, and the jagged bill of rock that marked the very top of Sìdh Chailleann, hundreds of feet above him.

He completed his first circuit of the cairn, needing sixty paces to do it.

The air felt alive around him. His skin crawled with it; with a mixture of anticipation and dread.

He was close. He could feel it.

Yes, the presence that had taken up root within him crooned, urging him on.

The muscles in his legs burned. His head swam from the exertion and from hunger. His vision blurred slightly, the landscape around him fogging, and for a moment he was willing to put that down to the same thing, but it wasn't. He had started his second ring around the stone cairn, and in doing so had passed through the first veil. His breath quickened. His heartbeat matched it, beating more and more erratically against his ribs. He forced himself to press on, feeling the wind rise to batter at his face and body as though the elements themselves were amassing to hold him back. He didn't know what he expected to find waiting around the next corner; an army of kirtled highlanders looking to spill blood, perhaps?

Alymere put his head down and pushed on into the storm.

And a storm it was.

The mist had become rain, and now lashed at him, stinging his face and hands. The wind howled, bullying him, but he refused to let it push him even a single step backwards.

Halfway around his second pass, he made the mistake of looking down at his hands. They were shaking, but that wasn't what unnerved him so badly. They had begun to fade, blurring around the edges. He reached out, holding his hands out before him, and saw that they lost a little more clarity and definition. He pulled them back sharply, wanting to turn and run and forget all about the Black Chalice.

You are my knight, Alymere, my champion. Bring me my grail.

He could not refuse the voice.

He did not *want* to refuse.

He walked on.

After six more paces, as he came around to the front of the cairn to complete the second lap, he heard the sound of a dog barking in the distance. He peered down the slope through the storm, but could see neither hide nor hair of the animal. He glanced back over his shoulder, but all he could see there was thickening white mist. With each step forward, the barking intensified; the dog had his scent now. He started to run. He could hear it bounding across the open ground, hear it slavering and panting between growls, but the animal was nowhere to be seen.

Then, between one step and another, the sky went black.

Somehow in that single footstep he had left the day behind and stepped into night.

He didn't have time to panic – a huge black hound came racing toward him, every powerful muscle visible beneath its slick pelt. Its eyes burned sulphurous yellow in the moonlight, and its teeth – long saliva-flecked fangs – gleamed wickedly. Alymere stopped dead in his tracks. For a moment he couldn't move; all he could do was stare at the animal. It was easily twice the size of any dog he had ever seen. Its huge gait devoured the distance between them. He drew his sword, for what little good it would do him against the monstrous hound.

Behind it, he saw the dog's master striding purposefully up the hill towards him. Like his beast, the man was black as night. He wore the shadows like a cloak, masking his face, and was big. Considerably bigger than Alymere. Broader at the shoulder, thicker at the trunk, and graced with forearms like huge ham hocks. As he drew closer Alymere saw that he was wearing some sort of blackened leather armour, with a skirt over his thighs in the Roman style. A huge double-headed axe rested against his shoulder, the blades demonic in the jaundiced moonlight.

"Call it off!" Alymere demanded, the wind stealing his words away.

The axeman gave no indication that he had heard Alymere's plea, and his face was unreadable, wrapped in black cloth.

And then the dog was on top of him, snapping and snarling as he brought his sword to bear. Alymere moved instinctively, ramming the blade between the huge animal's ribs even as its teeth raked his face, spattering the ground with blood. Even with his steel buried in its body, the black dog kept fighting, snapping its huge jaws as it strove to reach his throat and slashing his shirt with its claws, ripping fabric and flesh. Alymere strained to keep the beast at arm's length, but faltered as it lunged again; his scream curdled in his throat as the dog's teeth sank into the side of his face and tore his right ear off. Blood streamed from the wound, but the scarred flesh of his ruined face felt no pain.

That saved his life.

He rammed the sword in deeper, thrusting it up all the way through the dog's body until the animal jerked and spasmed on the end of it like a spit. And still he drove the sword deeper, twisting the blade until it scraped against bone.

Only then did Alymere wrench his sword clear.

He kicked the still twitching carcass away and turned to face the dog's master.

"Have you come to die as well?"

The axeman said nothing.

"Very well," Alymere sucked in a ragged breath and wiped away the blood from the side of his face with his free hand, "Best get on with it."

They came together. Still the axeman said nothing. There was a coldness behind his eyes that chilled Alymere more than anything else. He lunged forward, throwing himself off-balance in the hope that the sudden assault would end the duel before it had even begun. The axeman caught his blade on the long shaft of his double-headed axe and brought the butt of it scything around to sweep Alymere's legs out from under him.

The boy leapt back, barely avoiding the blow, and stumbled on the loose shale beneath his feet. He feinted low, to the right, drawing the black warrior's defenses towards a strike that, at the very last moment, he reversed and slashed upwards. The tip of his blade opened a shallow cut across the axeman's belly to his sternum, but even as it did, the wound sealed itself behind his sword and Alymere felt burning pain slice deep through his own belly and up towards his throat. He looked down at the gash that had opened up, and the blood soaking through his shirt, and staggered back before the axeman's silent onslaught.

He gritted his teeth against the pain and stuck again, this time slicing through the muscle and tendon of the axeman's left arm, feeling the muscle tear away on his own arm as he did so.

They fought bitterly in and out of the shadow of the towering cairn. Twice he had struck the axeman, twice the blows had bitten deep, and twice Alymere had come away wearing the wounds whilst the axeman remained unmarked. He staggered back another step, wondering how he could possibly best the warrior without slicing through his own throat.

The black warrior came on remorselessly, still saying nothing.

Alymere brandished his sword, holding it out before him and cutting at the air wildly in an attempt to keep the axeman at bay, but it occurred to him that all his opponent had to do was simply walk into his wild cuts and he'd cripple Alymere without having to lift a finger. He lowered his sword, letting the tip drag against the dirt, and stared at his opponent. There was no sign the man was winded, or that the exertion of running up the hillside had taken the slightest toll on him. There was no sign he was breathing at all, Alymere realised.

He circled his opponent warily, never taking his eyes off the huge double-headed blade.

The giant made no move to swing, though he could quite easily have cleaved Alymere's head from his shoulders.

Or could he?

Could he inflict any sort of hurt of his own volition? Or was he merely a mirror-soul?

There had to be a way around this thing – whatever it was, he was absolutely sure it was *not* a man, or not a mortal one – all he had to do was use his head and think.

Think.

His mind was the key that would set him free.

Could it be as simple as cutting himself? He tried it, running his thumb along the edge of his blade, and drew blood.

The axeman did not bleed. So that couldn't be it.

What was this thing, then? Perhaps the secret of its undoing lay in its true nature?

He could see nothing of its features, obscured as they were by the cloth wound around the axeman's face. His eyes were empty – no, not empty, he realised. They were obsidian, reflective. They only gave back what they were offered. So when Alymere saw emptiness behind them, it was his own emptiness he was seeing.

Alymere lashed out with his blade a third time, deliberately pulling the blow at the very last instant. He cut and parried, transforming the fight into a dance of cuts without ever delivering the final blow. The black warrior mirrored each blow perfectly, his wrists twisting to turn the axe-blade away from Alymere's flesh each time. The moves were more than merely familiar to Alymere; they were ingrained, the axeman mirroring his own technique perfectly. It wasn't just the way he used his weapon, but in the way he moved his body, how he leaned and shuffled his feet on the ground and how as he pushed off with his left foot the toe of his right scuffed. He was toe-to-toe with *himself*, or a version of himself. He didn't need to see the guardian's features beneath the woollen scarf. It didn't matter that he had never wielded an axe in his life. What was it the Crow Maiden had said? There were countless possibilities of the man he could be. This was one of them. He scrambled back, ducking beneath the warrior's final blow, and the silver heads of the huge axe passed inches from Alymere's face.

He was breathing hard now, thinking harder.

"Talk to me. Tell me what to do!" he called upon the voice, but it remained silent.

He cursed it. Hawked and spat into the dirt at his feet.

The Devil mocked him with his silence.

The axeman was a reflection, then? A ghost? An automaton?

Was he here to protect the Chalice? A grail guardian? Was he a true man? Good? Evil? Did such concepts even exist on this side of the veil? And even if they did, how could he kill something that he could not harm, or even strike, without injuring himself? Did he have to kill it to defeat it? Could Alymere simply throw down his own sword? Would that be enough to render this copy of him impotent?

He thought about it, but at the last moment couldn't relinquish his grasp on his sword.

The guardian came forward again, and Alymere realised it was trying to steer him away from the cairn. Alymere cast a quick glance toward the stones. The cairn now rose to almost five times his height, hundreds and thousands of stones gathered from about the mountainside and from the land hereabouts, laid one atop another, slate, granite, basalt. All hard, dark stones. But Alymere saw a shape picked out right in the very centre of the cairn's curved wall, formed out of pale stones that obviously didn't belong.

It was a cross.

The holy symbol for a god the pagan clansmen surely did not worship?

He licked his lips.

It could not be a coincidence. Indeed, just then the book pulled heavily on his shoulders.

Break the cross. Beyond it lies the great laird's tomb, where you will find my Chalice.

There was no way he could break the stone cross, not with his bare hands and not with his sword.

He looked back to see the axeman moving relentlessly towards him once more, and an idea began to formulate within his mind. He raised his sword, shuffling sideways and bringing himself in line with the stone cross.

He dropped his shoulder and feinted for the black warrior's legs, drawing it into a heavy swing for his head. Alymere pulled his blow, ducked under the swing, and backed away until he felt the stone wall of the cairn press up against his back. There was nowhere to run, but running was the furthest thing from his mind. Now he had to use his head. He had to press the advantage he had given himself.

Alymere forced himself to stand stock still, rooted to the spot, as his chest rose and fell. The blood flowed thickly from the shallow cut, which burned whenever he tried to move. He winced through the pain, hefting his sword in his right hand, knowing that in a moment the agony was going to be blinding, but it was his only hope.

The guardian wouldn't strike until he did, that much he knew. Alymere took a moment's respite, mastering his breathing. His vision swam. The world reduced to the thing before him, and beyond that mist and pain. There was nothing else.

"Come on, then," he muttered. "Let's finish this."

With that, he lunged forward desperately, cutting high from the left, then rocking back on his heels to block and thrust at the guardian's left shoulder, reversing at the last moment to deliver a sweeping cut across the thing's midriff, barely pulling back before disembowelling it and leaving his own guts to unfurl across the mountain top.

The guardian mirrored every move with unerringly silent precision; not making a sound as it threw the weight of the huge axe from hand to hand, twisting to sweep it through low scything arcs or bring it down overhead as though chopping wood. Amidst the manoeuvring, the scarf slipped down around the black warrior's neck, baring its face for the first time.

Alymere's breath caught in his throat. He was looking at *himself*, but not in any form he recognised: the beard was thick, the jaw square. Indeed, the man looked uncannily like Bors. *Was that the man I was meant to become?* Alymere thought, even as he rammed the point of his blade deep into the axeman's belly. The guardian's obsidian eyes flared, not in pain but in triumph, as Alymere drove the point through the boiled leather plates of his armour.

You are better, the Devil crooned inside his head.

And Alymere screamed, and held on. The blood bubbled out of his gut and out of his mouth. Had he guessed wrong? Had he just seen to his own killing? The pain was incredible. Everything inside him was on fire. He cast one frantic glance over his shoulder at the stone cross. It was now or never. Alymere reached down, grasping his sword with both hands, and shrieked as he drew it out of the axeman's gut, feeling his own innards unravel as the steel slid out. There was no blood on the blade; just a sickly ichor. He managed a twisted smile. This was all about sacrifice. He was giving himself to the Devil, trading his life, his soul, for whatever aid the Horned One could grant... it was a desperate gamble. He just couldn't believe that the Devil would allow him to die, not now, not so close to the black grail.

Alymere gathered every last ounce of strength he had and threw it behind a wild overhead slash at the guardian's bare head. If it bit, the fierce swing would have cloven halfway through the bone and brain and left the sword buried, while Alymere twitched and contorted in the dirt, dying before he could even remove the blade. At the last, Alymere threw himself sideways, sprawling in the dirt, the sword spinning harmlessly from his hand even as the axeman's huge swing chopped down where his head had been only a heartbeat before.

The massive axe slammed into the centre of the cross, shattering the keystone that anchored the entire structure together. The axe clove deep into the soft rock, which splintered with a sound like bones breaking.

As the core of the cross crumbled, so too did the stones it held in place. Alymere scrambled away, bleeding and in absolute agony as the cairn groaned and the first stones began to shift. He could barely see through the sting of tears. He felt everything, not merely the tears in his flesh, but the prickle of the wind, the brush of his shirt against the cuts, everything. He was dying. He didn't know how long he had left; minutes? Less? It was all he could do to crawl a few feet further away from Nectan's cairn. He needed to put distance between them before it came down. *If it came down*, he amended. And even if it did, what then?

The ground beneath his hands and knees shivered, trembling, and then the black warrior tore its axe free of the stone crucifix, wrenching a dozen more of the pale stones out of the wall. The cairn could withstand the odd stone being dislodged, but the crucifix anchored the entire structure. With its integrity destroyed, it was only a matter of time before the whole thing came tumbling down in an avalanche of jagged rocks.

Alymere rolled over onto his back, clutching at his stomach as the cairn came crashing down. The noise, as stone crashed and cannoned off stone, was hideous. It drowned out every other sound, rolling like thunder across the mountain.

Part of him had hoped that breaking the cross would be enough to vanquish the thing, but it wasn't. The two had to be linked though, surely?

The thing remained eerily silent as the falling rocks battered it, hammering off its armour and skin without any seeming effect. One huge piece of slate struck its shoulder and shattered; another broke at its feet. The axeman made no move to protect itself. It wasn't created to offer any resistance, Alymere realised. It existed purely to protect the Black Chalice.

With the destruction of the cross, the key to the cairn, the axeman had failed in its duty as the last defender of the Devil's Grail. If Alymere had guessed right, the cross in the wall had marked the spot where the Chalice itself was buried, like a treasure map. And now, as the Chalice was uncovered in the cairn's collapse, its guardian would be buried in its stead. There was a fearful symmetry to it.

It didn't offer any defence as the stones smashed off its chest and head. It simply held on to its axe, waiting for Alymere to attack again. It had no understanding of its own, and didn't grasp that the stones were Alymere's last, best weapon against it – a weapon he did not need to wield, at that.

The axeman was the last ward, the final protection for the Chalice. Anyone looking to steal it must first best *himself*, not as he was, but the best that he could have been. The axeman was all that Alymere might have become had he not strayed from the road into the Crow Maiden's glade and lain down with her in the snow as it melted around them, their embrace taking them to the kingdom of summer and back. What he saw reflected in the axeman's black eyes was the good he had lost along the way.

He would never recover it; he knew that. He had accepted it. It didn't matter.

All that mattered was finding the Chalice. If it truly was the Devil's cup and had similar properties as the legendary Grail, then one sup from it might save his life. Or damn him forever.

That was the risk he was just going to have to take. He was damned if he didn't, and most assuredly damned if he did.

Clinging to consciousness, Alymere lay on the damp grass, watching Nectan's cairn collapse, burying the thing even as it revealed the long dead clansman's tomb.

FORTY-EIGHT

HE CRAWLED THROUGH the rubble. It was all he could do to force himself to move. His blood streaked across the stones as he dragged himself forward. He couldn't control his legs; his left foot trailed uselessly behind him, dislodging the broken stones as he crawled toward the unearthed tomb. The rocks shifted beneath his weight, skittering away down the banked ruin that was all that remained of the high wall.

He could see into the hollow heart of the cairn and, laid bare despite the shadows, the coffin of the great laird.

Alymere's right foot slipped as he scrambled desperately down the other side. He collapsed onto his back, gasping, every muscle on fire. His entire stomach and chest felt as though it was being ripped open and peeled back on his ribcage.

In scaling the debris, Alymere's exertions had exposed the guardian's broken and twisted forearm. It lay there lifelessly amid the rest of the rubble.

Alymere watched it in horror, wildly fearful. His jaw hung open, each new breath a strain. He didn't have the strength to fight on; he barely had the strength left to drag himself to the tomb, and had no idea how he was going to open it. If the Chalice was not inside, he was a dead man, and even if it was the chances were he would never get it open to find out.

He dug his fingers into the dirt, using every ounce of strength left to him to pull himself forward, his eyes on the stone tomb.

His vision swam in and out of focus. His blood trailed slickly across the dirt as he reached up, desperately trying to snag the top of the tomb and claw himself up against it.

He didn't know what he had expected; perhaps to find the Black Chalice laid on top of the stone tomb, but there was no sign of it.

Alymere left bloody hand prints on the stone face and a smear of blood across the granite chest, trying to force it from its resting place. He heaved his weight up against its side, weakly, trying to crack it open, but it didn't give so much as an inch. He levered his body around, trying to push his shoulder against the stone lid, but it wasn't moving. Not for him, not for the Devil, not for anything.

So close, but, as with everything in his life so far, he was destined to fall tantalisingly short.

He slumped back, content to die.

There is life still in us, is there not? There is breath still in our lungs. Blood still in our veins. Use it. Use the last of that life, and the rewards will be beyond imagining. Let me fill you, let me lend you my strength to sustain you. We are one. We are Alymere. Now RISE!

Alymere pulled himself up, needing the tomb to support his weight, and took one step away from it on trembling legs. He saw the silver edge of the axeman's double-headed blade through the rubble and stumbled unsteadily towards it.

He sank to his knees, pulled at the stones burying the axe and threw them aside, dragged it out of the rubble, and hauled himself up once more to lurch back toward the stone tomb. With every step he found a little more strength returning to his limbs, a little more vitality, though whether it was the strength the Devil had promised him, or somehow came from the weapon, he neither knew nor cared. He revelled in the new-found strength surging through his veins.

Behind him, the stones stirred, but Alymere only had eyes for the tomb.

Grimacing, he raised the weapon overhead. He felt a brief, wild urge to bring the huge axe smashing down into the centre of the tomb's granite lid, but stopped himself, knowing it was a futile gesture – there was a marked difference between the soft pale rocks of the cross and the flawless granite slab that marked the laird's final resting place. Instead, he worked the edge of the axe's blade between the lid and the base, and used the shaft to lever it free. And as long as he kept his hands on the axe, strength continued to flood into him.

The grating of stone on stone, as the lid started to slide, masked the sounds of the guardian clawing its way out of its grave.

With one last colossal heave, the tomb opened far enough for him to see inside. The laird's old bones had been preserved, along with some scraps of decayed leather, but nothing else. There, clasped in the bony fingers, was a silver goblet, yellow-black with tarnish, a single chalcedony stone set in its side. The gem was a bloodstone, flecked with red.

He reached into the coffin to pry the Chalice from the dead man's grasp.

He lifted the fingers one at a time with a peculiar reverence, but the bones powdered beneath his touch. As they crumbled, the sudden cacophony of stones shifting and falling behind him caused Alymere to turn; for one panicked moment he thought the entire cairn was coming down on top of him, but then he saw the axeman stubbornly clawing itself out of the rubble.

Nothing would stop it. Not being buried, not being struck down. It just kept coming. Alymere had visions of the silent warrior chasing him all the way to Camelot.

Alymere reached for the axe, and then stopped himself. The warrior was a grail guardian. He would never defeat it with axe or sword. The only way to win, he realised, was to claim the grail.

Even as the massive warrior hauled himself silently out of the rubble, Alymere tore the Black Chalice from the dead man's clutches and lifted it out of the tomb.

Yes, the Devil whispered in his mind. *Yes, yes, yes... This is our destiny... Lift the cup to your lips and drink of me. Finish what you began. Seal yourself to me. Drink... sup of my blood.*

Alymere raised the cup to his lips, but there was only dust and the bitter tang of the tarnished metal on his tongue. There was no blood, no water.

Press the stone against one of your cuts... Drip your blood into the Chalice... Your blood is our blood... Our blood is my blood... Raise it to your lips and drink... Drink of me. Drink to me. Drink.

Behind him, the guardian rose to its feet and kicked its way clear of the rubble. Alymere hesitated.

Do it. Now. Drink. Seal our pact. Be mine. Forever. And I will be yours.

He pressed the lip of the tarnished silver cup – as black as its name suggested – against his stomach, collecting blood from the wound, and raised it to his lips.

Inside his head the Devil howled in triumph.

And Alymere fell.

FORTY-NINE

HE LOOKED UP, blood on his lips, to see the cracks that had already formed in the axeman's armour, the wrinkles in its flesh and the fissures in its eyes.

In taking that draught, swallowing the tainted blood, Alymere had killed the last spark of goodness in him. His wounds still bled but they no longer weakened him. He had become the Devil's Knight. He ran his tongue around the lip of the Chalice, licking the last of the blood clean, and then lowered the grail.

He held it idly by his side, a sneer forming on his lips, and watched as the axeman climbed free of the rubble. It didn't matter. Where Alymere was multiplied, the guardian was reduced.

He waited for the thing to claw its way free, then strode across the hard packed earth to meet it. He pressed his hand against the wound in his belly, and then reached out, placing his hand in the centre of the guardian's chest, leaving a bloody hand print, and in an alien voice said, "You have done well, guardian. The grail is returned to its rightful owner. Rest now; you have earned your eternity." They were the first words the Devil's Knight had uttered, and came purely from the voice of his master. Alymere was nowhere to be heard in them.

And the cracks in the leather around Alymere's bloody hand print widened and burrowed into the guardian's flesh, weeping dust instead of blood.

The axeman's eyes cracked and shattered like fine glass beneath a crude hammer blow. The axeman's body convulsed, wracked by spasms as the taint of Alymere's blood burned through its skin and hollowed out its innards.

"Go," Alymere commanded, and as the breath behind the word touched the guardian its shell simply crumbled, as though the years it had stood watch over the Devil's cup caught up with it all at once. Within moments, all that remained of the guardian was dust, settling over the scattered stones.

Alymere shucked off his pack, loosening the strings, and took out a small cloth, which he used to wrap the Chalice before stowing it alongside the book, and shouldered the pack again.

The huge double-headed axe was still wedged under the lid of the tomb. Unlike its wielder, it hadn't crumbled to dust. Alymere tested the edge – it was still wickedly sharp – took it and walked out of the tomb.

He walked three times around the ruined cairn, stepping from night back into day, and the world he had left behind.

He did not see the old witch, the streak-feathered crow perched on her shoulder, or the beautiful maiden hiding high in the crags. They watched him go silently. They had each witnessed him drinking from the tainted cup, and knew too well what it meant: he was lost to them; their hero had fallen. Unable to help herself, Blodyweth cried out his name, hoping against hope that he would hear and come back to her, but as Alymere left the Annwn, all he heard was the raucous caw of the crow, and it grated on his nerves.

FIFTY

His ʀᴇᴛᴜʀɴ ᴛᴏ Camelot was not the hero's homecoming he had always imagined. His arrival was as unremarked as his first had been, long months before. Not even Bors was there to greet him.

Alymere had been a child the first time he'd set foot in the great castle. He was a man now. As he walked beneath the portico, his journey was complete.

Pennons snapped in the wind. The lists had been decorated with all manner of devices, displaying the arms of every Knight of Albion. Brightly coloured tents were being assembled by sweating men. The sound of steel striking steel rang out from the smithy. Men with axes hewed branches from trees, that were in turn stripped and shaped into lances. To Alymere's left, people bustled around the carts and stalls, while to his right maids wound ribbons around the Maypole for the summer feast. The *scraw-scritch-scraw* of a prentice honing tools and arms provided a grating, atonal accompaniment to the rest.

Children laced garlands of flowers and laid them around the foot of the Maypole. Girls laughed and giggled at boys playing the fool. The air smelled of cinnamon and sweet mince, mulled wine spices and freshly baked bread. Camelot was filled wall to wall with life. No-one looked at him. Why should they? He had undergone a transformation since he had left Camelot with Lowick – he couldn't call the dead man *uncle* or *father*, as he was neither – and now he was unrecognisable, even to himself. He was a stranger in their midst. Their lives would go on without him after he made the short walk through their number and climbed the stairs to the castle door. He might just as well have been a ghost... Alymere stopped himself from finishing the thought.

He saw a familiar face as he crossed the outer bailey. The maid Bors had flirted with during that first visit to Camelot – the one who had brought his father's tabard to them in the armoury.

He struggled to recall her name. Caroline? Claire? Katherine?

Was that what Bors had called the maid? Katherine? He found his lips shaping her name, as though to call it.

As though she sensed his scrutiny, the woman looked up from the well where she was labouring to draw a pail of drinking water up. She was pretty, in a sensuous rather than sweet way, and every bit as dangerous as Bors had warned. He watched the way her body moved beneath the skirts, appreciating it.

Alymere saw recognition pass fleetingly across her eyes, but they clouded and quickly something else replaced it. Shock? Revulsion?

No. It was worse than either of those, he realised. It was pity.

He drew himself straighter, defiantly, and strode towards her.

She couldn't take her eyes off him. There was no lust in her gaze this time, though. Of course, she hadn't seen him like this before. She had only seen the pretty boy he had been, not the burned man he had become.

He stopped two steps before her. Alymere hawked and spat into the dirt at his feet.

"Not so pretty now, eh?" he said, by way of greeting.

Katherine looked away. "Beauty belongs on the inside as much as it does on the outside, my lord," she mumbled, eyes downcast.

He barked out an abrasive laugh. "Then perhaps this," he touched his cheek, "is my ugliness clawing its way out. Or maybe if you kiss me I shall transform into a handsome prince?"

She had no answer for that: no coy smile, no batted eyelashes, no flirtatious offer to make a man of him.

"I thought not."

He left her at the well.

A young girl ran up to him, a chain of daisies in her hands and a summer flower tucked behind her ear. He turned, snarling, but was stopped by her pretty little face, so full of happiness and excitement. He reached out to take the daisy chain and looked down at them, the perfect little flowers on his scarred palm, and as he did, the little girl caught sight of his face. Her breath caught in her throat, but she did not scream or run away from him. She seemed oddly fascinated by him. There was something uncannily familiar about the child, although he had never seen her before.

The daisy chain slipped through his fingers. Alymere stooped quickly, picking the flowers up from the dirt before they were ruined, and slipped the chain over his head. He smiled his thanks, earning an uncertain smile before he kissed the centre of her forehead and sent her back to play with the others. Rather than being frightened, she seemed delighted. He listened to her as she skipped away, singing the refrain of a madrigal he vaguely recognised. He caught the words "Kingdom of Summer," before she was too far away for him to hear the rest of her song.

He looked down at his left arm where Blodyweth's favour was tied around his bicep, and for just a moment, perhaps, the lost Alymere might have reached up from the darkness where the Devil had cast him, but then the moment was gone.

He rolled his shoulders and stretched before continuing the short walk across the bailey to the keep's doors.

No-one got in his way.

The two guards standing sentry over the main doors didn't block his entry into the castle itself. They looked at him from head to toe before lowering their pikes and stepping aside to let him through. They offered no hint of recognition.

He nodded to them.

He was back. It wasn't the allotted two years and a day, but with both Lowick and Roth dead, there was no-one left to see to his training. And besides, he was more of a man now than they had ever been, he thought bitterly.

His footsteps echoed hollowly through the passageways of the place.

He heard the strains of music – a piper – filling the distance. It was a pleasant enough tune, if made rather funerary in the echoing halls. The castle had not changed. He knew where he was going without knowing where he was headed; he paused at the stairway that led up to the aviary where he had first met the king, turned and set off in the direction of the great hall.

The huge double doors groaned heavily on their iron hinges as he opened them. He hesitated a moment on the threshold, as though unsure he could enter the heart of Albion, but then he smiled without warmth and strode into the hall. He felt himself growing in stature with every step as he marched down the aisle toward the Round Table.

He was no longer a child. He was Alymere, Killer of Kings.

There was nothing left of the young man he had been.

We are not here begging for approval, nor are we hoping for freedom from old ills done to loved ones. This is our right, our destiny. We are here to claim our destiny. And if the fool king dares refuse us, we shall take it. There was no doubt in the voice of the Devil. It filled him. It thrilled him.

He commanded the chamber in a way that Sir Bors never could.

This time he was not awed by the kite shields hanging on the walls. He didn't care that the devices belonged to Sir Dodinal le Savage and the brothers Sir Balan and Sir Balin, Sir Helian le Blanc, Sir Clariance, Sir Plenorius, Sir Sadok, Sir Agravaine of Orkney and Sir Ywain of Gore or any of the other brother knights. His own device would sit amongst them soon enough, once they took down Lowick's leaping stag. He only had eyes for a single seat at the table, the Siege Perilous.[12] His face twisted from a smile into something approaching a sneer as he walked towards it, determined to break whatever bond the sorcerer, Merlin, had set upon it and claim it for himself.

It was only the first of many things he intended to claim, including Camelot itself and, in time, the kingdom beyond its walls.

---

[12]The vacant seat at Arthur's Round Table, reserved for the knight who would find the Holy Grail. It was said that any other knight who sat in it would suffer a terrible fate. Galahad eventually takes the seat, in Book XIII of *Le Morte D'Arthur*.

He knelt at the foot of the chair, as though in worship, and pressed his hands flat against the cold stone floor. He could feel the power of the earth flowing through the stones, the sheer thrill of it coursing through his veins. His expression as his head came up had passed beyond supplication into the realms of adoration. The weight of the book and the Chalice, wrapped carefully and stowed in his pack, pulled on his back; the chair was the heart of the chamber, which in turn was the heart of the castle, which in turn was the heart of Albion, making the Siege Perilous the centre of all things – and there was magic in the symmetry of that.

Alymere breathed it in, and then rose to his feet.

He reached out for the chair, though whether to steady himself or claim it for his own it was impossible to say – but before he could lay a hand upon it, a voice rang out across the chamber. "You think to claim the seat even before you take the Oath?" The quiet question reverberated in the stone hall. "Did your time with Lowick teach you nothing then?" Arthur's voice was resigned, almost wistful.

Alymere wheeled on his king, snatching his hand back, and for the second it took for him to master his face, his eyes burned.

"No my liege," he said, forcing himself to sound meek. "I was overcome, sire. It is an extraordinary thing, is it not?"

"It is."

"It is not often in my life that I have come face-to-face with something worthy of legend. My apologies."

For a moment he was sure the king would not be so easily mollified, but he need not have worried.

"I heard about your uncle," Arthur said.

"Anyone would think I was cursed," Alymere said.

"Not words to say lightly, b–" he had been about to say *boy*, but caught himself. "So, tell me, what have you learned about yourself?"

Alymere's smile was genuine. "It is safe to say I am not the man I was."

"That is good to hear. So, tell me then? There is much I would hear."

And so, for the best part of an hour, the king and the Devil sat side-by-side in the great hall of Camelot, while the Devil spun a tale as full of lies as any that had ever been spoken.

It began in the snows of the borderland and the reivers' pillaging as they sought their prize, the Black Chalice, the Devil's Grail.

The Devil remembered lying in the snow with the maiden, making promises to save the world, and could not help but smile at his naïvety. The very best lies had their roots in the truth. He tapped the intense love that had fired Alymere's soul, his fear for Arthur and Camelot, and his desire to be a true man, and used it as the foundation for his lies. What fiercer passion could there be to fire the memory of Medcaut's inferno and the slaughter of the monks at the hands of the reivers? He touched his ruined cheek once during the entire telling but otherwise barely mentioned his injuries, highlighting the knightly qualities a true champion of the unfortunate ought to have. The lies he told may have mirrored the path Alymere had walked, but where each step had in truth led him deeper into darkness, he retold it now as something heroic.

It was the classic quest against insurmountable odds, where, still, somehow, the hero returned with the spoils, the day saved. More than that, it was what the king wanted to hear. Arthur sat silently, attentive.

The king wanted to believe that his judgment had been right – that, in sending Alymere off to learn from Lowick he had made a man of him – so Alymere gave him what he wanted, a tale filled with damsels in distress and selfless heroism, burning buildings, battles to the death, honour, and, at the end, the triumph of good. He transformed Lowick into a valiant knight, and twisted the story of the book and the Chalice until it was a tale worthy of Lancelot himself. And, at the tale's height, he withdrew the book from his pack, opening it and spreading flat its pages, knowing that the king couldn't read a word that it said.

Arthur studied it for a moment, running his fingers over the unintelligible text, mouthing the shapes of words that didn't exist in his mother tongue, and then looked up at Alymere. "I don't understand. How could this lead you to the cup?"

"It is a treasure map, my lord."

"But how could you decipher it? Do you read this script? Is it a language known to you?"

"Aye, sire. It is a tongue common to the Saracens. Baptiste schooled me in it. I must admit I am unfamiliar with its subtleties, but I can muddle my way through most of it, given time."

"Incredible. And these heathens knew the secrets of the dark grail?"

It was an easy lie to tell; how the Devil's cup had been smuggled out of the Holy Land and delivered to a Saracen prince, only to be lost during the wars with the Crusaders and taken to Byzantium as spoils. They knew it as the Cup of the Threskeians – the Deceivers.

"And what properties did the Saracens believe the grail to hold?"

"It is the Devil's Grail, my king, the very antithesis of the cup of Our Lord. And the Devil is the Father of Lies."

"To drink from it brings death?" the king asked sharply.

"Not so literally, sire. The Devil was always a creature of subtlety. It is more insidious, creeping root and branch into every aspect of the drinker's life and twisting it, corrupting and withering it to the point that it bore no resemblance to the life it had been." His words were so close to the truth, but like all great lies, it left one telling 'truth' out – that the drinker must sup of human blood if he was to be spared death.

"And the book told you this?"

Alymere nodded. "It is all in there, my king. All you need is a willingness to believe."

"Where the Holy Father is the key to creation, and his blessing grants life, the Devil's gift is subversion, deceit, and all that is wrong with the world."

The king nodded solemnly.

Alymere continued, warming to his tale. "To sup from the Black Chalice once is to taste the lie. When those around you are hiding the truth, you can see to the heart of the matter. To sup twice from the cup is to live the lie, allowing the drinker the gift of tongues, the Devil's language, allowing him to spin the most plausible lies that speak to the heart of their listeners."

"A dangerous *gift*," Arthur acknowledged.

"But worse, by far, should the drinker drain the cup of every last drop. The Chalice will grant the drinker the power to conjure the ultimate lies, to bring to life the heart's desire. Imagine: whatever it is the listener needs, the drinker can fashion out of nothing. That is the true power of the Black Chalice; deception. Planting seeds in the needy mind so that they believe what they see and hear is real."

"Sorcery!"

"Of the most heinous kind, my king."

"Then this *treasure* must not be allowed to fall into the wrong hands. You have done well, Alymere. Very well."

The greatest king Albion had ever known believed every word of it. He could see it in his eyes. It was like telling a story for a child.

He had planted the seed.

One sip was all it would take. Arthur would not be able to resist. He was surrounded by people who told him what he wanted to hear, which was not necessarily the truth. His was a court of equals, but who could he really trust? What man wouldn't want to know when he was being played for a fool by the people he thought of as allies and friends? More to the point, what king wouldn't want to sit at the Round Table and listen to the arguments of his knights and know who among them was dissembling, who harboured selfish motives, and who was driven by lust and other impurities. Who, in other words, might have their sights set on the throne?

It was the perfect trap for a king, no matter how great he was.

Alymere's smile spread.

"And now," he concluded, lowering his head diffidently, "I have returned with both the book and the Chalice, prepared to take the Oath, if you would still have me as a knight, my liege?"

"It would be both a pleasure and an honour to see you take your seat at the Table." The king rose slowly from his chair and held out his hand to shake.

Alymere grasped his forearm, sealing the bond, and then

started to kneel, but the king stopped him, hauling him back up to his feet with one strong arm.

"No. Not like this. A feat like yours deserves more. Tonight, after the feast when everyone's bellies are bloated and they've shed a tear at the crowning of the May Queen, let us make a proper celebration out of it." He looked over Alymere's shoulder. No words passed between them, but the younger man knew the king was looking at the white stag and recalling a lost friend.

It was only fitting that it should end here tonight amid the revels, Alymere thought.

Let them drink and dance and sing in celebration of his triumph. Let them fete him and shout his name as the bonfires crackled and pretty maids danced around the Maypole. Let them toast his rise to the Table with the poisoned Chalice, let them call him the hero of the feast. Let them cheer his knighthood and mourn for the dead Arthur both at once. "I owe that to your father at the very least."

"Then so it shall be, my king," Alymere said, his voice thick with anticipation.

FIFTY-ONE

A NEW MOON lit the sky.

Men gathered around the bonfires, waiting for the signal to light them. Flaming brands, held aloft by smiling page-boys, bathed people of every station – from the poorest to the most noble – just the same, making them equals for one night. Standing side by side, the knights and farriers, smiths and serving girls, dukes and priests, were all swept up in the spirit of the evening. As far as they were concerned, the only person counted higher than any other that night waited to be crowned Queen of May.

The sickly-sweet smell of roasting chestnuts drifted over to Alymere. He smiled at the gap-toothed girl standing beside him as she fumbled in her skirts for a coin to pay for the treat. He looked her up and down, seeing the ground-in grime and the threadbare cloth. "Allow me," he said, inclining his head slightly in the direction of the roasting tray. He flipped a coin over the smoking chestnuts. The roaster snatched it out of the air and shovelled a small handful of the nuts into a wooden bowl. He handed it Alymere, who in turn handed it to the gap-toothed girl with a smile. "Please, enjoy, my treat."

She curtseyed clumsily. "Thank you, Sir Knight."

"Just plain 'Alymere' for a few minutes yet, my lady."

He left her to chew on the hot nuts, mingling with the throng of revellers. All around him people were laughing and joking with each other. He saw maidens flirting outrageously with all manner of men, lifting their skirts and tossing back their heads; the moonlight made them all beautiful. No doubt, nine months down the line, more than a few houses would wake up to the shrieking and wailing of new life. After all, that was part of the whole ceremony, wasn't it, the wine, ale and song given in offering to the fertility of the land? He smiled at a young girl with bluebell eyes and skirts that trailed in the mud as she skipped by, followed by three boys who were obviously her brothers, and nodded to a broad-shouldered man about to try his hand against one of the knights in a roped-out wrestling ring. Quite a crowd had gathered to watch the bout. Alymere skirted around the edge of it, going to collect an ale to quench his thirst.

He was very much an outsider here. He did not belong. It wasn't so much the the years the dancers and revellers had grown up together, or that his face was ruined, or that his voice marked him as coming from the north, or even that he had been raised the son of a noble. It was something far deeper than that. Each one of these people was, in their own way, innocent. It had been a long time since Alymere had known that. He could smell it every bit as thickly in the air as the sweat and lust and chestnuts.

The air had grown thick with the milling people's musk; beneath that heavy scent he caught the stink of a woman's menses, of beeswax and of a festering wound that would soon turn gangrenous, of a splash of urine and – he sniffed, trying to isolate the smell – of wet fur. One of the animals had been playing in the river. There were so many other scents. They were unique, overwhelming. And yet he seemed to be the only one aware of them.

By the ale tent a troubadour had taken up residence, planting himself on an upturned log and resting his lute across his knee. Alymere listened to his jaunty little song for a moment. All he could think was that, in a few short minutes, everything would change. The singing would become screaming, the dancing would become panicked flight. They wouldn't know where to turn or who to trust, and then they would see him, Alymere, Killer of Kings, the Black Chalice in his hands, and they would know the true glory of what they had just witnessed, the coming of their new king.

He felt immensely powerful. Mighty. He closed his fist and knew that he had the strength within it to crush Arthur's face – his mouth, his nose, his windpipe – to beat the life out of him, if he chose.

A ragged cheer went up.

Alymere turned to see the girl who would become the May Queen emerge through the gates of Camelot. She was accompanied by three young girls, who barely came up to the belt of flowers she wore around her waist. She wore a garland of daisies twined through the curls of her long black hair, and a simple white fine linen dress that hugged the curves of her body. All four of them carried sprigs of hawthorn. She wasn't a girl, he realised, aware that he was staring; she was without doubt the most beautiful woman he had ever seen. There was something uncannily familiar about her, although he knew he couldn't have seen her before.

His breath quickened, and his head swum with voices of his past, voices of people who had meant something to him: his mother, Lowick, Roth, Baptiste. He heard Bors' booming voice, and the blind monk from Medcaut begging for his life. He heard other voices, less familiar, voices that in many cases he had forgotten he had ever heard. Alymere's soul glimmered briefly, and the Devil stamped it down, hard, asserting himself once more upon the borrowed flesh.

He watched the soon-to-be Queen walk toward the Maypole. Her smile lit up the night.

Had her voice been one of the clamour? How could that be possible? He looked at her again, and as he did so he idly touched the favour tied around his left bicep. His eyes drifted down to the hem of the woman's white dress.

It was torn, a strip of cloth missing.

She walked toward the king, curtseying as she reached him. The revellers formed a circle as they gathered around the Maypole, hushed, expectation bright in their eyes.

Alymere pushed his way toward the front of the circle, his thirst momentarily forgotten. He felt his skin crawl as he brushed up against a fishwife, every fibre raw enough that the slightest touch made him want to cry out. He gritted his teeth against the pain and pushed between a tallow girl – the wax still thick on her skirts – and a butcher's boy who had been making eyes at her. A horde seemed to stand between him and the coronation.

He was minutes away from the kingship. He had thought it through meticulously, utilising Alymere's skills of reasoning; thinking through each possibility and outcome as though preparing a strategy for an upcoming battle. The Devil savoured the irony that, in effect, Arthur had forced this flesh, this mind, to learn the skills that would prove to be the king's ultimate undoing. It was delicious. Had he not meddled – had he simply granted Alymere his wish, freeing him from his ties to Lowick and his northern estates and instead offered him a place in Camelot – none of this could have happened. In trying to prove how fair and just a ruler he was, Arthur had condemned himself. He was a living, breathing dead man, and like all of the damned his breath was about to run out.

Alymere had contemplated poisoning the well – the idea had come to him when Katherine had refused to look at him. He had watched the pail rise slowly, sloshing water over its brim, and realised that by emptying a single cupful of water from the Black Chalice into the drinking water he could have killed every man, woman and child in Camelot. For the devil told Alymere that water from the cup was lethal to those who had not drained it of his hellish blood. The only thing that stayed his hand was how indiscriminate it was. Arthur himself might live while all those around him died, if he wasn't thirsty. And even should Arthur have been the first to fall, the water would have been fouled for years, the poison seeping down into the underground lake that fed the well and killing all who drunk from it, so who then would have remained for him to rule over? A king needed his subjects, his knights and his servants, otherwise he was just a fool living in an empty castle.

No, it needed to be much more exact than that – and public. That was paramount. He wanted the world to see Arthur fall, and him rise to take his place. They would toast his rise to the Round Table, each taking a sip from the tainted cup. By drinking his own blood from the cup he had let the Devil in. It was a part of him now. He was immune. Arthur was not. One sip from the Chalice was all it would take.

He could see it now, the mighty Excalibur touching his shoulder, Arthur shouting "Arise, Sir Alymere!" Taking a swig from the Chalice together, before everyone, to toast his triumph. It was glorious in its simplicity, like all the best lies.

He breathed in deeply, savouring all of the stinks that he inhaled.

This was it. His time was now.

Alymere walked into the back of a callow-faced boy, who was gazing straight ahead. The lad grunted and Alymere leaned in close. "Do me a service, lad, and you'll earn a good coin or two. Understand?" The boy nodded. Alymere pushed back his cloak and untied the small cloth pouch holding the Chalice from his belt.

He felt his heartbeat race and his mouth dry. He clenched his fist.

He struggled to keep his breathing steady. Parting with it, even for a few moments, and even with his triumph so close at hand, was difficult. More difficult than he had anticipated. But needs must as the Devil drives...

"Bring this to me when I call for it. Do not open it. Do not touch it. Your life depends upon it, boy. Do you understand me?"

The woman behind him looked aghast when she saw his scarred face and heard the threat, before recognising him as the man about to be knighted, and therefore beyond reproach. She struggled to smile at him. The boy didn't seem to care; he reached out for the pouch, delighted with the chance to earn a few coins. Alymere pushed a copper penny into his palm. "Do as I've asked and there are five more where this one came from."

The boy's face lit up. He nodded eagerly, shuffling his feet in the dirt. He clutched at the cloth pouch as though it were the most precious thing in the whole world – which, of course, it was.

Alymere said, "Come with me," and worked his way to the front of the crowd. He made sure the boy was beside him. It was going to be a night both of them would remember for the rest of their lives.

He was mighty. He was Alymere, and in just a few moments he would kill King Arthur.

Arthur held a crown in his hands. This was the May Crown. It wasn't made of gold or precious metals and stones, but of flowers woven around briar twigs, hundreds of tiny perfect blossoms crammed tightly together. Each petal was a thing of beauty, like the girl about to wear it. But Alymere only had eyes for the torn hem of her dress.

The girl curtseyed, spreading her skirt and stooping so low she nearly knelt at his feet, and lowered her head, dark curls trailing on the grass. The king smiled down at her, then lifted his gaze and addressed the onlookers. "Friends, we are here this night to join in two-fold celebration. First, to revel in the richness of the land and the renewal of spring as the cycle of life begins once more; and second, to welcome a brave knight, a true man, as he swears the Oath of chivalry and takes his seat at the Round Table." A cheer went up at this. Alymere inclined his head slightly, acknowledging the adulation of the crowd. "Make that three-fold, my friends, for then we shall revel in good company, drink and make merry 'til the sun comes up!" Arthur proclaimed, and the cheers that greeted his words were twice as loud.

"But first we need a Queen!" Alymere watched as the king's smile widened and his gaze drifted toward his own beloved queen, Guinevere. She was beautiful, of that there was no doubt, but beside the soon-to-be-crowned Queen of May she was at best merely pretty, at worst plain.

The king leaned forward, placing the briarwood crown on the girl's head, and moving a stray curl away from her brow.

"The Queen is crowned!" someone in the crowd shouted. The boy beside him took up the cry, "Long live the Queen!" and others joined in. Again and again it rang out around him, voices raised in jubilation. Alymere studied the woman's face as she looked up, and found that he could not look away from her eyes. Instinctively his fingers drifted toward the favour tied around his arm. Something passed between them; a connection. Not between himself and the woman, but between her and the man he had been.

He flinched, pulling his hand away from the favour as though burned.

The May Queen drew herself up to her full height and turned to face the cheering crowd, and the three younger girls ran forward with baskets of petals for her to cast on the wind. Her smile could have melted the stoniest heart as she moved barefoot through the crowd, bestowing her smile, and the softest brush of her lips on cheeks and foreheads, on her worshippers, who loved her all the more. Dirt and grass stains smeared the soles of her feet. She was skipping, a trail of petals strewn across the moonlit grass in her wake, by the time she took the ribbon from the outstretched hand of a grinning lad, and running by the time she finished circling the Maypole. It was all part of a well-rehearsed ritual that ended in the one great truth of life: what comes from the earth needs must return to the earth.

The May Queen stood with her back against the pole, breasts heaving, curls of hair matted flat to her scalp, and looked around until her eyes found Alymere in the crowd.

She blew him a kiss, much to the delight of the women in the audience.

Her smile widened. And in that moment her eyes, her smile, together, were the most beautiful he had seen. He felt his body stir, aroused by her scrutiny.

He was burning. He reached up instinctively to touch his ruined cheek.

She waved a signal to the other dancers, who each held a trailing ribbon in their hands, to start the dance, around and around the Maypole, until the ribbons had bound the May Queen completely to the pole at her back. And still they twisted and twined the ribbons around her until they smothered her completely, and not a trace of her white dress or porcelain skin was exposed.

Alymere stared at her, watching the shallow rise and fall of her breast beneath the shroud of ribbons, and thought of her fighting for breath, suffocating under there. Of course, the ribbons were not wound so tight that she couldn't breathe. And soon the men would rush from the crowd and cut her free, but it would be 'too late,' and they'd bear her down to the river where they'd lay her down on a raft on a bed of spring flowers, and sail her down the river. But not yet. Her release would come at the end of the feast.

First, Alymere had to kneel and swear the Oath to Arthur, and then the king must die.

He broke the circle and walked toward the king.

FIFTY-TWO

"KNEEL, LAD," ALYMERE recognised the voice, and for a moment thought it was another hallucination. He turned to see Sir Bors de Ganis place a meaty hand on his shoulder. The knight smiled reassuringly, as though their fight of a few days before was forgiven, or at least forgotten. Perhaps it was. Still, his presence unnerved Alymere; he had not allowed for it. He sank to one knee and lowered his head, thinking desperately. Did the knight's presence at Camelot change things? Had he come looking to stop Alymere from fulfilling his destiny? He looked up at Bors. There was pride in his face, not anger. He had no intention of stopping the ceremony. Far from it, he was here to watch Alymere fulfil his destiny. Despite the arguments, despite the harsh words and threats, two years and a day from when they had first met, here on this open field, Bors had returned to watch Alymere be knighted. He was the closest thing the young man had to family.

If he hadn't sensed the threat the big man posed, Alymere might have been touched by such loyalty.

As it was, he hated the big man. He would be the first to die.

Second, he amended. Arthur would be the first; in just a few moments they would toast his triumph together, and the screaming and dying would begin. But first he had to mouth useless platitudes and empty promises.

Bors stepped aside to make room for the king.

Alymere looked around at all of the expectant faces.

Arthur held Excalibur, the tip of the great blade piercing the ground between his feet. He braced both of his hands on the cross-guard. The king smiled broadly at him. "Do you recall the code?"

"I do, my liege," Alymere said. *Oh, I do, I do,* the voice inside crooned expectantly.

"Good, for on this hallowed night, and in the presence of all Camelot, beneath the skies of God, I would hear you swear to uphold it."

"I swear to uphold the honour of Albion, my liege."

Arthur nodded. "With these words you will not only become a true man, but a Knight of Albion. Think on, before you speak. These are no rash promises you make tonight; you will bind yourself to me, and to Camelot, for the rest of your days. Now, Alymere son of Roth, tell me, do you swear to hold life sacred above all else?"

"I do so swear," Alymere said, releasing the breath he hadn't known he was holding.

"Do you swear that treason shall have no place in your heart, and that you will honour and serve the will of Camelot above all others?"

"I do so swear," Alymere said.

"Do you swear that you will offer mercy to all deserving of it?"

"I do so swear."

"Do you swear that you will offer succour to those in need if it is yours to offer?"

"I do so swear," the words came easily to him now.

"Do you swear never to take up arms in wrongful quarrels for love or worldly goods?"

"I do so swear."

"Do you swear never to stand by idly whilst such evils are perpetrated by others upon the weak and innocent?"

"I do so swear."

"And do you so swear to be noble, worshipful and just in all things?"

"I do so swear," Alymere concluded, the lie tripping easily off his tongue.

The king raised Excalibur. "I will hold you to this oath, Alymere, for now you are no longer the son of Roth, but a Knight of Albion, witnessed before all here present. Serve your king and your country well, Sir Knight." He touched the blade first to Alymere's right shoulder, then to his left, and bade him, "Arise, Sir Alymere."

The applause was rapturous, heady. He breathed it in. They loved him. He closed his eyes, savouring it for a moment more before he stood. He rose slowly, and turned to summon the boy, but before he could, the king clapped him on the back and put an arm around his shoulder. "I think it only fitting that your first duty as my knight should be to save the fair maiden. What say you?" he called out to the gathering, who met his question with a roar of approval. "Go, Sir Alymere, cut the Queen free from her prison."

"But our toast? The Chalice?" Alymere hated the way he sounded, like a whining child, but the words were out of his mouth before he could stop himself.

"There will be time enough for that later, Sir Knight. The night is still young. Right now there is a damsel in need of saving. And what sort of man would my newest knight be if he left her trussed up like some prize pig? Besides, it is customary for the hero to claim a kiss, is it not?" Arthur offered a crooked smile.

Alymere had no choice but to cut her down. He couldn't force the king to drink.

Once again his hand moved to touch the linen favour tied around his arm, and he pulled it away sharply. The boy took the sudden motion to be his signal and came scurrying forward with the Chalice clutched in both hands.

FIFTY-THREE

Alymere was torn.

He started to call out to the boy to stop, raising his hand, but saw the way the king eyed the Chalice in his hands expectantly and stopped himself. There was nothing he could do, the die was cast. Now it was down to the Fates.

"Is that it?" Arthur breathed beside him.

"It is," Alymere said, nodding. His mind raced. He needed to think through the alternatives open to him, even as they were rapidly diminishing. He could always snatch the Chalice from the boy, he realised, but before he could reach out for it, the king said, "I'll take that, boy," and, coins or no coins, there was no way a guttersnipe was going to disobey his king.

Alymere's heart sank. He clenched his fist and ground his teeth, then turned his back. It was out of his hands now, literally and metaphorically.

The king had the Chalice.

It would work its pervasive magic on him, just as the book itself must have done. He had been canny in allowing the king, even encouraging him, to feel the curious flowing script inked deep into the pages, just as Alymere had after taking the book from the blind monk. Touching the book gave strength to its voice, allowing them to soak into the reader and draw them back to the pages, again and again until they utterly possessed him. And then, likewise, he would be driven to possess the book, which would mean killing Alymere.

Arthur was damned if he drank from the Chalice, and damned if he didn't. But he had no desire to die. He liked this body.

He had to trust that the seed he had planted – that one sip from the Devil's cup would grant Arthur the perception to see through lies – would be enough to make the king willingly choose to drink from the Chalice.

It didn't need to be a public spectacle; as much as he wanted to savour the king's humbling, an unseen death served him just as well. The thought raised a bitter smile. Indeed, there were several advantages to privacy, the most obvious being that there would be nothing to link Alymere to the deed, and he wouldn't have to partake in the wailing and gnashing of teeth as the commoners mourned. There was only so much lying even the Devil was prepared to do.

He turned his back on the king, allowing a smile to spread across his face. He had no need to mask his excitement anymore, he realised. He could be himself. More fool them, if they believed he was sharing their high spirits.

The crowd parted around Alymere as he walked to where the maiden was tied to the Maypole.

He strode confidently through them, offering a smile here, accepting a hearty back-slap there, until he stood before the bound woman. He started to pull at the streamers, tearing them away from her face and body. Others came up to join him and soon there were ten men crowded in around the Maypole, shredding the ribbons. Once she was free, with nothing to support her, the May Queen slumped forward into Alymere's arms. She was surprisingly light. He looked down at the woman, her name bubbling up in his mind, along with a bewildering rush of recollections and desires.

She opened her eyes, done with playing dead, and looped her arms around his neck to draw him down into a kiss. As the kiss broke, much to the delight of the crowd, she breathed the words "Do you love me?" into his mouth, and Alymere's buried voice cried out: *Yes! Yes!*

Before he could say anything, the other men claimed her, taking the May Queen into their arms and carrying her away from him.

Alymere touched his lips. The taste of her lingered there; the taste of summer.

A meaty hand clamped on his shoulder. He didn't need to turn to know it was Sir Bors; the big knight was always there when he least wanted him. "So, Sir Alymere, am I to take it you are smitten with our new Queen?" He said it lightly enough, but the ghostly *Yes! Yes!* of that buried voice still answered him.

Alymere lowered his hand from his lips self-consciously. "She is quite something," he said, even as the inner voice mocked him with the promise that had started it all, and the gift with which she sealed their pact, *so that I am always close to you, wherever you may be.* But he could not remember her name. He clenched his fist until it hurt; he struggled to impose his will upon the voice, but it wouldn't be silenced.

"*Enchanting* is the word you are looking for my young friend. She is a woman worth pursuing, eh?"

Enchanting... Witchery...

No, Sir Bors was wrong. The word he was looking for was *love*.

He had said it to her before, he now knew with shocking clarity. He had said those very words to the girl with the daisies in her black curls, even as he had lain with her, and again, after, as they lay spent. He had sworn to love her. And he knew this now because her kiss had set him free, providing the spark within him the fuel it needed to burn once more, in the engulfing darkness where the Devil's cup had banished him.

He looked around for the woman, the May Queen, but she was gone, swallowed by the revellers.

That didn't stop the sense of turmoil rising in him. Alymere sniffed the air as though he might smell her on it – her briarwood, her hawthorne and spruce, her daisies and bluebells and buttercups and all the flowers of spring – but all he could smell was sweat and ale.

And then he heard it. An ear-splitting *caw*. He spun around, scanning the skies.

They were all involved, the hag and her damned bird, the maiden, all of them, one and the same.

It took him a moment to find it in the oppressive sky, a single speck, blacker than black, flitting across the moon, but he knew beyond any doubt that it was the crow with the streak of white feathers, watching from afar. He watched it bank and turn and expected to see it swoop closer but it was gone, lost in the black sky. It didn't cross the moon again.

He lowered his eyes and scanned the faces in the crowd instead, looking for the hag. Surely if the crow was here, the old crone couldn't be far removed? They were bound.

"Where are you?" he demanded harshly. "Where are you, woman? Face me!" He yelled, shrilly. "What game are you playing, witch? Damn you! Face me!"

The people closest to him looked at Alymere as though he had lost his mind. Bors tried to reassure him that the pretty young thing who had obviously stolen his heart was fine, and that he'd have the rest of his life to plight his troth, if that was what it took. Alymere shook off his hand.

"Ignorant whoreson!" Alymere roared, startling Bors with the vehemence that drove his words. "Get out of my sight, or so help me G –" he stumbled over the word *God*, and instead raged: "Go! Go, damn you! Leave me be!" Alymere placed his hands flat against the big man's chest and pushed him, hard.

For a moment it looked as though Sir Bors was going to strike him – his entire body quivered with barely supressed rage – but as quickly as it had flared, he mastered his temper.

Alymere didn't care. She was here. He felt her presence before he saw her, hovering around the edge of the gathering. He saw her crooked back, and her hair, wild with thorns and briar twigs. She watched him intently, a mocking smile on her leathery face.

"You!" he yelled, levelling a finger at her accusingly.

Help me! Alymere's true voice cried out suddenly, filling his mind so completely there was no room for the Devil. They locked gazes in that moment, as though she had heard his plea, but she turned away. The hag disappeared back into the crowd before he could stop her.

He felt trapped; people crowded in on all sides. He couldn't breathe. He couldn't move. He wanted to scream. He spun around again and again, clutching at people's clothes, at their throats, yelling: "Where is it? Where is the Chalice? *Bring me the cup!*" Each demand more maddened than the last. He would drink from it once more. He would spill his blood into the cup and banish this damned voice once and forever so that he was free of it. "Bring me the Chalice! Now!"

And with the true soul of Alymere rising inside him, clamouring to be heard, he ran blindly forward, arms outstretched, yelling for the Chalice. He pushed at the front rows of people, trying to force his way through them, and when they didn't immediately shrink away from him, screaming at them. They flinched away from the madness in his face. He was burning.

Be my champion. Save me. But this wasn't Alymere's voice. It was hers. The woman. The Queen of May. The Summer Maiden. The Crow Maiden.

He remembered her name then: *Blodyweth*.

And with that, he remembered what it was that she had given him to seal their pact. He clawed at the favour tied around his arm, trying to rip it off, but the damned knot wouldn't give. He tugged at it, working his fingers into the stubborn knot.

The boy appeared at his side, clutching the Black Chalice, and pressed it into Alymere's trembling hands. "Where are you, my king?" he bellowed. "You owe me a toast! Drink with me, Arthur! Drink!"

Giving up on the knotted favour, he spun, waving the Chalice in the air above his head. "This is it, the Devil's cup! Just one drink! Drink with me, my king!"

Someone pushed into his back. He spun around, snarling at the woman who'd had the temerity to touch him as he tried to fight his way free of the maddening crowd. Startled, she gathered up her skirts and bolted.

She wasn't important. His world had reduced to two things: The Black Chalice and Arthur.

Then Sir Bors stood where she had been.

Alymere stared for a moment too long, uncomprehending, as

Sir Bors looked Alymere straight in the eye, the disappointment writ plain on his face, cocked his fist and punched him square in the jaw.

Alymere tasted blood in his mouth as the shock of the blow rang from his chin to his toes. He stumbled, swaying on his feet; for a moment the world spun away beneath him.

Then it went black.

FIFTY-FOUR

HE OPENED HIS eyes.

"Shhhh, drink this."

The king tried to part his lips to pour water down his throat, and Alymere shook his head.

He regretted it instantly as a wave of nausea welled up within him. He rolled over onto his side and vomited onto the grass. His stomach heaved again and again until there was nothing left to come up save for bile.

Cradling him in his arms, Arthur pressed the Chalice to Alymere's lips, forcing him to swallow a mouthful of water. He emptied the rest of the water before Alymere could take a second gulp. Then he gripped Alymere by the jaw and turned his head left, then right, studying him. "You'll be fine. A little bruising, a few loose teeth for a while, and of course, sore as hell in the morning, but fine." He waited a few moments, studying Alymere's face, and then asked, "So, tell me, am I lying?"

Alymere looked up at the king, taking his time to collect himself. Everything hurt. He rolled his head slowly on his neck, feeling the muscles and tendons stretch and throb with the tentative movement. His head did not fall off, which was a small mercy. "No, sire."

Arthur smiled. "Excellent. Now perhaps we ought to get you somewhere more comfortable before Bors decides to smack you again for your impertinence. That's quite a tongue you have on you for one so young, Sir Knight. It is fortunate he is not one to hold a grudge. Quick to anger, quicker still to forgive, that is Bors."

"I deserved it," Alymere said, rubbing at his jaw.

"That you did, boy. That you did." It was the first time the king had called him *boy* since his return to Camelot.

Alymere didn't feel himself. He looked around at the Maypole and the concerned faces of the few bystanders who had gathered around after the commotion. He tried to rise, but his body was having none of it. The bonfires were burning bright now, turning night into day. Every bone in his body rattled.

"I have made a fool of myself," he said eventually; but mercifully, beyond the punch, the details of it refused to come back to him.

"People will forget it soon enough."

"The day Sir Bors knocked out the newly knighted Sir Alymere with one punch."

"Or when you put it like that, perhaps not."

"Where is Bors?" Alymere asked. He felt a shadowy presence at the back of his mind, clawing at his consciousness. Struggling to be free.

Arthur didn't answer him immediately. Instead he gestured for someone to come forward from the crowd. Katherine. The maid hurried forward and knelt at his side. Again there was pity in her pretty eyes, but this time it had nothing to do with his disfigurement. She pressed a wet rag to his chin, and pulled it away red with blood from where his teeth had cut into his gums. He hawked and spat blood into the grass beside him.

And the voice inside his head whispered insidiously: *I will not give you up without a fight, Alymere, Killer of Kings. You are mine. You are me. We are.*

And he shivered. *Leave me alone. I do not want to kill the king. I do not. I. Do. Not. I...*

Do... the Devil whispered.

FIFTY-FIVE

In the end it was simple.

He had no need of elaborate schemes; the king had already held the Chalice and dribbled water into his mouth with it. All Alymere needed to do was get the man to place the tarnished goblet to his lips and take a single sip.

"My liege," he said, leaning on Katherine slightly. "Before this series of... ah... unfortunate events, I had been about to buy myself an ale. Might I make up for my behaviour by sharing a draught with you, by way of a peace offering?"

"There is no need," Arthur said.

"Then humour me, sire. Please."

"Very well. I promised you a toast, and a toast you shall have. But hurry or we will miss the May Queen's voyage down the river."

They walked together to the ale tent. The smell of hops and barley was strong in the air as the barmaid brought two overflowing mugs over to the table they had taken. The tent was all but empty; a few hardened drinkers remained, but most had gone down to the river to watch the May Queen's farewell. It wasn't the grand humbling he had hoped for, but it would do.

Arthur drank deeply, wiping the foam away from his lips with the back of his hand, and slammed the half-empty tankard down on the table. Alymere matched him, licking his lips.

"What of the Chalice?" He asked, leaning forward conspiratorially.

The Chalice was on the table between them. They were alone. There was no-one to save the king, once desire got the better of him. "One sup to see through the lies of men; two to be given the gift of tongues; three to become Lord of Illusions? Will you drink?"

"Honestly," Arthur said after a moment, "I do not know if I want to know every lie I hear. Sometimes, perhaps, it is better to live in blissful ignorance."

"But more dangerous, surely, my king? With so many people eager to see you fall."

"Indeed? Who is eager to see me fall?" Arthur said, a wry smile touching his lips.

"Your enemies, sire," Alymere said, without a hint of irony. "And you cannot know them, not for sure, because you cannot see into the heart of a man. No-one can."

"You can," the king corrected him. Alymere frowned, and Arthur gestured toward the cup. "You have supped from the Devil's Grail."

Alymere nodded slowly. He *had* supped from the Devil's Grail, and survived. Not once, but twice. The blood had sustained him; the water had revived him. He emptied what remained of the ale from his flagon into the Chalice and pushed it across the table toward the king. Arthur didn't take his eyes from it, but neither did he reach for it.

"How do I know *you* aren't my enemy?" he said, finally.

Alymere steepled his fingers and inclined his head toward the Chalice. "All you need to do is drink, and you'll hear the truth of my words," Alymere said. "Ask me any question. I shall tell you the truth, and nothing but."

"A convincing argument – but a man would be foolish to treat with the Devil, a king doubly so. I do not like this cup you have brought me. More, I do not trust this cup."

"And yet you had me drink from it, and by your own hand."

"I am the king. Your life is mine anyway," Arthur said, matter-of-factly. The off-hand manner of the comment – the callousness of it, and the blatant disregard he had for his knight's life – rankled.

"You live to serve. That is the nature of the oath you just took, is it not? Camelot is all. When we are long gone, Camelot will endure. It is more than just stone walls; it is an ideal. Our lives are pledged to that ideal, and if we should die upholding it, then so be it. That is the will of God and who are we, mere mortals, to argue?"

We are Alymere, Killer of Kings, the voice barked in his mind. *That is who we are! That is our destiny!*

"I will not drink," Arthur said. "Not from the Devil's cup. I will give you your toast, but I will not willingly sup from something so obviously tainted with evil. He is the father of lies. There is something wrong about it. Can't you feel it?" *I feel nothing except the pulse of blood pumping through the thick vein at your neck, the pounding of it through your temple, and I know what it means. You are afraid.* "How can you know that every word in the book you found is true? How can you know that he had not sown the seeds of discord and discontent in the lies therein?" *I know because I know,* he wanted to scream. *I know because I am he and he is me and we, together, are the end of you!* "No, I will not drink. Tell me, why are you so eager that I drink? That, to me, is a far more interesting question."

Alymere licked his lips and leaned forward, taking his hands from the table.

He had to battle down the urge to snatch up the Chalice and swallow down a second and a third gulp, merely to put the fear of the Devil into the king.

Beneath the table, Alymere felt himself reaching for his sword, and clenched his fists. He couldn't draw steel on the king – his head would roll before he was halfway across the table. Arthur was the greatest swordsman in all of Albion; Excalibur and its wielder, the stuff of legend.

Just drink it, damn you!

But he knew the king was not going to. Not without... help.

I do not want to kill the king. I do not. I do. I do not. I do. I do not. I do... not! I do... not. I... do... not...

And again, louder than all the denials, shouting him down, the Devil's voice cried: *I do!* And there was nothing he could do to silence it. All he could do was try to claw back control of his own body. It didn't matter who his father was; Alymere, son of Corynn, was still in there, fighting for his very survival. Both Lowick and Roth would have been proud of the boy they had raised, regardless of which of them was his father.

His hand trembled violently.

"You have no answer for that? Curious. I would have thought you would."

"Have you heard the voice yet?" Alymere asked. He had no control of the words as they left his mouth. It was as though the other part of him was speaking. The buried part.

"What voice?" The king asked sharply. Something in his frown betrayed the fact that he had. In the hours since he had come into contact with the book, the voice of the Devil's Bible had wormed its way insidiously into the king's mind, and it wouldn't stop worming away at him until it had complete and utter control.

"The book. The Devil. Have you heard the voice yet?"

"Oh, dear God," Arthur said. And then nothing more. With no words there could be no lies.

FIFTY-SIX

SIR BORS APPEARED behind Arthur's shoulder.

He drew back a stool and sat himself down. "You've got a skull like granite, lad," the big man said, rubbing his fist, his familiar affable grin on his face. It was as though nothing had ever happened between them. But that was what the king had said, wasn't it? Quick to anger, quicker to forgive.

"I don't mind saying I've worked up a devil of a thirst. Ah," the big man reached out for the only full goblet on the table. "You truly are a wonder, lad," he said to Alymere. "Every time I think I understand you, you go and do something utterly idiotic..." He trailed off, grimacing. "It's a bad habit, lad, and one that could get you in an awful lot of trouble." Sir Bors rolled his head on his bull-thick neck, and worked his shoulders. There was an enviable affability about the man, even now. He truly could never hold a grudge for more than a few minutes.

"Now, I believe a toast is in order to mark this auspicious occasion. So, if you will allow me, I think there is one in particular that lends itself to the situation. Never has a young man been so loved: Corynn, Roth, Lowick, all good people, good friends – even that old bugger Baptiste would have died for you, lad – and to look at you now would make them so proud. You have grown into a good man. A true man. And for that, we all owe them a debt of thanks." His meaty fist closed around the stem of the Black Chalice and he lifted it to his lips. "To absent friends!"

Alymere reacted without thinking.

And this once it wasn't the book, or the Devil, or well-crafted schemes that controlled his actions. It was simple instinct, rising from the Alymere of old, driven by anguish. By loss.

No! He had lost too much in his short life; he would not lose any more. He sprung from his seat, dashing the Chalice from Bors's lips even as they parted to drink from the poisonous cup. Ale sprayed everywhere: down Bors's shirt, across his face and the table in front of him. The Chalice struck the table, spilling what was left of its contents over the king as it rolled away and fell to the dirt.

Alymere, breathing hard, loomed over Bors. The big man couldn't look away from the war going on behind the new Knight's eyes.

"What is happening to you, lad?"

"The Devil," Arthur said, staring at the damned cup where it lay on the ground. "That is what is happening to him."

Kill the king! Do it. Now! Snatch up our sword and drive it through his withered heart! Do it! Gut him! It is our destiny!

Alymere drew his sword in a single smooth action. The blade shone deadly in the moonlight.

Kill him!

No! I will not! I will not kill Arthur! Alymere's heart screamed in protest, and his entire body shook. The tip of the sword wavered.

His eyes darted from the king's exposed chest, to Bors, and back to Arthur. No-one seemed capable of moving, trapped as though by a spell. Out of the corner of his eye he saw Blodyweth's ragged linen favour, still stubbornly tied around his arm. It had slipped down to his elbow, where he could ease it down and be free of the damned thing, and whatever hold it had upon him.

"Blodyweth," he said, tasting summer on his lips again as he did, and drawing strength from her name. "Blodyweth," he repeated. His chest heaved. His arm trembled violently, the sword's tip swinging wildly between Arthur and Bors. And he heard her again, in that moment when he most needed her. *Be my champion. Save me. Stay true. Save me, my champion. Save me, or the Devil take both our souls.*

I will not kill! I. Will...

And then with one triumphant surge of will, Alymere hurled the sword aside. *Not!*

He collapsed to his knees. "You will not have her," he said, having barely the breath to say the words. "And you will not have me."

And then Bors's thundering right fist hit him again.

A MAN REDEEMED

FIFTY-SEVEN

"THIS IS BECOMING something of a habit," Bors said, looking down at him.

Alymere didn't know where he was. The only thing he could remember was asking the king if he had heard the Devil's voice. Before that, nothing; after that, nothing.

There was nothing familiar about the room. It was dark, the single source of light a torch guttering in a sconce behind Bors's shoulder. It was cold; looking down, he realised all he had to fight the chill was a thin blanket. It was the most uncomfortable bed he had lain on in years. The wooden slats of the cot dug into his back and side.

"Where am I?" he asked, groggily. He rubbed at his eyes with his knuckles.

"Ah, well, hmmm," Bors said uncomfortably, shuffling from foot to foot. "You did draw a weapon on the king..."

Alymere eased himself around so that he sat on the low cot, and in doing so saw the thick timber door and the week-old straw scattered across the cold stone floor. He knew where he was: one of the dungeon's cells beneath the castle.

"This wasn't how I dreamed I'd spend my first night as a knight," Alymere said, nursing his tender jaw.

"Not the most auspicious of starts. What possessed you to –" Bors stopped, lost for words.

Alymere held his head in his hands. He felt like himself for the first time in ages, all thanks to the ruined favour still tied around his left arm. She had saved him.

Had she always known of the weakness in his heart that the Devil might exploit?

Surely she had, and that was why she had given him her favour.

"Take me to the king. I need to see him. Please."

"I don't think that would be such a good idea, lad. Let him cool down first."

"Please," Alymere pleaded.

Bors shook his head. "I don't think so."

Frustration welled up within Alymere. There was no vile voice driving it, this time. The frustration was his own. He knew what he had to do.

And then it hit him.

The Black Chalice was only part of the threat. It was the book; that was where the real danger lay. The book could transform a man, letting the Devil into his soul.

The king had handled the Devil's Bible. He had run his fingers over those tainted whorls of ink. And, when Alymere had asked if he had heard the voice, Arthur had not denied it.

"The book," he said. "Where is it?"

"What book? What are you talking about?"

"The Devil's Bible. The book. Where is it?" Alymere demanded, rising unsteadily to his feet. The entire cell pitched and rolled around him, and he reached out for the wall to stop himself from falling. "Does Arthur have it? Please God, tell me he doesn't." But he knew that he did. That would explain the silence in his head.

Bors reached out a hand to steady him. "Slowly, lad. Slowly. Now, tell me what this is all about."

And he did, confiding his fear – that the Devil had found a way into the king, and it was his fault. Bors paled, his usually jovial face strained as Alymere explained how the voice whispered its demands and insinuations until they became irresistible. How it became a part of you, slowly driving your sense of self down until it was buried in the darkest recesses of what passed for your soul. And the more he talked, the sharper the memories of confinement in that Hell became. He was trembling by the time he finished, a fine sheen of sweat peppering his brow.

But it was his eyes that convinced Bors he was telling the truth: they were haunted. Alymere had seen things no man ought to see, things that had changed him. That much was obvious. And it explained his behaviour these past weeks. That, in itself, was almost a relief, until Alymere asked again: "Does Arthur have the book?"

"He keeps it with him at all times now."

"Lord give me strength. I have to do something," Alymere said. He pulled away from the big knight's grip, only to be confronted by the barred door. He stared at it helplessly, wanting to beat it down with his bare fists, but he was weak. "This is my fault. I gave him the Chalice, and now he has the book. I have to stop him. I have to save him. Please."

"If I let you out of here he'll have my head, lad."

"And if you don't, the Devil will take Arthur's soul and it won't matter a damn if you have your head or not."

"I can't," Bors said, torn.

Alymere turned away and slammed his fist against the wall, venting his frustration.

"But," Bors said, thinking quickly. "I can take the book. If it is as dangerous as you say I can take it and destroy it."

And for a moment Alymere dared to hope that it would work, that Bors could cast the damned book onto one of the smouldering bonfires outside and the flames would eat it. But then he remembered Medcaut. It wouldn't burn. The book had its own defences.

"No. It won't work." But an idea began to form in his mind, and he knew he had no choice. This, at last, was how he would redeem himself, and how he would become a true man. "But, but – Let me think. Let me think. Yes. Right. Yes. You have to bring me the book. It's the only thing you can do. You have to bring it to me here. I will do the rest."

Bors looked at the young knight sceptically. "But won't that put you at risk?"

Alymere looked at him. It would have been easier to lie, but lies were the Devil's way. He was not one of his creatures now, so he summoned the courage to tell the truth. "Yes. But I know what I have to do. You will have to trust me. Please, my friend, do not fight me on this. Let me become the man I was always meant to be. Let me become someone my father – God rest his soul – can be proud of."

Bors nodded slowly, then grasped Alymere with both of his meaty hands and drew him into a fierce embrace.

He didn't let him go for a full minute. He whispered in Alymere's ear, "God be with you." And left him.

Bors did not return for hours.

The cell door opened twice before he did. The first time it was a young, gangly maid, come with a tray of food. The prisoner would get to eat a hearty meal, at least, before the king decided his judgment. She had long dirty blonde hair and round cheekbones, and a slightly elfin quality to her face, with bright blue eyes. She blinked against the darkness. The cutlery on the tray rattled against the plate. She looked as though she were wearing her mother's clothes, like she had just come into womanhood and was uncomfortable in her new body. There was something appealing about her gaze; something familiar.

"You look familiar. Tell me," Alymere said, taking the tray from her, "have we met before?"

"Yes, my lord, though in truth I did not expect you to recognise me like this."

"Where?"

"I was the May Queen this year. You cut me down from the Maypole so the men could carry me to the river."

He looked at her then, trying to see her properly in the low light. He shook his head slowly. "What is your name, girl?"

It wasn't Blodyweth. It had never been Blodyweth.

She left him with the food, but he didn't touch a morsel of it. He sat on the edge of the cot, waiting for Sir Bors to return with the book.

The second time the door opened it was another one of the maids come to retrieve the tray. She looked down at the untouched plate, shrugged her shoulders as though to say *suit yourself*, and left him.

The torch burned out an hour later, leaving him alone in the dark.

It was deep in the night when the door finally opened a third time to let the big man in. He clutched the Devil's Bible close to his chest with one hand, and held a burning brand overhead with the other. The guard who had opened the cell door shrank back into the shadows. Alymere didn't move from the bed; for the longest time Bors simply stood silhouetted in the doorway, looking at him.

"Give it to me," Alymere said, looking up.

He didn't hold his hands out for it.

If he had, Bors would have been able to see him shaking.

The big man moved cautiously into the room and closed the door behind him with his foot. "I have it," he said unnecessarily.

Alymere felt a thousand warring emotions surge up within him then, this close to the book, but it was fear that won out. He closed his eyes.

"Leave it with me. I will do what has to be done."

"I don't know..."

"Trust me, please. This once. Trust me."

He couldn't look up. He couldn't meet the big man's gaze. He didn't want to remember him like this, clutching a burning brand in a dank cell. He wanted to remember him striding confidently through Camelot, flirting outrageously with Katherine, making Maeve the cook laugh by stealing food. Being larger than life. If he looked at Bors now, he knew he wouldn't be able to go through with it.

Bors put the Devil's Bible down on the bed beside Alymere.

"Be careful, lad."

"Don't worry about me, my friend. I know what I am doing. It is the only way."

Bors rested a hand on his shoulder. "I meant what I said last night. Roth, Corynn, Lowick, they would have been proud of you, lad."

"I hope so," Alymere said. When he looked up, tears were streaming down his face. The big man said nothing, but left him. He switched the brand for the burnt-out torch in the sconce, leaving Alymere the light.

Beside him, the book spoke straight into the darkness of his heart.

You can hear me, can't you, Alymere? You know I am still here. I am always in the darkness, and always will be. You can't escape me. You and I, we are one. Our time together is not over until I am done with you. You are my creature.

"No," Alymere said aloud. "I am your keeper. There is a difference."

He looked at the linen favour on his arm.

It was the last thing he ever saw.

With that, he lifted the brand from the wall and put his own eyes out, welcoming the darkness.

FIFTY-EIGHT

Come dawn, Bors opened the door to the cell, unsure what he expected to find.

Alymere lay huddled in the corner of the room, clutching the Devil's Bible to his chest.

He looked up. Tears of blood caked his cheeks.

Bors stared at the young man's ruined eyes, unable to accept what he saw.

He rushed to Alymere's side, cradling him in his arms. "You foolish boy. What have you done?"

"What I had to," Alymere said, tilting his head unerringly toward Bors, as though, despite the deep holes where his ruined eyes lay, he could see him. "It is the only way. I cannot stop the voices, but no matter how seductive they become I can never read the book. He cannot crawl his way back inside me. I have won."

"But at what cost?" Bors said, aghast.

"It was the only way," Alymere repeated, remembering his promise to the Crow Maiden. *There is nothing you could ask of me that I would not willingly do, without a second thought.* This is what it meant, to be her champion. Sacrifice. The willing offering of everything he was and everything he could ever have been. "Now, one last favour, my friend."

"Anything. You need only ask," Bors said, unhesitant.

"Take me away from this place. Take me somewhere I will never see another living soul as long as I live. Take me to Medcaut."

Bors understood. Isolated, the book's vile voice could not worm its way inside another man. "And that will be the end of it? How will you live? How will you eat?"

"The book will sustain me," Alymere said, thinking of the blind monk, and finally understanding.

"And the Chalice? What of it?"

"It can't stay here."

FIFTY-NINE

SHE WAS WAITING for them in the forest. He did not need to see her to know she was there.

She smelled like summer.

"My champion," Blodyweth said. She leaned close, kissing his cheek, and he smiled. He could not help himself. Despite everything, despite the savagery of his wounds and the ugliness of the scars they left behind, she could still be tender towards him. Loving.

He offered her the Chalice. "The Kingdom of Summer is safe, my lady. I have kept my promise. I will live out all of my days doing so."

"I never doubted you, my love."

*Here endeth the first part of the
Second Book of King Arthur
and his Noble Knights...*

ABOUT THE TRANSLATOR

STEVEN SAVILE (NEWCASTLE University) has written more than twenty novels and short story collections, including *The Hollow Earth, Temple: Incarnations, Laughing Boy's Shadow, Houdini's Last Illusion, Angel Road*, and the graphic novel *Fragrance of You* (with artist Robert Sammelin).

He was a runner up in the 2000 British Fantasy Awards, a winner of a 2002 Writers of the Future Award, and was nominated for the inaugural 2006 Scribe Award for best novel adaptation for his novel *Sláine: The Exile*. His novel *Primeval: Shadow of the Jaguar* was nominated for the 2008 Scribe Award for Best Young Adult Novel.

His translation of Sir Thomas Malory's "The Tayle of Sir Alymer and hys Queste for the False Grayle," the first part of *The Second Book of King Arthur and his Noble Knights*, is his first project for Abaddon Books.

APPENDIX I

The Salisbury Manuscript

JUNE, 2006. THE vestry of the nine-hundred-year-old parish church of St. Barbara and St. Christopher in Salisbury has been in need of a new roof for years; swathes of irreplacable parish records have been destroyed by leaking rainwater, not to mention mould and the various pests which enter through the cracks to nest in the room. A collection, several church fetes and a fundraiser thrown by the local school have finally raised the £16,000 needed to carry out the repairs, and work starts in the beginning of August.

Before work can begin, the countless documents lying stacked and boxed at the rear of the room need to be removed, which has turned out to be a more complicated task than expected. Students from Salisbury University, working side by side with Church volunteers, need to open and inspect every box *in situ*, identify, index and catalogue every document, and transfer them to new, more secure archive boxes before removing them from the building. Many of the boxes haven't been opened in decades – some, according to Canon Arthur Drake, since before World War I – and few of Drake's forerunners made any attempt at organising them.

On the third or fourth day, a remarkable find is uncovered by one of the students.

"I remember Lily [Evanson, the Church secretary] had just come back with about the seventh tea run of the day, and I had my back turned to the kids while I selected a biscuit," says Drake. "Suddenly, one of the girls from the university – I honestly can't remember which – started shouting and carrying on."

What the unnamed student had discovered was a large bound manuscript, purporting to be a second book of Arthurian tales by the writer of *Le Morte D'Arthur*.

"Work more or less stopped for the day," reminisces the canon. "Who am I kidding?" he laughs. "For the week. I just about managed to keep the kids from just running out of there until they'd logged it and cleared everything up for the night, and it was rushed off to the university."

At the university's Middle English department the next day, the job of identifying and analysing the extraordinary book is begun, and *The Second Book of King Arthur* is set to sweep the academic world.

The Book

BRITISH LIBRARY MS Add. 1138, now better known as the "Salisbury Manuscript," holds 504 sheets, including a title page apparently added in 1863. All the leaves are 287mm by 205mm. The original sheets are written on French paper stock from the late fifteenth century, and the later title sheet in English paper stock from Liverpool, from the mid-nineteenth century. The whole is bound in goatskin, apparently around the time of the added title page in the nineteenth century.

The added title page reads "The Second *Booke* of Sir Thomas *Malory*, donated to the Library by the Hon. Mr. Wm. Landsdowne. MDCCCLXIII." Which library, and who Mr. Landsdowne is, and how the book entered into the possession of St. Barbara's and St. Christopher's, are all still unknown.

The second – original – title page reads "The Seconde Boke of kyng Arthur and also His noble Knyghts, as writen by Sir Tomas

Malorye before hys deth." Several truncated marks at the bottom right-hand corner of the page show where further text has been lost when the leaf was trimmed.

The text is written by a single scribe, writing consistently in a secretary hand. Arabic figures are used to number the leaves. Comparison of the hand with the scribes who wrote the Winchester Manuscript of *Le Morte D'Arthur* has ruled out the possibility that either of the latter scribes worked on *The Second Book*.

Ink smudges on several of the pages suggest that printed sheets from the 1485 Caxton edition of the *Morte* were rested on sheets of the Salisbury Manuscript to dry, as with the Winchester, which confirms that Caxton had both manuscripts in his possession, and that the Salisbury is contemporary with the Winchester.

Authorship

THERE IS SOME debate about the authorship of the Salisbury Manuscript, in spite of its age and its connection to William Caxton.

"I'm convinced this is not only Malory, but Malory's own hand," says David Moore (Queen Mary, University of London). "He wrote the *Morte* while he was imprisoned, on poor stock and over some years; the Winchester was rescribed for clarity, possibly by scribes in Caxton's employ. He wrote much of the *Second Book* at the same time, but piecemeal, without collating and organising it the same way he had the first book. These are essentially the stories he cut out. When Caxton purchased the *Morte*, Malory set about redrafting the *Second Book* and rescribing it. I would guess Caxton's death in 1492 prevented him from going ahead with publication, and [Caxton's successor, Wynkyn] de Worde lost or sold it."

By contrast, Charlotte Hill (De Montfort University) argues, "The Salisbury was thrown together by Caxton himself or one of his clerks, hoping to 'cash in' on the *Morte*'s success. Keep in mind the *Morte* itself was published thirteen years after Malory's death. Caxton evidently decided against publishing, for fear of Malory's family bringing suit."

Whether Malory's own work or a contemporary forgery, the Salisbury Manuscript is a hugely important find, and academics around the world have studied and discussed the text.

Malory's Knights of Albion

DISCUSSION OF A modernisation of the *Second Book* has been bandied about since a few months after its discovery. Canon Drake asked those involved in studying the text to hold off on a mainstream publication until he had a chance to discuss an edition with several publishers. Following talks with Jason Kingsley, CEO of Rebellion Publishing, Ltd., and Jonathan Oliver, Editor-in-Chief of Abaddon Books, Drake gave the imprint the go-ahead to develop a series of novelisations in modern English in early 2010.

"I'm a great fan of Abaddon's work," said Drake. "I usually have one of their zombie or steampunk books tucked into my pocket – once, I realised, I had one tucked into my cassock when I was conducting a wedding – and I think they'll do a brilliant job with the new Malory stuff."

Speaking for Rebellion, Oliver said, "We're very excited to be involved with bringing this work to the world. Whether it's an original Malory book or a fifteenth-century forgery, it's still an immensely important work, and it's brilliant to have our authors involved in it.

"Besides, the stories are great fun. There's a rich vein of chivalric tradition in these books, and I think the public will enjoy a chance to escape to a nobler time of heroic knights, evil monsters and virtuous maidens."

APPENDIX II

The Black Chalice

*"Good Alymere ne hadde no treasoun in his heerte whan
he stepyt across the bridge into Camelout."*

THUS BEGINS ONE of the most controversial documents to enter the
world of academe so far this century: Sir Thomas Malory's *The
Second Book of King Arthur and his Noble Knights*, sequel to *Le
Morte D'Arthur*, written towards the end of the good knight's
life. Unless, that is, it was written alongside the *Morte*, was only
ever the collected excisions from his original work, or wasn't
written by Sir Thomas at all. This remarkable book has been the
subject of more papers, started more arguments, and launched
(and ended) more academic careers in four short years than
many very worthy texts manage in a century or more.

Like the *Morte*, the *Second Book* is episodic, relating a number
of separate stories of figures from King Arthur's court at Camelot.
Unlike the *Morte*, which presents the stories in chronological order
and ties them together into a whole, the *Second Book* appears to
be a haphazard collation of disconnected stories. Benedict Smith
(Glasgow University) has suggested that they represent the stories
that Malory "cut out"; tales that he collected while compiling the
Morte, and which he ultimately dropped from the final work for

various reasons, generally because the central characters were not important enough to the overall story.

Enter Sir Alymere. What's perhaps most interesting about the hero of "The Tayle of Sir Alymer and hys Queste for the False Grayle" is that, in spite of being almost unknown – he's mentioned only once, in the *Alliterative Morte Arthure*, as a loyal knight on the side of the king in the final battle with Mordred – he is one of the twenty-five names on the famous Winchester Round Table. Why would Henry VIII have placed such an obscure knight alongside the likes of Gawain, Lancelot and Pellinore? And if he wasn't as obscure in Henry's time as in ours, why hasn't his story survived to the modern day? Why didn't Monmouth, or Wace, or Malory leave us his tale?

Perhaps because the story is original to Malory? The Devil's Bible mentioned in the story (formally the *Codex Gigas*, currently on display at the National Library of Sweden in Stockholm) was completed in 1229; *The Second Book*, assuming it was collected by Malory, before his death in 1471. Unless the Bible was a later addition, Alymere's story must have been written in the intervening years – and later rather than sooner, to allow for reports of the "Devil's book" to reach England from its native Bohemia. It's quite possible that Alymere's story was written in Malory's life, possibly by Malory himself, and that he, or Caxton, decided against including it in the *Morte* as it lacked authority.

Alternatively, perhaps, it was not included because of the nature of the story. *The Black Chalice* tells of a young knight's descent into corruption and evil in pursuit of a tainted reflection of the Grail. In the end, the knight is redeemed, but he is also blinded, incapable of taking part in Arthur's war with his son. If the story of Alymere's life conflicted with the *Alliterative Morte* as to which battles he took part in – if a knight otherwise remarked only for his loyalty is noted as having once dreamed of assassinating the king – then perhaps Malory wasn't the only Arthurian editor to have been troubled as to how to deal with him. Alymere had no treason in mind when he first entered Camelot, as the narrator tells us, nor when he last left her; that he dreamt of treason in the interim may have been deeply troubling in a time when he was regarded as an icon of loyalty.

Unless the story was an exploration of loyalty and duty. Malory was fascinated by the challenges of chivalry and piety, and by the choices the knights must face in striving to adhere to the Oath. Lancelot, the greatest of the knights, is an adulterer, and even Arthur is guilty of tyranny and cruelty. These worldly heroes are always conflicted by their choices; far from suggesting hypocrisy, Malory is apparently exploring the practical impossibility of a truly chivalrous life, and the very human weaknesses that undermine it. *The Black Chalice*, then, can be seen as an exploration of duty in the same light, in which the famously loyal Sir Alymere is first tempted to treason, and his struggle with the Chalice is a spiritual battle, in which he stands beside his king. As a symbolic piece, Malory may have felt it did not belong in the collection.

Themes from *The Black Chalice*

THE THEME OF corruption and redemption is common in grail literature, usually focusing on Lancelot's adultery with Guinevere, but here, the hero's fall and rise is the whole point of the story. The recurring corrupting force is *ambition*: Alymere is driven by his ambition to prove himself the greatest knight, as the long-dead monk Harmon was by his ambition to complete his book. In turn, Alymere gambles on Arthur's ambition to prove himself a great king, and is nearly vindicated. Only humble Bors, it seems, who desires nothing more than to serve, is above the influence of the Devil's book.

Malory's anxiety about family is addressed as well. Alymere is an orphan, progressing through a series of father-substitutes – his father's servant Baptiste, Sir Bors, his uncle Lowick – each of whom dies or turns on him. The death-bed reconciliation with his uncle prompts further tragedy, when he discovers that Lowick is his father, and that he is a child of rape (and, in the eyes of Malory's society, of incest). The parallels with Arthur's own story – himself a child of rape, who fathers his own killer on his sister – are obvious. Alymere flees into the arms of love, but even then, his relationship with Blodyweth, who rests his head on her breast as he sleeps, is described almost in terms of a son's with his mother. In many ways, Alymere's quest is a quest for belonging. Malory regularly presents comradeship as nobler than family ties, and here, Alymere's relationship with Sir Bors is the only one that is never undermined or perverted. It is Bors's intervention – twice – that prevents Alymere from killing the king, and Bors who helps him to accept his duty as the book's guardian at the end of the story.

Love in Malory is redeeming, but it is also troubling. Chaste love drives a knight to greatness, but physical love – especially if it is incestuous, violent or adulterous, but even at best – is always accompanied by a loss of grace. On the one hand, we see Lowick's rape of his sister-in-law, which haunts him his whole life, and on the other Bors's obvious love for Katherine, which he refuses to take beyond a courtly romance. When Alymere passes judgement on Craven and Isaiah, he stresses the importance of a loving life, but he rules in favour of the law, causing Josephina to take her own life. In that light, the Maiden's sexual love for Alymere is challenging; it is offered as a blessing, even as redemptive, but in the end it is not enough to protect him from the Devil's influence.

Finally, sight and perception are recurring themes in *The Black Chalice*. The monks at Medcaut have blinded themselves to protect themselves from the Devil's Bible's corrupting effects, but see all the more clearly as a result. Conversely, it is while blinded by a snowstorm that Alymere is led to the bower of the Crow Maiden, who deceives and misleads him the whole time he knows her. Thus, when blinded one is deceived, but by choosing to blind oneself one sees. Amidst the various examples of fairy illusions, symbols and misunderstandings, and Alymere's claims about the Chalice's powers over insight and illusion, the most important illusion in the story is Alymere's resemblance to his supposed father, Roth. His father, of course, is Roth's brother Lowick, but the two men are similar in appearance, so in Alymere people see his supposed father. The similarity is observed repeatedly, but the irony of the observation is only brought home when Lowick confesses on his deathbed. "You are my ghost," he tells his son, "You look like your father." In blindness, as the story closes, Alymere is not only protecting himself from the Devil's book, but from appearances that have betrayed and damned him all his life.

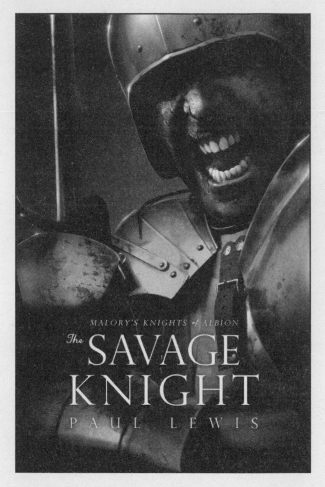

UK ISBN: 978 1 907992 33 9 • US ISBN: 978 1 907992 34 6 • £9.99/$12.99

Sir Dodinal the Savage is more at home in the wild forest than in the tilting yard or the banquet hall.
Keenly attuned to the natural world, but burdened with a terrible rage, he turns his back on Camelot
to find peace, or a just death.

In a quiet village on the Welsh border, Dodinal believes he may have finally found a home, but the village is
struck by child-stealing raiders from the hills, and he must take up arms once again in his new friends' aid.
His quest will take him into the belly of darkness, as the terrible secret hidden in the hills comes to light...